CLIVILIUS
WHERE CREATION MEETS INFINITY

© 2024 Nathan Cowdrey. All rights reserved.
First Edition, 20 March 2024
ISBN 978-1-4461-0681-5
Imprint: Lulu.com

Step into Clivilius, where creation meets infinity, and the essence of reality is yours to redefine. Here, existence weaves into a narrative where every decision has consequences, every action has an impact, and every moment counts. In this realm, shaped by the visionary AI CLIVE, inhabitants are not mere spectators but pivotal characters in an evolving drama where the lines between worlds blur.

Guardians traverse the realms of Clivilius and Earth, their journeys igniting events that challenge the balance between these interconnected universes. The quest for resources and the enigma of unexplained disappearances on Earth mirror the deeper conflicts and intricacies that define Clivilius—a world where reality responds to the collective will and individual choices of its Clivilians, revealing a complex interplay of creation, control, and consequence.

In the grand tapestry of Clivilius, the struggle for harmony and the dance of dichotomies play out across a cosmic stage. Here, every soul's journey contributes to the narrative, where the lines between utopia and dystopia, creator and observer, become increasingly fluid. Clivilius is not just a realm to be explored but a reality to be shaped.

Open your eyes. Expand your mind. Experience your new reality. Welcome to Clivilius, where the journey of discovery is not just about seeing a new world but about seeing your world anew.

Also in the Clivilius Series:

Gladys Cramer (4338.204.1 - 4338.214.3)

In a world frayed by tragedies, Gladys Cramer seeks solace in wine, her steadfast refuge amid life's turmoil. Tethered to a man ensnared by duty and love, she stands at a pivotal crossroads, her choices poised to weave the threads of her fate. Each glass of wine deepens her reflection on the decisions looming ahead and the silent vows brimming with untold consequences. Amidst tragedy and secrets, with wine as her guiding light yet potential harbinger of misstep, Gladys's journey veers onto a path set for an inevitable collision.

Beatrix Cramer (4338.205.1 - 4338.211.6)

Beatrix Cramer's life is a delicate balance of contradictions, her independence and keen intellect shadowed by her penchant for the forbidden. A master of acquisition, her love for antiques and the call of the wild drives her into the heart of danger, making her an indispensable ally yet an unpredictable force. When fate thrusts her into the clandestine world of Guardians, Beatrix must navigate a labyrinth of secrets and moral dilemmas. Caught in the crossfire of legacy and destiny, she faces choices that could redefine the boundaries of her world and her very identity.

Luke Smith (4338.204.1 - 4338.209.2)

Luke Smith's world transforms with the discovery of a cryptic device, thrusting him into the guardianship of destiny itself. His charismatic charm and unpredictable decisions now carry weight beyond imagination, balancing on the razor's edge between salvation and destruction. Embracing his role as a Guardian, Luke faces the paradox of power: the very force that defends also threatens to annihilate. As shadows gather and the fabric of reality strains, Luke must navigate the consequences of his actions, unaware that a looming challenge will test the very core of his resolve.

Karl Jenkins (1338.209.1 - 1338.214.1)

Plunged into Tasmania's most chilling cases, Senior Detective Karl Jenkins confronts a string of disappearances that entangle with his clandestine affair with Detective Sarah Lahey. As a dangerous obsession emerges, every step toward the truth draws Karl perilously close to a precipice threatening their lives and careers. "Karl Jenkins" is a riveting tale of suspense, where past haunts bear a perilous future.

4338.204.1 - 4338.212.1

CODY JENNINGS

CLIVILIUS
WHERE CREATION MEETS INFINITY

"Clivilius may be powerful, but the human heart is an unpredictable force that can change the course of destiny."

- Cody Jennings

4338.204

(23 July 2018)

GUARDIAN ATUM

4338.204.1

Leaning over the ageing wooden railing, I found myself lost in the vast, endless sea that stretched before me. The last rays of the setting sun cast a magnificent tapestry of purple and orange across the horizon, transforming the sea into a canvas of fleeting beauty. The waters beneath Glenelg Jetty danced in the light, each ripple reflecting the day's final glow with a grace that belied the violence of the deep. The rhythmic lull of the ocean kissing the wooden pillars beneath me was a familiar tune, a melody that whispered of home and simpler times. Yet, the comforting cadence was a stark contrast to the memories of Belkeep's waters, a realm known for its ruthless currents and lifeless embrace.

My contemplation of the serene spectacle was abruptly shattered by a deep, resonant voice that echoed from behind, slicing through the tranquil ambiance like a ship's bow through calm waters. "You're looking old." The words, though blunt, carried a warmth that only familiarity could breed.

"Jeremiah!" I exclaimed, my voice tinged with a mixture of surprise and delight. I turned slowly, almost reluctantly, to face the man behind the voice. As my eyes found his, time seemed to stand still for a moment. Jeremiah, with his imposing presence, surged forward, closing the distance between us with a few purposeful strides.

His embrace was like a harbour in a storm, a safe haven from the uncertainties that had become my constant companions. "It's so good to see you again," he said, his voice muffled against my shoulder. The pat on my back was comforting, yet, beneath the warmth, there was a weight to his gesture, a heaviness that spoke of the unspoken stories and hardships etched into the lines of his face.

As Jeremiah and I stepped back from our embrace, I allowed myself a moment to really look at him. His long, wiry hair, once a uniform shade of deep black, now played host to strands of grey, betraying the passage of time. These changes framed a face that had become almost a stranger to me, concealed beneath a thick, scraggly beard. I forced a twisted grin, attempting to mask my growing concern for the toll that time, and perhaps the burden of our duties, seemed to have exacted on him.

"You look like you've seen better days," I teased, my voice carrying a lightness that belied the undercurrent of unease swirling within me. It was our way, Jeremiah and I, to cloak our worries in banter, a dance of words that had always served to ease the seriousness of life.

"Ain't that the truth," he admitted, his voice tinged with a resignation that seemed to weigh heavily on the air between us. Our laughter was a familiar tune, a customary exchange between Guardian Atum and Guardian Atum Ra, yet beneath the surface joviality, a sense of foreboding gnawed at me.

Jeremiah, only a few years my senior at fifty-three, seemed to carry the world on his shoulders. His visage, marked by the passage of time and the scars of Guardian life, spoke of a weariness that went beyond physical exhaustion. The scruff, the ragged attire, all seemed to tell a story of relentless strife, of a life spent in the shadow of constant threat.

Three years had elapsed since our paths last crossed. In that time, the world had grown only more perilous for those of our calling. The huntings had intensified, necessitating a distance between Guardians not just for our own preservation but for the safety of the settlements we vowed to protect. Whispers of cities fallen, of Guardians slain or vanished into the abyss of self-preservation, filled the air with a sense of impending doom.

Observing Jeremiah now, his rugged appearance, the lines of hardship etched deep into his features, I couldn't help but wonder about the choices he had made in the intervening years. *Had he, like some of our comrades, chosen the path of solitude, hiding from the ever-present threat that stalked us?* The thought unsettled me, casting a shadow over our reunion.

Despite the comfort of our shared history, the reality of our situation lingered at the edge of my consciousness. The world we had sworn to protect was fracturing, its Guardians reduced to shadows of their former selves, scattered and isolated in the face of an overwhelming darkness. As I stood there, facing Jeremiah, I was acutely aware of the delicate balance we maintained, a balance that seemed ever more precarious as the days wore on.

Jeremiah's sombre expression set a grave tone to our conversation. When he uttered the words, "Port Stower has fallen," it was as if a cold hand had gripped my heart. The gravity of his statement, the loss of a city that had thrived with over 2.7 million souls, was a blow that reverberated through the very core of my being.

"Shit," escaped my lips, a feeble attempt to voice the myriad of emotions that welled within me. My response was a whisper in the face of an unimaginable storm, laden with a sorrow that seemed to suffocate the very air around us.

"How can that be?" The question was more a plea for some shred of misunderstanding, a hope that perhaps the reality was not as dire as it seemed. The idea that such a bustling metropolis could be reduced to ruins, its vibrant life extinguished, was a concept my mind struggled to grasp.

Jeremiah's eyes, red and swollen, locked with mine, bearing the brunt of grief that words could scarcely convey.

"It's all but gone," he whispered, his voice a soft echo of despair. His revelation painted a grim picture of a city lost, its people either fled in search of sanctuary or fallen victim to the cruelty of adversaries.

As he recounted the fate of Port Stower, the details of the tragedy unfolded like a dark tapestry before me. The image of over seven thousand souls clinging to the remnants of their city, while the majority lay scattered across desolate regions, was a vision that pierced the very fabric of my soul. The thought of many, in their desperation, seeking refuge in neighbouring cities only to overwhelm the fragile sanctuaries that struggled to support them added layers to the tragedy.

Jeremiah spoke of the Guardians, forced into dangerous liaisons with Earth to procure supplies, only to be hunted down, tortured for information, or mercilessly slaughtered. Each word he uttered was a testament to the sacrifices made and the relentless assault we faced from those who sought to extinguish the light we guarded.

As he spoke, a tear escaped my eye, a solitary witness to the grief that swelled within. My heart ached for the lost, for the city that had once been a beacon of hope and prosperity. The reality of war, its ruthless, unforgiving nature, was not foreign to me. Even my island fortress, a haven I had believed impregnable, bore the scars of conflict.

"Cody," Jeremiah's voice broke through the tumult of my thoughts, softer now, carrying a weight that seemed to tether the very air around us. "Clivilius is in chaos." His words fell like stones into the still waters of my mind, sending ripples through the calm I had fought so hard to maintain.

I cast my gaze downward, a silent acknowledgment of the turmoil that was not confined to distant realms but echoed in our own. "And Earth is no different," I confessed, my voice barely above a whisper. The admission felt like a surrender, an acceptance of the disharmony that had seeped into every corner of our existence.

In a moment that seemed to suspend time itself, Jeremiah extended his hands towards me. The deep scars of iron shackles etched into his wrists were a chilling testament to the hardships he had faced, to the sacrifices made in the name of a cause that seemed increasingly insurmountable. "I need help," he implored, his plea cutting through the veil of my own struggles, reaching out to me with a vulnerability that was both rare and profound.

Those words, "I need help," transported me back to a time before the weight of the world had settled upon my shoulders, to a pivotal moment that had unknowingly set the course for our intertwined destinies. I was swept into the vivid hues of an evening sunset, not as a mere observer but as a participant in a journey that had begun on October 29, 1987.

I was nineteen, my life rooted in the hard soil of my parents' farm near Gawler, the oldest country town on Australia's mainland. The farm was more than just land; it was a legacy of hard work and perseverance, a testament to the values that had been instilled in me from a young age.

That day, after toiling in the fields, I had ventured into the local pub, seeking the simple comfort of a cold beer. It was there, amid the hum of conversation and the clinking of glasses, that fate intervened in the form of Jeremiah. Our initial encounter was anything but auspicious—a collision at the bar that resulted in spilled beer and a momentary flare of tempers. Yet, what could have escalated into conflict swiftly transformed into an unexpected camaraderie.

As Jeremiah insisted on replacing my spilled beer, a gesture of goodwill that bridged the gap between strangers, we found ourselves embroiled in conversation. The beers flowed, and with them, stories of my life on the farm, of days governed by the rising and setting of the sun, of a life defined by the rhythm of the seasons. It was a connection forged not just in shared drinks but in the recognition of shared values—a bond that had only deepened in the years that followed.

Amid the ebb and flow of family life, with its trials of siblings, the watchful care over ageing parents, and the sting of my brother's silent departure to Sydney, the farm had become my sanctuary. It was here, among the rolling fields and under the vast skies, that I found not just solace but a sense of obligation. The land demanded my attention, offering in return a grounding presence amidst the disruption of change. Into this world of mine, Jeremiah entered—a figure shrouded in mystery, his reluctance to speak of his past only deepening the enigma that surrounded him.

Despite the veil of secrecy that clung to him, there was an undeniable connection, a mutual respect that seemed to bridge the gap between our vastly different lives. His admiration for the simplicity and authenticity of farm life resonated with me, offering a glimpse into a soul that, despite its scars, sought something pure and steadfast.

Jeremiah's past, as much as he chose to reveal, painted a picture of a life marked by loss. An orphan, he had been cast adrift in a world that showed little mercy, with the last six months spent surviving the harsh realities of street life. The resilience he must have mustered to navigate such a path was something I could scarcely comprehend.

On a whim, driven by a compassion that surprised even me, I invited Jeremiah to stay with my family. It was an impulsive offer, born from a place of empathy and a desire to extend a hand to someone who, for all his mysteries, had sparked a sense of kinship within me. Little did I know, this simple act of kindness would set us on a path from which there was no turning back.

Later that night, curiosity piqued by my sister's guiding Jeremiah to his temporary quarters, I found myself standing before his door, drawn by a sense of intrigue. A vibrant flash of light seeping from beneath the door halted me in my tracks. My knocks, tentative at first, grew more insistent when they went unanswered. Compelled by a mix of concern and curiosity, I entered the room, only to be met with a sight that defied explanation—an entire wall pulsating with a swirling mass of colourful energy, the room devoid of any sign of Jeremiah.

The moment he emerged, the extraordinary vision dissolving into the ether, I was caught in the intensity of his gaze. His voice, when he spoke, carried a weight that seemed to anchor the very air. "Cody, I need your help," he declared, a conviction underlying his words that left no room for doubt.

Standing there, confronted with the undeniable reality of something beyond my understanding, I was at a loss. The farm, with its predictable rhythms and tangible challenges, had not prepared me for this. Yet, as I met Jeremiah's gaze, I felt a resolve stir within me. This was more than an appeal for assistance; it was a call to step beyond the boundaries of my world, to embark on a journey that would challenge everything I knew.

Uncertain but irresistibly drawn by the mystique of the moment, I found myself nodding in acquiescence to Jeremiah's silent request. He placed a small, rectangular device in my hand, its surface cold and foreign, yet somehow inviting. As he guided my actions, instructing me to point and press, I was momentarily taken aback by the simplicity of the mechanism. Yet, when my finger depressed the button, a sharp prick startled me, and in an instant, a burst of energy erupted from the device, transforming the wall before us into a canvas painted with a kaleidoscope of swirling colours.

Jeremiah's encouragement to step through the vibrant threshold was met with a mixture of fear and fascination. The decision to cross into the unknown was a leap of faith, one that propelled me from the familiar confines of my world into the embrace of an intense darkness. My heart hammered in my chest, a frantic rhythm that mirrored the tumult of my thoughts. The voice that greeted me in that darkness, though not audible in the traditional sense, resonated within the very core of my being. "Welcome to Clivilius, Cody Jennings," it intoned, a greeting that was both an introduction and a confirmation of the journey I had embarked upon.

The immediate surroundings, barely visible in the oppressive gloom, hinted at the presence of water lapping against unseen shores. An eerie silence, so complete it felt like a physical presence, enveloped me, amplifying the sense of isolation. As minutes stretched into what felt like hours, the cold began to seep through my clothing, a creeping chill that spoke of an environment alien to the warm, familiar climes of Gawler. The soft crunch beneath my feet, a sound out of place and time, revealed a terrain covered in snow—a stark contradiction to the natural order of my South Australian world.

Mindful of Jeremiah's warning, I hastened my steps back through the swirling portal, the vibrant hues giving way to the dim familiarity of the room. The relief of return was palpable, a tangible thing that I clung to as I recounted my surreal experience to Jeremiah. His attentive silence, a testament to the gravity of what had transpired, eventually gave way to an explanation that would unfold the mysteries of Clivilius before me.

In the hours that followed, Jeremiah unveiled a narrative so vast and complex, it seemed to stretch the very boundaries of reality. Clivilius, a world parallel yet profoundly connected to our own, was now an integral part of my destiny.

Unbeknownst to us at that moment, danger lurked on the horizon, a shadow that would chase us through the years.

In the thirty-five years since that first night, my life had changed irrevocably. The journey that began in a room bathed in the light of an impossible portal had led me down paths fraught with challenges and sacrifices. Yet, amidst the chaos and the danger, there was also a sense of purpose, a conviction that what I fought for transcended the limits of individual lives. The bond forged between Jeremiah and me in those early days, tested by time and adversity, had become my anchor, a constant in a sea of change.

"Cody? Are you okay?" Jeremiah's voice, tinged with concern, broke through the fog of my memories, anchoring me once again on the weathered timbers of the jetty. The transition from the depths of recollection to the present was jarring.

"Yeah," I responded, my voice a touch too quick, perhaps betraying the tumult within. I shook off the remnants of the past, forcing my mind to focus on the here and now. "What can I do to help?".

Jeremiah's gaze upon me was one of cautious intensity, as if he were weighing the sincerity of my offer against the backdrop of unsaid truths. "How is your settlement doing?" he asked, his question seemingly simple yet laden with the weight of unspoken implications. It was a query that sought not just an update but an understanding of the resilience and spirit of those I had sworn to protect.

"We're struggling," I admitted, the honesty of my response laying bare the vulnerabilities of our small community. "Only three-hundred-and-twenty-six of us left." The number was a dire reflection to the challenges we faced, each loss a blow to the very heart of our settlement. "We still haven't found any other settlements. People are desperate to escape the islands. Last week, sixty-two died at sea." The admission felt like a confession, the weight of the losses a burden that seemed to grow heavier with each passing day. "The seas around the islands are rougher than anything I've ever seen on Earth." The comparison to Earth underscored the severity of our plight, the isolation that compounded our despair.

Jeremiah's reaction was a solemn nod, an acknowledgment of the gravity of my situation. Yet, beneath the surface, I sensed a purpose, a reason for his sudden appearance that went beyond mere reunion. Impatience, borne of desperation and the need for action, crept into my tone. "What do you want, Jeremiah?" I asked directly, my patience frayed by the uncertainty that clouded our reunion. The question was not just a plea for clarity but a demand for honesty. In the face of our shared struggles, the time for obfuscation was past. We stood on the brink, and if Jeremiah had come seeking aid or offering a glimmer of hope, the moment for revelations was now.

The sudden shift of our conversation towards the personal caught me off guard, his eyes widening with an intensity that spoke volumes of his underlying intentions. "You've been seeing someone for several months now. Don't you think it's time you did something about it?" he prodded, his words slicing through the air with a precision that unsettled me.

"She's not ready," I found myself replying almost instinctively, a defensive edge to my voice that I couldn't quite mask. The relationship in question was one of intricate complexity, a delicate balance of emotions and circumstances that I doubted Jeremiah could fully appreciate.

Jeremiah's frustration was palpable, his voice tinged with an urgency that seemed to stem from a place of deep concern. "Since when are any of us ever ready for the responsibility?" he challenged, invoking the welfare of my children into the discourse—a low blow that sent a ripple of unease through me. "Think of your children."

An uneasy chuckle escaped me, a reflexive response to what felt like an absurd line of questioning. *Why was Jeremiah pressing this issue now, of all times?* "The twins are young adults now," I countered, attempting to steer the conversation away from personal waters that were too turbulent to navigate in this moment.

"Yeah. I know," he conceded, yet his gaze remained unyielding, penetrating in a way that seemed to search the very depths of my soul. "But you've been trying to support the settlement yourself for years. How many since the last Guardian was killed?"

The weight of his question settled upon me with a heaviness that was hard to bear. "Eighteen. Sylvie Sprake. Killed twenty-third of December, Two-Thousand," I answered, each word laden with the weight of memories and years of solitary struggle.

"Why are you trying to do it alone? You know I still have two more devices. Let them help you," Jeremiah's plea was laced with a desperation that belied his usual composed demeanour. His words revealed not just a concern for my well-being but an understanding of the enormity of the burden I carried.

Deflecting his inquiries, I questioned Jeremiah's sudden reconnection after years of silence. "Why now? Why after all these years? Why now reconnect with me?" The questions spilled from me, a cascade of confusion and suspicion that seemed to hover in the air between us.

"So many questions," Jeremiah mused, his response accompanied by a head shake that seemed to carry a mix of amusement and resignation. It was a reaction that did little to quell the rising tide of my frustration.

"Don't start that obedience bullshit with me, Jeremiah. You were the one who taught me to question everything," I asserted, my voice sharp, the tension between us escalating like a gathering storm. It was a tension born not just of the moment but of the years and experiences that lay between us, a complex tapestry of mentorship and camaraderie, now fraying at the edges.

Jeremiah's response was immediate and physical, his grip on my arm tightening in a manner that bordered on alarming. "What the hell! Have you gone mad?" I exclaimed, the shock of his action sparking a visceral reaction as I sought to free myself from his grasp. It was a moment that teetered on the edge of conflict, a precipice we had never before approached in our years of acquaintance.

"Luke Smith has been found. He's been given a Portal Key and has now activated it," Jeremiah revealed, his tone hushed and erratic, as if the words themselves were laden with danger. The revelation sent shockwaves through the foundations of my reality.

"What!" I erupted, the implications of this news reverberating through my being. "The Luke Smith? The one Clivilius has told us to watch for?" The question was rhetorical, a verbal manifestation of the turmoil that churned within me. The mention of Luke Smith, a name entwined with prophecies and warnings, was a harbinger of change, a signal that the fragile balance we had been struggling to maintain was about to be irrevocably altered.

Jeremiah's confirmation came with a grin, a simple affirmation that belied the complexity of the situation. "Yes." His smile, in the face of such monumental news, was disconcerting, yet it spoke volumes of his acceptance of the path that lay before us.

The gravity of the moment sank in, and with it, a shift in my demeanour. The confusion and suspicion that had clouded my thoughts gave way to a sense of purpose, a clarity that had been elusive until now. "Then it's time," I declared, the words a solemn vow, a commitment to the challenges that awaited us.

"Yes," Jeremiah agreed, his nod a silent echo of my resolve.

From the depths of my jacket pocket, I produced a small, white plastic card, its surface smooth and unassuming under the dim light. Handing it over to Jeremiah, I watched as his expression morphed from one of mild interest to outright curiosity. He turned the card over in his hands, inspecting it as if it might reveal its secrets through touch alone. "What's this?" he asked, his voice tinged with intrigue.

"It's an access card for Killerton Enterprises," I responded, the words hanging between us like a veiled promise. The card was more than a piece of plastic; it was a key to a door we had only speculated about, a piece of leverage in a game much larger than any we had played before.

Jeremiah's reaction was as swift as it was intense. "What? How did you get this?" he stammered, his composure momentarily slipping. The shock in his voice mirrored the weight of what I had just revealed.

"The how is not important," I deflected, unwilling to divulge the intricacies of my acquisition. The origins of the card were a shadowed path best left unexplored, at least for now.

Our stares locked, a silent exchange of caution and curiosity. "Have you seen the facility?" Jeremiah finally broke the silence, his question laced with a mixture of fear and fascination.

Dropping the bombshell, I admitted, "I've been inside." The confession felt like a gamble, revealing a hand that could either save me or condemn me.

"What!" Jeremiah's exclamation was a mix of shock and concern. "You need to be careful. They'll kill you if you're found out," he warned, his voice laden with the weight of implications my actions carried.

"No!" The volume of my shout surprised even me, a spontaneous burst of emotion that echoed our precarious situation. I quickly moderated my tone, seeking to soften the impact of my outburst. "It's not what you think," I assured him, hinting at the layers of complexity that Killerton Enterprises harboured.

"What do you mean?" Jeremiah's confusion was evident, his brow creasing as he struggled to align my revelations with his understanding of the world.

"Killerton Enterprises isn't what we thought. It can help us," I disclosed, a statement that bordered on the heretical given what we had been led to believe.

Jeremiah's disbelief was palpable, morphing into caution as he processed my words. "Help us? But Clivilius said..." his protest began, rooted in the teachings and prophecies that had guided us.

"I know what Clivilius said. But what if Clivilius was wrong?" I interjected, daring to question the infallibility of our guide. The suggestion was blasphemous, yet it was a seed of doubt that needed planting.

"Wrong?" Jeremiah echoed, the word foreign, almost unthinkable in the context of his beliefs. "Clivilius is never wrong."

"Are you sure about that?" I pressed further, challenging the foundation of our faith. It was a pivotal moment, one that demanded we reevaluate our convictions in the face of new evidence. The access card to Killerton Enterprises was more than a tool; it was a symbol of the potential for change, for a path divergent from the one Clivilius had laid before us. In this exchange, fraught with tension and disbelief, lay the possibility of a new direction, one that required us to question everything we thought we knew.

The silence that followed my proposition hung heavy, a dense fog of contemplation and conflict enveloping Jeremiah.

Seizing the momentary pause, I pressed on, the urgency of the situation lending weight to my words. "You need to get that to Luke," I urged, my finger directed at the access card as if it were a lifeline that could alter the course of our future.

Jeremiah's reaction was immediate. "I don't think it's a good idea. This is treason you're talking," he insisted, his hand extending the card back towards me as if it were a live grenade. "If Killerton Enterprises doesn't kill you for this, Clivilius most certainly will." His words were a stark reminder of the perilous tightrope I walked, yet my resolve remained unshaken.

Refusing to take the card back, I implored him, desperation threading through my voice. "Please, help me get this to Luke." It was a plea, a call to action that transcended our fears, anchored in a mutual understanding of what was at stake.

Jeremiah's response was a shake of his head, a gesture of resignation rather than refusal. "I'm not in a position to make contact with him," he admitted, his words spawning a sea of suspicion within me. The puzzle pieces didn't fit, the narrative he presented incomplete.

"But then how did you know..." I began, my query cut short by his interjection. "But you are," he declared, his hands pressing the card against my chest with a firmness that left no room for argument. The gesture, so definitive, so final, left me grappling for comprehension.

"I don't understand," I confessed, the confusion manifesting plainly upon my face. The situation, already mired in complexity, seemed to warp further with each revelation.

"Gladys Cramer," Jeremiah solemnly revealed, as if the name itself were a key to unlocking the enigma that lay before us.

"Gladys?" I echoed, the name stirring a mix of familiarity and bewilderment within me.

"Yes. Gladys knows Luke Smith very well." The simplicity with which he delivered this piece of information belied the magnitude of its implications.

Accepting the access card once more, a whirlpool of frustration and curiosity swirled within me. *How had Jeremiah come by such critical information, information that had eluded my grasp?* His hand, now resting reassuringly on my shoulder, seemed to anchor me amidst the storm of revelations. "Let me bring her to Clivilius, my dear friend. You need her," he spoke, his voice imbued with a certainty that brooked no argument.

Looking down at the access card in my hand, then back at Jeremiah, my features were a canvas of concern and determination. The path ahead was fraught with uncertainty, yet the decision was clear. "Okay," I conceded, the word carved from a resolve solidified in the crucible of our shared trials. "Let's do it."

4338.205

(24 July 2018)

PERSUASION

4338.205.1

Taking those final two strides with a deliberation that mirrored my resolve, I found myself perched atop the low wall that served as the verandah's boundary. Positioned here, my legs dangled freely, the gentle warmth of the mid-morning sun enveloping me, casting sharp relief on the contours shaped by my navy shorts. It was a moment of brief respite, the calm before the storm of revelations I was about to unleash.

Beside me, a bottle of Gladys' preferred shiraz stood as a silent witness to the importance of the conversation that awaited. Its position on the ledge was precarious, much like the balance I sought to maintain in the dialogue ahead. The sunlight, filtering through the amber contents of the bottle, lent an air of promise to the setting. It was an odd sort of peace offering, chosen with care despite the insistence of the morning hour that perhaps it was too early for such gestures.

The distinctive sound of a silver Honda Civic navigating the steep driveway snapped me back to reality, marking Gladys's arrival with an understated, mechanical fanfare. The car's journey ended atop the driveway, a plateau that mercifully offered level ground. The sight brought a mixture of anticipation and trepidation, a silent acknowledgment of the complexities that our meeting would entail.

"You're out early," I called out, my voice carrying a depth that belied the casual observation. The moment Gladys emerged, my involuntary eye roll betrayed my thoughts. Observing her approach, a bottle also in her grasp, underscored the symmetry of our intentions, if not our expectations.

"Cody," Gladys greeted, her gaze lifting to meet mine as I remained perched on the verandah's wall. The tone of her voice, tinged with surprise yet underscored by a thread of annoyance, hinted at the complexities of our relationship. "What a pleasant surprise. You haven't been by for a few weeks; I thought you'd moved on." The words, though spoken lightly, carried a weight, the implication of neglect hanging between us like an uninvited guest.

"Looks like I shouldn't have bothered," I retorted, the words slipping out more sharply than intended. I held up the bottle of shiraz, its dark contents glinting in the sunlight, a gesture of peace, albeit a fragile one, encapsulated in glass.

Her response was swift, a hurried ascent up the concrete stairs that belied the casual nature of our encounter. "Come inside," she urged, her voice laced with a haste that seemed out of place for such a sunny, languid morning. "I've told you before not to be so obvious," she scolded, her words carrying the weight of a warning, as if our meeting were an act requiring discretion.

"Perhaps you should give me a spare key then," I suggested half-jokingly, closing the distance between us in a few strides. My attempt to lighten the mood was met with resistance, both in her refusal to relinquish her own bottle of shiraz and in her brisk dismissal of my proposal. "Perhaps another day," she replied, her tone final, as she entered the house, the prized bottle still in her grasp.

I hesitated at the threshold, half-expecting the door to shut in my face, a silent rebuke to my unannounced visit. Yet, the finality I anticipated never came. Instead, Gladys continued into the living room, her actions leaving a trail of ambiguity in her wake. *Was this still an invitation, or had I overstepped?*

The question lingered, unanswered, as I contemplated my next move.

Deciding to interpret her actions as a tacit invitation, I shrugged off the uncertainty and stepped inside, quietly closing the door behind me. "Gladys," I called out, a gentle announcement of my presence, seeking to bridge the gap her earlier words had created.

Inside, the sound of Gladys dumping her handbag onto the kitchen bench broke the silence, a soft thud that seemed to echo the tension between us. Beside the bag, she placed her bottle of wine, a silent sentinel amidst the undercurrents of our unspoken discord. The scene echoed the delicate dance we navigated, a balance of familiarity and distance, connection and isolation.

"Gladys, I've missed you," I found myself whispering, the words barely escaping as I drew her into an embrace that felt both familiar and charged with the tension of our recent estrangement. My hands settled lightly on her waist, a touch meant to convey the depth of my sentiment without overwhelming her. A subtle smile, fleeting and delicate, teased the corners of her mouth, softening the serious set of her lips. It was a dance of emotions, her irritation at my absence mingling with an unspoken appreciation for the independence she so fiercely valued. Gladys had always been a beacon of self-sufficiency, revelling in her autonomy, yet the span of weeks without contact seemed to stretch the fabric of our connection just a bit too thinly.

"Where have..." she started, her voice trailing off.

In that moment, propelled by a mixture of desperation and desire, I bridged the distance with a kiss. It was a gesture laden with all the complexities of our relationship—a firm yet tender testament to the history we shared. My tongue delicately traced the outline of her lips, a silent plea for entry, for a chance to communicate in ways words had failed us.

Gladys's response, a soft parting of lips, was a concession, an invitation to delve deeper into the embrace that spoke volumes of our tangled emotions.

As our kiss deepened, my hands ventured further, tracing the contours of her back, memorising the curve of her spine with a reverence reserved for moments of profound connection. Yet, as quickly as the moment had ignited, it was extinguished by Gladys's withdrawal. The sudden lack of her warmth, the absence of her closeness, felt like a cold splash of reality on the flickering flame of our reunion.

"I'm sorry," I found myself saying, the apology a reflex to the abrupt end of our intimacy. "I've had to travel for work this past week. I should have contacted you." The words were technically true, a veil of half-truths to cover the myriad responsibilities that my role as a Guardian entailed. The duty, though noble, had erected barriers in my personal life that I was now scrambling to dismantle. The resolve to improve our communication, to lessen the chasms created by duty and distance, was a promise I made to myself in that moment of silence. The journey back to each other, I realised, would require more than the bridging of physical distances; it necessitated a mending of the emotional gaps that had widened in the wake of my absence.

Gladys's shrug was an enigma, her expression a puzzle I couldn't solve. *Does that mean forgiveness?* The thought fluttered in my mind, a hopeful whisper amidst the tumult of emotions. Leaning in, I sought another kiss, a silent plea for the reassurance her words had yet to provide.

"Cody, stop," she asserted, her voice firmer than before, her palms a gentle barrier against my chest. The rejection stung, a forlorn look swiftly crossing my face as the reality of our strained connection settled heavily upon me. This moment, fraught with vulnerability, was the one I had chosen to unveil the truth about Clivilius. Her anger or dismissal was the last thing I needed.

"What's wrong?" I asked, my voice laced with concern, probing the silence that hung between us.

Gladys shook her head, a gesture of dismissal or perhaps avoidance. "Nothing. I just have a lot on my mind at the moment, that's all," she offered, her voice a mixture of weariness and evasion.

I couldn't let the moment pass, couldn't let her withdraw into herself. My fingers traced the curve of her spine, a touch meant to soothe, to reassure. "You can talk to me, Gladys," I urged gently, hoping to coax her into sharing the weight of her thoughts.

A heavy sigh was her initial response, a sound laden with unspoken troubles. "I'm sure it's nothing," she replied, her voice betraying the heaviness of her 'nothing.'

"With a sigh like that, it doesn't sound like nothing," I countered softly, encouraging her to unveil the thoughts that clearly troubled her. Yet, she slipped from my grasp, distancing herself physically as she had emotionally, moving towards the cupboard with a determination that seemed to shield her vulnerability.

"It's a bit early for that, isn't it?" I remarked, trying to inject a lightness into the air that had become dense with unspoken tensions. My attempt to halt her progress towards the wine glasses was met with a silent acknowledgment of the morning hour's inappropriateness for such indulgences.

Gladys paused, her hand massaging her left temple in a gesture of discomfort or perhaps contemplation. "I suppose it is just a little early," she conceded, her back to me, a wall of silence erecting itself with her turned shoulders.

As I nestled the bottle of shiraz I'd brought onto the middle shelf of the pantry, it took its place among an eclectic collection of other varietals, a silent testament to the moments we'd shared and those yet to come. Gladys's voice broke through my reverie, her question catching me off guard. "But hang on," she paused, turning to face me with a mix of curiosity and surprise, "Didn't you bring wine too?"

Peeking out from the pantry, I felt a momentary flush of uncertainty. "I thought we could share it later," I said, the words slipping out smoothly, though they masked the turbulence of my thoughts. The truth was, now didn't seem like the right time to delve into the deeper, more tumultuous topics that lay between us, least of all the notion of leaving her world behind.

"Hmm," she mused, her gaze drifting past me, as if searching the pantry's contents for answers to unasked questions. She started to speak again, only to stop abruptly, the unfinished sentence hanging in the air like a promise unkept.

The silence that followed was heavy, charged with anticipation and an undercurrent of worry that seemed to etch deeper lines into Gladys's forehead. Her solemn expression, one that spoke volumes of the internal debates raging within her, prompted a frown of disappointment from me. I craved her trust, yet my own secrets loomed large, a barrier to the honesty and openness I so desperately sought.

Retreating further into the pantry, I scanned the shelves for any semblance of a welcome distraction, anything to bridge the gap widening between us. Then, out of the blue, she shared, "I just had a rather strange conversation with Jamie's partner."

The surprise at her sudden divulgence widened my eyes. Since my reunion with Jeremiah yesterday, I had combed through my memory, cataloging names and relationships Gladys had ever mentioned. The realisation that Luke Smith might be more closely connected to Gladys than I had imagined sent a jolt through me. *Was it possible that he, someone from her circle, was entwined with the very dilemmas Jeremiah and I were grappling with?* The thought that he could replace me, or worse, take Gladys away from the world we shared, was a cold splash of fear. My mind reeled, grappling with the implications of her words and the roles we each might play in the unfolding events. The revelation added another layer to the complex tapestry of our relationship, a new angle to consider as I navigated the precarious path of honesty, duty, and the possibility of love.

"Ah, Luke?" I ventured, my tone casual as I feigned a continued interest in the pantry's contents.

"Yes," she confirmed. "You're starting to remember them all, then."

Her voice held a hint of a smile. *Finally, a silver lining,* I thought, emerging from the pantry with a broad grin. "And what did Luke say?" I asked, eager for more details.

"He said that Jamie was sick," she relayed. My initial reaction was one of mild confusion—sickness was hardly unusual. "Well, that hardly seems strange," I remarked, trying to keep the conversation light. "I'm sure Jamie has been sick before."

However, the look of concern that clouded Gladys's features told me there was more to the story. Watching her rush to retrieve a folded piece of paper from her handbag, I felt a knot of anticipation tighten in my stomach. "But then he gave me this really weird list," she explained, her voice laced with unease as she passed the paper to me.

As I unfolded the paper, my mind raced. The contents were far from ordinary—a list that seemed to suggest preparations of a sort. My eyes scanned the items: *concrete, sheds... Immediate storage and protection,* I surmised. My thoughts drifted to the struggles I had faced in Clivilius, the harsh winds that had ravaged my own settlement time and again. The devastation was a bitter reminder of our vulnerability to the elements, of the countless times we had been forced to start over, with every shred of progress erased by nature's fury.

I recalled the biting cold, the relentless wind, and the ferocious snowstorms that had driven us to seek shelter in the caves among the cliffs. Each word on the list echoed my own experiences, resonating with a familiarity that was both comforting and alarming.

Holding the list in my hand, I looked up at Gladys, my expression a mixture of concern and determination. This was no ordinary list; it was a scramble for survival, reminiscent of the measures we had taken to safeguard our own community against the capriciousness of nature in Clivilius. The realisation that Luke's message carried implications far beyond a simple illness was a jolt to my system, a reminder of the broader connections and challenges that lay outside the confines of our immediate world.

"Looks like he has plans to build something," I remarked, striving to maintain a veneer of calm despite the turmoil churning inside me.

"Luke said it was a surprise for his birthday," Gladys explained.

"But he didn't say what he was building?" I probed further, hoping for some detail that might offer a clue to his intentions.

"No," Gladys replied, her pace quickening as if eager to move past the topic. Yet, what she shared next stopped me cold. "And he also gave me his brother's credit card."

I looked up at her, my expression betraying my shock. "And where was his brother?" The implications of Luke's actions, the careless entrusting of a credit card, the absence of his brother—all of it painted a picture far from ordinary.

"No idea. I didn't see him. But I didn't think to ask until after I'd already left," she explained, her words trailing off into the charged silence that enveloped us.

A realisation dawned on me, dark and foreboding. If Luke's partner and brother were now entangled in Clivilius, then Luke's nightmare was indeed just beginning, unfolding on multiple fronts. My own experiences echoed this harsh truth. Initiating someone into the mysteries of the Portal without adequate preparation invited chaos, a relentless scramble for survival amidst the unyielding realities of a new world. The deceit required to mask their true circumstances, to prolong the secrecy of their whereabouts, was a web of lies that became increasingly complex and fragile with each passing day.

I sighed, a sound so faint it barely disturbed the air. The Luke we had awaited, the one shrouded in prophecies and expectations, seemed to be veering dangerously off course. I had harboured hopes that he, of all people, would navigate the intricacies of his situation with foresight and wisdom. Yet, the unfolding scenario suggested a lack of preparation, a naiveté that could have dire consequences not just for him but for all involved.

As I stood there, absorbing the implications of Gladys's revelations, I was struck by the weight of the journey ahead. Luke's actions, seemingly innocuous in the context of a birthday surprise, hinted at a larger, more complex play unfolding—a play in which we were all unwitting actors. The challenge now was not just to support Luke through his ordeal but to mitigate the fallout, to safeguard the fragile balance between our worlds.

"That is quite odd," I found myself agreeing, my attention fully recaptured by Gladys. "I think you should help him," I suggested, the idea forming as I spoke, a spontaneous solution to an increasingly convoluted problem.

Gladys's reaction was immediate, her mouth dropping open in a mix of surprise and disbelief. "What? Help him? Why?" Her confusion was palpable, a mirror to the chaos that Luke's actions were, no doubt, beginning to sow.

"So many questions," I couldn't help but chuckle gently, the irony of the situation not lost on me. I was echoing the words of a dear friend, the same friend who had once chided me with them. "I'm sure Luke had a good reason for it all," I tried to reassure her, despite the uncertainty that clouded my own understanding.

The silence that followed was thick with contemplation, our gazes locked in a silent standoff. My look was a challenge, daring Gladys to question the logic behind my suggestion, to find a reason strong enough to counter the pull of curiosity and concern that I knew tugged at her just as it did at me.

"You've already got the week off work anyway, don't you?" I probed further, a gentle nudge towards the direction I believed she was already considering, even if subconsciously. The mention of her scheduled time off seemed to be the push she needed, a reminder of the opportunity that lay before her.

"Yeah, but..." she started, her voice a testament to the internal conflict she faced, the 'but' hanging in the air like a barrier to the unfolding path.

I shrugged, the gesture an embodiment of nonchalance, designed to ease the weight of the decision. "May as well," I concluded, my voice light, attempting to infuse the moment with a sense of simplicity. "It's not like you're spending your own money." The words were the final nudge, a gentle push towards acceptance, wrapped in the logic of practicality and the unspoken allure of adventure.

As I reached out to Gladys, she yielded to the pull, stepping into the circle of my arms. The closeness, a comforting embrace amidst the whirlwind of uncertainties, was a silent affirmation of our connection. I planted a light kiss atop her head, a gesture of affection and solidarity. In that moment, it wasn't just about persuading Gladys to embark on a peculiar errand; it was about reaffirming the bond that held us together.

"You can stay here and wait for me to get back," Gladys's voice, muffled against my chest, carried a warmth that contrasted sharply with the coolness of the situation at hand. "The cats would like it." Her words, light yet laden with an unspoken trust, drew a wide smile across my face. It was a rare moment of domestic simplicity in the midst of the swirling complexities.

Gladys, with her layers of depth and shadows of past demons, often seemed like a puzzle I was only beginning to piece together. Her struggles, though largely unspoken, were a reflection of the resilience that underpinned her generous spirit. Holding her tighter, I was reminded of the delicate balance between her independence and the interconnectedness of our fates. The desire for her to join me in Clivilius clashed with the knowledge of the risks such a move entailed. The prospect of losing her, not just to the physical distance but to the unpredictable currents of our intertwined destinies, was a thought I could barely entertain.

As Gladys disentangled herself from our embrace, her actions were decisive. Ignoring the bottle of shiraz that sat unattended on the kitchen bench—a symbol of normalcy we both knew was far from our grasp—she reclaimed Luke's list. The urgency with which she snatched it from my grasp, coupled with the swift retrieval of her handbag, spoke volumes of her resolve. "I'll be as quick as I can," she promised, her voice a mix of determination and haste. The finality of the door closing behind her marked the transition from shared warmth to solitude, leaving me to navigate the silence of her absence.

Left alone, my thoughts wandered to the possibilities that Luke's arrival in Clivilius could herald. The hope that it might signal a change, perhaps even a positive one, for our world lingered in the back of my mind, a faint beacon amidst the uncertainty. The complexity of my own situation, with its blend of personal desires and the broader challenges I faced, was a constant balancing act. As I stood there, contemplating the quiet space Gladys had vacated, I was acutely aware of the thin thread that connected us all. The decisions we made, the actions we took, they rippled outwards, touching lives in ways we could scarcely predict. The waiting game began, a test of patience and faith in the unseen forces that guided our destinies.

❖

For those few moments after Gladys's departure, the silence of the house seemed to amplify, each tick of the clock a reminder of the situation unfolding beyond the confines of these walls. I stood there, staring at the door she had closed behind her, lost in a tumult of emotions. Taking a deep breath, I sought to centre myself, to push aside the disappointment of not sharing the significant news I harboured about Clivilius. The reminder of my decision, though tough, felt right. Understanding the precariousness of Luke's situation, especially if he had indeed initiated others into our world, underscored the necessity of Gladys's involvement. The grim reality of the challenges ahead, particularly the inevitable occurrence of the first death, weighed heavily on me.

Snowflake, with her timely interruption, seemed to grasp the severity of the moment as much as any human could. Her affectionate nuzzle against my shin, accompanied by a loud meow, was a welcome distraction, a momentary reprieve from the heaviness of my thoughts. "You're right," I found myself speaking to her, the words more for my own benefit than hers. The idea that helping Luke might inadvertently prepare Gladys for the realities of Clivilius offered a sliver of hope in the complexity of my plight.

Snowflake's reply, a meow that seemed to carry more weight than usual, prompted a smile from me. Her presence, comforting and familiar, brought a sense of normalcy to the whirlwind of thoughts and emotions. "Excellent point, Snowflake. I agree. Luke clearly hasn't told Gladys anything about Clivilius or Guardians. He would be unlikely to take her through the Portal until he had told her," I mused aloud, the conversation with the cat a grounding exercise, a way to sort through my tangled thoughts.

Her emphatic meow, more insistent this time, seemed to echo the urgency of the situation. As I picked her up, her soft fur a comfort under my fingers, I found solace in the simplicity of the moment. Snowflake's continued vocalisations served as a reminder of the immediacy of my concerns. "That's true too," I responded, considering her 'input' seriously. The question of timing, of how long I had until Luke might reveal the full truth to Gladys, loomed large. It was a race against time, one whose outcome could alter the course of our lives in unforeseeable ways.

"Meow," Snowflake agreed, her voice a mix of comfort and urgency.

"Sorry, kitty," I said finally, setting her down gently. The call of my responsibilities, of the people who relied on me in Belkeep, could not be ignored. The brief respite Snowflake provided was a necessary balm, but the reality of my duties remained.

Short on blank wall spaces and under the pressure of necessity, I directed my Portal Key toward the fridge. The small, bright ball of light that shot from the device, colliding with the stainless-steel door, erupted in an explosion of colours—a spectacle that never ceased to amaze me, no matter how many times I had initiated it. "Stay," I instructed Snowflake, my tone firm yet gentle, pointing a finger at her as a visual command.

Snowflake, ever the obedient feline, settled on her haunches, watching me with intense, curious eyes. "Good girl," I praised her softly, my heart swelling with a mixture of affection and apprehension. I knew all too well the inexplicable allure the Portal's energy held over animals, much like its effect on people. Their instinctual curiosity, unhampered by the rational fears that might restrain a human, made them unpredictably brave—or perhaps recklessly so.

As I prepared to step through the swirling colours, Snowflake's sister, Chloe, a bundle of feline mischief and curiosity, made a sudden dart toward the anomaly. "Chloe! Stop!" My command came out as a growl, a protective reflex as I leaped in front of the fridge, blocking her path. The last thing I needed was for one of Gladys's "children" to inadvertently wander into Clivilius.

Snowflake's tail began to wiggle, a sign of her growing excitement or perhaps confusion at the unfolding drama. With my arms outstretched, creating a barrier no curious cat could bypass, I cautiously moved backward through the Portal, my heart racing with the fear of unwanted followers.

The moment my foot touched the cold, stone floor of the Portal Cave, I commanded the Portal to close, sealing off my world from theirs. A deep breath escaped me as I scanned the area anxiously for any sign of Snowflake or Chloe. Relief washed over me as I found no trace of them having followed. "Shit," I exhaled, the tension draining from my body. "That was too close. Gladys would never forgive me."

The thought lingered, festering with implications. While Gladys's forgiveness was a concern, the darker musing of a "carefully orchestrated accident" wormed its way into my thoughts—an insidious suggestion that Gladys wouldn't, couldn't leave her pets behind. The idea was a dark insight to the desperation I felt, a measure of how far I might be willing to go to ensure her safety, and perhaps, her presence in Clivilius.

I slapped myself across the face, a sharp rebuke to the dangerous path my thoughts had wandered down. "Don't be a fool," I scolded myself, the sting of the slap a physical reminder of the fine line I was teetering on. The moral quandaries of my role, the sacrifices and decisions it entailed, were a constant battle—a struggle between what was necessary and what was right. In that moment, standing alone in the cold embrace of Clivilius, I was reminded of the weight of my responsibilities, not just to the people I sought to protect, but to the moral compass that guided me.

HOPE

4338.205.2

Standing on the jagged embrace of the rocks that bordered Lake Gunlah, I couldn't help but reflect on the stark, unyielding landscape that had defined my existence in Belkeep for nearly three decades. The lake, its surface a mirror nearing the brink of freezing, lay encased in the desolation that had come to symbolise our fight for survival in this relentless terrain. Lewyyd Drikarsus, our steadfast Chief, had seen in this harsh vista a final battleground for our people. Here, on the edge of survival, we made our stand against Clivilius' merciless embrace, a last bastion against the oblivion that threatened to consume us should we falter again.

Belkeep, a land more stone than soil, offered little in the way of nurture. The dreams of cultivation and growth were continuously dashed against the reality of its barren heart, the weather a constant adversary to our endeavours. Guardians, myself included, became the lifeline of our community, our efforts focused on erecting structures to shield our precious, hard-won provisions from the bitter clutches of the cold.

Looking across to the far side of the lake, the stone cottages there stood as silent sentinels to both our hopes and our desolation. Grey smoke, the breath of life within, curled into the sky, a stark contrast to the promise of prosperity that had once been envisioned for this place. The vision of a thriving lakeside community, one where the settlers could fish and live off the land, remained just that—a vision, elusive and unattained.

As the first snowflakes of the day began their descent, a soft, cold caress against the backdrop of the never-ending winter, I drew my large brown fur coat closer around me. The chill of Belkeep was not just physical; it seeped into my bones, a constant reminder of the life I had left behind. My mind wandered to Earth, to memories of a sun that warmed the skin and a sky of the deepest blue.

Yet, it was not just the harshness of Belkeep that anchored me to this place. Responsibility, a bond as unbreakable as the rock beneath my feet, held me fast. The twins, my charge, were bound to this land, and in turn, so was I. Their safety, their future, was intertwined with the fate of Belkeep, a burden that weighed heavily on my shoulders. In the solitude of the lake's edge, amidst the quiet fall of snow, I grappled with the reality of my duty and the longing for a world left behind, a tether to both realms that I bore with a weary heart.

The rhythmic approach of heavy winter boots against the unforgiving rocks was a welcome distraction from my introspective musings. The movement was lively, almost dancing, accompanied by the soft hum of a melody that seemed to weave through the chilled air, infusing it with a warmth all its own. My lips curved into a broad smile, my heart lifting in response to the familiar sound. In all of Belkeep, there was only one person whose presence could pierce the veil of gloom that often settled over us.

"Aren't you cold, Krid?" I asked, amusement colouring my tone as I took in the sight of her short, skinny legs and bare arms, seemingly impervious to the cold.

"I'm never cold!" Krid proclaimed with the kind of cheerful defiance only a six-year-old could muster. Her hands flew above her head as she twirled, a physical embodiment of her words.

Laughing softly, I crouched to her level, opening my arms in anticipation of the hug I knew would come. "It's good to see you," I told her, and as our embrace tightened, I was reminded of the unique place Krid held in the fabric of our community. Born to the harsh realities of Clivilius, she had no frame of reference for Earth, no concept of a life beyond the struggles and rugged beauty of this world.

The loss of Guardian Sylvie had cast a shadow over us all, plunging many into a darkness from which they couldn't escape. The burden of sustaining the community, once shared, became almost unbearable in the wake of the collective despair that followed. The decision to halt the passage of new arrivals through the Portal was one borne of necessity, a grim acknowledgment of our limitations in the face of overwhelming loss. As some chose the tragic escape offered by the cliffs, the community was left to reckon with the voids left behind.

Krid's resilience in the face of such adversity was nothing short of remarkable. Orphaned at a tender age, she had become the collective charge of a community grappling with its own survival. Yet, it was her unyielding positivity, her innate cheerfulness, that marked her as a beacon of hope in our often bleak existence. In Krid, I saw the promise of a new generation, one perhaps better equipped to navigate the challenges of Clivilius, to find joy in the midst of hardship.

"I've brought you back something," I whispered to Krid, as I reached into the depth of my back pocket. The anticipation in her eyes, that spark of unbridled curiosity, was a light against the backdrop of Belkeep's harshness.

"Another surprise?" Krid's voice was a mix of excitement and wonder, her gaze fixed on me with an intensity that made the moment feel all the more significant.

"I thought you might like to add this one to your collection," I said, my voice softening as I slowly opened my hand to reveal the treasure it held—a small magnet, intricately shaped like an island. The reveal was slow, deliberate, a moment suspended in time between the giver and the receiver.

"What is it?" Krid inquired, her delicate fingers taking the magnet from my palm with a gentleness that belied her youthful enthusiasm. She examined it closely, her face a picture of concentration and awe.

"It's a place called Tasmania," I explained, watching her reaction closely. "It's where our next Guardian will come from." The weight of that statement, the promise it carried, seemed to hang in the air between us.

"It is?" Her response was one of pure wonder, her eyes growing wider with the realisation of what this small piece of metal represented.

"Yes. It is." My chuckle was soft, a sound that barely rose above the gentle whisper of snowflakes. My gaze drifted past Krid to Freya, who approached with an unconscious rub of her arms against the chill. "Honestly, Freya. You're as bad as Krid here," I called out, a playful reprimand that belied the warmth I felt at the sight of them together.

Krid, ever eager to share her newfound treasure, wasted no time in dashing over the uneven terrain towards Freya. "Freya!" she exclaimed, her voice carrying across the distance. "Look what Guardian Cody gave me," she beamed, presenting the magnet with all the pride of a seasoned collector.

Standing back, I observed the interaction between my daughter and Krid. The bond they had formed in the wake of tragedy was nothing short of remarkable. Krid, who had lost so much so early, had found in Freya a sister, a mentor, a friend. And Freya, along with Fryar, represented the continuation of a legacy, the hope of a future that their mother and I had dreamed of. The loss of their mother at their birth was a wound that time had softened but never fully healed. Watching them now, strong-willed and resilient, a swell of pride mixed with a poignant ache filled me. I hoped, more than anything, that she would be proud of the individuals they were becoming—of their strength, their compassion, and their unyielding spirit. In them, I saw the best of what we could be, a testament to the enduring power of love and the indomitable will to forge ahead, even in the face of Belkeep's relentless challenges.

"It's beautiful," Freya's voice, tinged with sincerity, pulled me back from the edge of my worries. Her eyes, when they met mine, held a warmth that felt like a balm to the cold uncertainty that had settled within me.

I smiled, a gesture that felt both reflexive and genuine in the moment. The habit of collecting small mementos from my travels, or in this case, a discreet souvenir from the side of the fridge, was a practice I found comfort in. Each item, like the magnet shaped like Tasmania, held stories, memories, and sometimes, promises of hope for the future. The thought that Gladys would never miss it wasn't just a justification; it was a small testament to the two worlds I navigated, the many lives intertwined with mine.

"Chief Lewyyd wants a word with you," Freya's voice, now carrying a note of gravity, shifted the atmosphere. Her standing up was a physical echo of the importance she placed on her message. "He's waiting for you in the Council Cottage." The mention of the Chief and the Council Cottage instantly signalled the seriousness of the matter at hand, a reminder of the responsibilities that came with being a Guardian in Belkeep.

"And Fryar?" The concern for my son, barely contained beneath my guardian façade, surfaced with my question.

"He hasn't returned," Freya's gentle head shake was a visual confirmation of my fears. The absence of Fryar, coupled with the ominous signs of an approaching storm, cast a long shadow over my heart, magnifying the anxiety that buzzed like an undercurrent beneath my skin.

As the darkening sky hinted at the impending tempest, Freya voiced the unspoken concern. "Aren't you worried about him?"

"Of course I am," came my immediate response, the admission heavy with the burden of leadership and fatherhood intertwined.

"Then why not send a search party?" Her suggestion was pragmatic, a beacon of action in the paralysis of worry.

"Is that what Chief wants me for?" The question lingered in the cold air, my thoughts tangled with the possibility that Chief Lewyyd's summons was a prelude to a search for Fryar.

Freya's soft chuckle, tinged with the wisdom born of understanding the intricate web of our community's dynamics, caught me off guard. "Chief doesn't need your permission for such things. If he wanted to do it, he would." Her words, though light, carried the weight of truth—a reminder of the Chief's autonomy in decision-making.

"But he doesn't want to?" I sought clarification.

"No," Freya replied, her tone sobering. "He says we've already lost too many. Fryar should never have tried to rescue them from the boat. Nobody has ever survived those seas." The finality in her statement, the acceptance of a grim outcome as an inevitability, settled heavily upon us.

"You sound like you've convinced yourself he's dead," I noted, my gaze shifting between Freya and the young child, probing the depth of despair and denial that wove through their responses.

"I know he's —" Freya began, her voice faltering.

"Not dead," Krid interjected with a certainty that belied her years, her small voice a beacon of hope in the gathering gloom.

Her assertion drew my attention, her childlike innocence standing in defiance of the harshness that defined our lives. Crouching to meet her gaze, I sought to understand the foundation of her belief. "How do you know that?"

"Probably the same way I do," Freya answered before Krid could respond, her admission adding layers to the mystery.

"And that would be?" My curiosity deepened, intrigued by the connection they seemed to share, a bond that hinted at knowledge beyond what was physically known.

"I don't know how to describe it," Freya admitted, her words trailing off into uncertainty. "I can just —"

"Feel him," Krid completed the thought, her simple yet profound assertion echoing with a truth that seemed to transcend logic.

"Exactly!" Freya confirmed, her agreement solidifying the shared sentiment.

Observing them both, skepticism mingled with a begrudging acceptance within me. Freya's connection to Fryar, as his twin, was understandable—a bond that perhaps facilitated a deeper, intuitive understanding. But Krid? Her inclusion in this shared certainty puzzled me, defying logical explanation. Yet, the islands, with their labyrinthine caves, provided ample shelter. I clung to the belief that Fryar, resourceful and resilient, would find refuge from the storm.

"So, if it's not about Fryar, what does Chief want to see me about? I'm very busy," I stated, my voice laced with a hint of irritation. My role in this community was one I took seriously, often putting the needs of Belkeep above my own. Yet, my patience for Chief Lewyyd's sometimes drawn-out deliberations was wearing thin, especially with the pressing concerns weighing heavily on my mind.

"He wants to go over the next phase of the development plan with you. I believe he has —" Freya began, her explanation hinting at yet another lengthy discussion that awaited me. But I couldn't afford to get entangled in another one of Chief Lewyyd's exhaustive planning sessions—not now, not with Fryar still missing and my heart torn between duty and personal anguish.

With a hand raised to halt her words, I sighed deeply. This sigh was not just one of resignation but also a recognition of the burdens that leadership entailed. "Tell Chief I'm on my way." My words were a concession, an acknowledgment of the responsibilities that I could not, in good conscience, ignore.

Freya's disbelieving gaze fixed on me, her eyes a mirror reflecting a challenge unspoken. It was as if she dared me to demonstrate the commitment I so often professed, a silent accusation that perhaps my actions didn't always align with my words. "Well, if you're on your way, you can come with me and tell him that yourself," she countered, her challenge laid bare.

"I just need to do something first," I found myself saying, an attempt to straddle the line between the immediate needs of our community and the pressing, personal duty that clawed at my conscience.

"So, I'll tell Chief you're not coming then," Freya declared, her voice firm, her decision to leave no room for further discussion. Her steps away from me were decisive, a physical manifestation of her disappointment.

"Freya!" The call was a plea, laden with a mix of desperation and resolve. "I will come." My assurance was a promise, not just to her but to myself. As I watched her retreating figure, the sway of her dark hair, so reminiscent of her mother, stirred a well of emotion within me. The reminder of what we had lost, and what we still stood to lose, was a poignant undercurrent to our interaction.

Looking down at Krid, who remained steadfastly by my side amidst the shifting currents of our conversation, I noticed the gleam of curiosity in her dark, thoughtful eyes—a testament to the depth and insight far beyond her years. "You'd better get yourself indoors too," I advised, my tone gentle yet firm, subtly nudging her towards the safety and warmth that Freya's presence promised.

"When will she be here?" Krid's question, delivered with an earnest gaze lifted towards me, momentarily caught me off guard. Her inquiry, seemingly innocent, carried an undercurrent of expectation that piqued my interest.

"Who?" I found myself asking, the confusion evident in my voice.

"The new Guardian," she clarified, her voice steady and sure. The awareness in her statement, the assumption of not just a new Guardian's arrival but the specificity of her gender, surprised me. It was a revelation, a piece of knowledge that I hadn't anticipated her to possess or ponder.

Taken aback by her insight, I pressed further, curiosity now fully piqued. "How do you know she's a woman?" My question was more than mere curiosity; it was a probe into the depth of Krid's understanding, a quest to comprehend the source of her conviction.

Krid's response came as a simple shrug, a gesture that belied the complexity of the knowledge she seemed to hold. The simplicity of her action, devoid of explanation, only deepened the mystery that surrounded her, a reminder of the unique perspective she brought to our intertwined lives.

I couldn't help but smile softly at her, a mixture of admiration and wonder stirring within me. Krid's untainted curiosity, her innate sense of knowing, was an elusive riddle that I couldn't answer. "Well, off you go then," I encouraged, gently steering her towards home. Her presence, her questions, had ignited a spark of curiosity within me, a reminder of the many layers and secrets that our small community harboured. Yet, I recognised that now was not the time, nor the place, to delve into an inquisition.

❖

As I cinched the coat tighter, the fabric's rough texture offered scant consolation against the biting chill that seemed to seep into my very bones. My legs, aching from the cold and my own inertia, served as a reminder of the time spent in vigil at the cavern's mouth. The wind, a relentless force, tore across the entrance with a ferocity that seemed to mock our attempts at shelter, its howl a constant companion in this desolate landscape. Snowflakes, caught in the tempest's embrace, swirled and settled momentarily on the hard rock surface before succumbing to the inevitable melt, a fleeting resistance to the freeze soon to claim the land.

Inside, the cavern's attempt at warmth was a battle half-lost to the omnipresent cold. The kerosene lamps, scattered and flickering, cast long shadows that danced eerily against the walls, their light struggling to pierce the pervasive chill.

The two large translucent screens along the cavern's highest side, stood as silent gateways of my domain. One screen, in particular, held a significance that weighed heavily on my heart—a reminder of the Guardians' dormant state, a visual testament to the once-vibrant force now stilled. This screen, a portal, stood an unmoving testament to the memories and legacies of those who had stood watch over Belkeep, now served as a poignant marker of what I had lost and what I still fought to preserve.

Reflecting on the early days of my guardianship, the rationale behind choosing such a desolate, frozen, and isolated place for our settlement often plagued my thoughts. The barren, unforgiving landscape of Belkeep seemed an improbable choice for a community. Yet, any questions regarding the decisions of Clivilius were met with a firm doctrine—Clivilius made no mistakes. This belief, instilled within me, served as a cold comfort amidst the challenges we faced.

I sighed deeply, a melancholic gaze fixed on the two vacant Portal screens that stood as silent witnesses to a once vibrant connection. One of these screens, now dormant, had once buzzed with the life force of two Guardian companions, their energy a beacon in the bleakness of our surroundings. Their absence left a void, a palpable silence where once there was the comforting hum of camaraderie and shared duty. They, like me, were natives of South Australia, a detail that lent an additional layer of connection and loss to their absence. This shared origin had fostered a sense of familiarity, a bond that had transcended the mere coincidence of birthplace to become a cornerstone of our shared identity as Guardians.

I sighed deeply, looking forlornly at the vacant Portal screen. It had been dormant for many years now. The memory of Jeremiah's words echoed in the hollows of the cavern and the hollows of my heart. "I've been watching them closely for a long time. Just as I have you," he had said, his voice imbued with a knowledge that seemed to stretch beyond the confines of our present circumstances. "You will be good for each other." His assertion, spoken with the certainty of one who had peered into the depths of fate, had been a guiding light. Soon after, he had equipped them, as he had equipped me, with a device, a Portal Key—a tangible link to the duty we were bound to and a symbol of the trust placed in us.

The arrival of Freya momentarily pulled me from the depths of my reverie. Her presence, marked by the shedding of her winter cloak's hood, and the cold air, playing across her flushed cheeks, served as a stark reminder of the harshness of our environment, a reality we all bore with a resilience born of necessity.

"Can you get these things for Chief?" Her voice, breaking through the solemn quietude of the cavern, brought my focus back to the immediate challenges we faced. The list she handed me was a small, yet significant, testament to our continued efforts to thrive in an environment that offered little concession to human habitation.

I couldn't help but scoff at the request, a reaction not directed at Freya but at the broader situation. The list in my hand was a bitter reminder of our technological backwardness, a jarring juxtaposition to the advancements I knew Earth continued to make—a reality unknown to those like Freya, who had never seen anything beyond the rugged confines of Belkeep. Tucking the list beneath my coat, I felt its weight as a symbol of our enduring struggle, a tangible representation of the gulf between the world I came from and the world I was trying to sustain.

Jeremiah is right, I found myself reflecting, the thought of the two remaining Portal Keys weighing heavily on my mind. The decision to let Gladys choose the recipient of the final device lingered as a strategic move, a part of a larger plan that required careful manipulation. *Anyone but Beatrix*, I resolved, understanding the necessity of keeping the two sisters apart for the plan to succeed. It was a calculated effort to coerce Luke into finding us, a manoeuvre that carried both risk and potential reward.

"Our settlement is struggling to survive. We are at the worst that I have ever seen," Freya's admission, laden with a grave sincerity, mirrored my own perceptions. Her words were a sobering affirmation of the dire circumstances we faced, a reality that demanded action, resilience, and hope.

"Luke Smith will find us. I promise," I assured her, my voice heavy with a conviction I needed her to believe in. The certainty in my declaration was not just for her, but a mantra for myself, a beacon of hope in the challenging times we navigated.

Freya's reaction, however, was a mixture of frustration and resignation, her belief in my assurances waning. "Go listen to Chief. He has a good plan," she pushed, her tone carrying the weight of weariness interlaced with a sense of urgency. It was clear she held little faith in the promises of guardians yet unseen, her patience thinning against the backdrop of her reality.

I couldn't help but frown at my daughter, the complexity of our relationship deepening in the moment. Freya, who had once hung on my every word, captivated by the stories of my past and the world beyond our harsh existence, had shifted. She had grown resistant to the prophecies, to my promises of a time when a new Guardian would unite the Clivilius world. The resilience and wonder that had once defined her were now marred by the scars of loss and the relentless fight for survival. She had grown, not just in age, but in perspective, becoming a figure of pragmatism born from the ashes of disillusionment.

"It's time," I found myself saying, an announcement that felt both monumental and heavy with the burden of what it entailed. My hands rested on her shoulders, a gesture meant to ground both of us in the moment.

Her shoulders tensed under my touch, rising in a shrug that spoke volumes of her internal struggle. "Time for what?" Freya's voice was tinged with a sadness that cut through me, a reminder of the innocence lost to the trials we faced.

"It's time to complete the team," I stated, the words ringing with a sense of finality and resolve.

Freya's gasp cut through the cavern's chill like a knife. "Is it safe?" Her question, laden with fear and the desire for reassurance, echoed the internal conflict that raged within me.

"No," I found myself admitting, the truth heavy on my tongue. "It's never safe." The reality of our existence, fraught with danger at every turn, was a bitter pill to swallow, yet it was our reality nonetheless.

"Then why?" Her frustration, a mirror to my own internal turmoil, demanded an answer. "Haven't we seen enough death already?"

The weight of her questions compelled me to shed the layers that shielded me from the cold, a symbolic disrobing that felt almost ritualistic in its intent. My winter coat, a barrier against Clivilius's unforgiving chill, was discarded over the rocks, revealing the stark contrast of my attire—jeans and a polo shirt, ill-suited for the climate yet emblematic of a connection to a world beyond. This act of shedding my coat was a transition, a preparation for the journey back to Earth.

Turning to face the silent Portal, I paused, the weight of my Guardianship pressing down on me. Glancing back at Freya, her eyes searching mine for an explanation, a justification for the risks, the pain, and the uncertainty that shadowed my every step, I realised that there was none to offer, no way to halt the inevitable cycle of life and death. Yet, I carried within me a burning ember—hope.

"Hope," was all I could muster, the word barely a whisper, yet it carried the entirety of my conviction. Approaching Freya, I placed a gentle kiss on her forehead, an act imbued with the promise of a future, of possibilities yet to unfold.

With my mind set on the destination, *Gladys Cramer kitchen*, I silently invoked Clivilius's power. The dormant Portal sprang to life, its screen a canvas of swirling colours, a gateway to a world beyond the harshness of Belkeep. Casting a final look at Freya, I stepped through the Portal, the vibrant hues enveloping me, as the gateway closed behind me, leaving behind the cold, the uncertainty, and the promise of hope that fuelled my perseverance.

DESPAIR

4338.205.3

The large kitchen, once bathed in the ethereal luminescence of the Portal, succumbed to an eerie darkness as the glow ebbed away, plunging me into a sensory void. The abrupt shift sharpened my senses, drawing them towards the remnants of the evening's revelries. I inhaled deeply, my nostrils flaring as they picked up the unmistakable meld of burnt ash and red wine—a scent that wove visions of intimacy and camaraderie into the fabric of the night. Before me, on the cold, hard surface of the bench, stood two empty bottles of shiraz, their labels dulled by the absence of light. They were flanked by a pair of wine glasses, their crystal rims stained with the echo of shared laughter and whispered secrets.

A simmering anger began to coil within me, its heat searing through my veins, a visceral response to the betrayal unfolding before my eyes. With a hand that trembled with the force of my burgeoning wrath, I reached for the second bottle, turning it to catch the faint light filtering through the window. It was unmistakably mine—a bottle reserved for a moment of celebration, for a toast to difficult conversations and a Guardian life revealed. The realisation that Gladys had uncorked this symbol of personal triumph to share with another was a blow, a sharp stab of treachery that constricted my chest and made it hard to breathe.

The house, which had been a sanctuary of warmth and welcome, now felt like a mausoleum, its halls draped in shadows and its silence oppressive, suffocating. I moved through the living room, each step heavy with the weight of my disillusionment. The archway that led into this space, once an invitation to comfort and laughter, now loomed like the entrance to a tomb. As I paused, a soft moan, barely perceptible, drifted from the direction of Gladys's bedroom. The sound, laden with implications, clawed at my already frayed nerves. Doubts, like voracious beasts, gnawed at my mind. *Was Gladys in the arms of another? Was this the reason behind her insistence that I remain hidden away, a secret kept from the world?* Her earlier explanations, veiled as concern over her parents' disapproval, now unravelled, threadbare and insubstantial.

My heart pounded against my ribcage. She was meant to be my Guardian, my partner in navigating the complexities of a world that demanded vigilance and strength. To my daughter, I had pledged the gift of hope—a promise that now felt as burdensome as the world itself upon my shoulders.

The sounds of more moans, soft yet profoundly disturbing, sliced through the silence, each one a blow to my already fragile state. I closed my eyes tightly, as if the mere act could somehow barricade my heart against the pain. Despite the absence of physical intimacy between us, the mere thought of its possibility with another gnawed at my already battered heart. Memories, like spectres from a past I struggled to keep at bay, surged forth. Grace, my beacon of light, whose life was snuffed out far too early, leaving behind a void no amount of time could completely fill. My fingers clenched, the knuckles white against the wooden frame, while my other hand pressed hard against my mouth, a futile attempt to silence the sobs that clawed their way up from the depths of my soul.

"It's not true. You're just being irrational," I murmured to myself, a desperate attempt to stem the tide of despair. *You're a good man, Cody. She just doesn't understand you. If she did, she'd choose you,* I reassured myself, clinging to this thought like a lifeline in the stormy sea of my emotions.

The voice within urged me on. *You have to help her see.* My gaze drifted down the hallway, fixating on the bedroom door that stood ajar, a sliver of space that felt as insurmountable as a chasm. "I have to show her," I whispered, the words barely leaving my lips.

With each quiet step towards the door, my resolve flickered like a candle in the wind. A sudden clap of thunder, distant yet ominous, mirrored the turmoil within me. Doubt, like a shadow, crept into my mind, whispering words of caution against the recklessness that threatened to take hold. This moment of hesitation, charged with the electricity of the gathering storm, was a crossroads. The path I chose next could either lead to reconciliation or further into the abyss of misunderstanding and pain.

Don't be a fool.
But I have to help her.
She will hate you if you do.
I have to take her.

My heart was a drumbeat of chaos, pounding against the walls of my chest with a ferocity that mirrored the tumult within. A tempest of pain and anger whirled through my veins, a heady and dangerous concoction that threatened to overwhelm my senses. Yielding to this relentless tide, I found myself crossing the threshold into Gladys's sanctuary, a space now charged with a palpable tension where emotions ran rampant and the threads of fate seemed perilously entwined.

As I entered, the moans grew louder, a discordant symphony with the shifting shadows on Gladys's bed. A flash of lightning, brief yet blinding, tore through the darkness, illuminating the room in stark relief. My breath caught in my throat as the light laid bare the unexpected truth—Gladys was alone, her distress unshared.

The night air was split again by the sound of thunder, each clap more menacing than the last, as if the very heavens were bearing witness to the drama unfolding below. A stifled cry broke from Gladys's lips, her form a tangle of limbs and linen. Panic, swift and sharp, pierced my heart. *Was she in the grip of a seizure?* The possibility of her coming to harm under my watch spurred me into action.

I rushed to her side, my intentions pure, yet my efforts to disentangle her only served to tighten the snare. The room was intermittently lit by the fierce dance of lightning and thunder, each flash a momentary beacon in the storm of our turmoil.

"Cody!" Gladys's voice pierced the darkness, laden with terror. "They're coming!"

In my haste to reach her, the heavy blanket became an unexpected adversary. My balance faltered, and my hands, in their misguided attempt to save, instead pushed Gladys further into the fray, one inadvertently sealing her cries. Desperation clawed at me as I fumbled for the edge of the blanket, my mind racing with the fear of causing her harm.

The sudden, sharp pain of teeth biting into my hand broke through the frenzy. "Gladys!" I hissed, a mix of pain and urgency in my whisper. "Stop!"

Her movements ceased, and for a moment, time stood still. Her eyes, wide with fear, met mine, and in them, I saw a reflection of terror. A cold realisation washed over me, chilling me to the core. *Was it me she feared?* The intimacy of our entanglement, the confusion of the moment, had morphed into a tableau of misunderstanding and fear. The weight of her gaze bore into me, a silent accusation that left me grappling with a profound sense of dread.

"Don't scream," I urged, my voice a mixture of concern and desperation. "You were having a nightmare, thrashing about. I was worried you'd hurt yourself." Yet, as I withdrew my hand from her mouth, a part of me bristled at the necessity of such a measure.

Gladys's response was immediate and forceful. "What the fuck are you doing here? How did you get in my house?" Her words, sharp as daggers, pushed me both physically and emotionally. The shove, though not unexpected, sent a jolt of panic through me. This wasn't how I had envisioned our encounter; her fear and confusion were palpable, mirroring my own internal turmoil.

I was cornered, caught in a maelstrom of emotions and circumstances far beyond my control. The urgency of the situation bore down on me, demanding immediate action, yet my options were limited. "I can't stay long," I whispered back, urgency lacing my voice. The plea for trust was a gambit, my last card to play. "You have to trust Luke. Clivilius is real. Do whatever he asks you to do." My words hung in the air, a desperate attempt to bridge the chasm of misunderstanding between us.

Her hazel eyes bore into me, a mix of incredulity and defiance, barely illuminated in the dim light that fought to pierce the darkness. "Trust me, Gladys. The lives of a thousand people are at stake. We need Luke." The gravity of the situation weighed heavily on me, a burden I hoped to share, if only she would believe me.

Her skepticism was evident. "We? How do you know about Clivilius?" she pressed, her voice a blend of curiosity and suspicion. It was a question that deserved an answer, one that I couldn't afford to give. Time was a luxury I didn't have.

"I have to go," I stated, a mixture of regret and resolve propelling me to my feet. The temptation to linger, to explain, to justify my presence and actions was strong, but the risk was greater. I couldn't afford to delve into the complexities of our situation, not like this.

Without a backward glance, without waiting for her response or understanding, I sprinted out of the room. The question of her companion's identity lingered in my mind, a thorn of curiosity and jealousy, but I pushed it aside. If I couldn't be the one at her side, then at least I could steer her towards someone who might protect her, someone who might make a difference.

In a final act, a message of sorts, I grabbed the empty wine bottle from the bench, its presence a bitter reminder of the evening's revelations. With a swift motion, I illuminated the fridge door with the colours of Clivilius, a silent beacon of my visit and a cryptic sign of the truths I couldn't voice. Then, in an instant, as if swallowed by the very shadows that filled the room, I was gone, leaving behind a whirlwind of confusion, fear, and the faintest glimmer of hope that my message would find its mark.

❖

Collapsed upon the cave floor, the soft snow beneath me offered no comfort against the biting chill that seeped into my bones. The wind's mournful howl navigated the craggy expanse of the Portal Cave's entrance, a frigid breeze that seemed to carry the weight of my despair. My body convulsed with shivers, each tremor a testament to the cold and the tumultuous storm of emotions raging within. Tears, indistinguishable from the melting snowflakes on my cheeks, were my silent companions as I clutched the empty shiraz bottle—a symbol of lost promises and shattered dreams—in my quaking hands.

The intensity of my emotions crescendoed into a surge of rage and despair, a force so overwhelming it eclipsed even the agony of losing my beloved Grace. Driven by this tumult, I found the strength to rise to my knees, my spirit fuelled by a blend of anguish and defiance. With a cry that seemed to tear from the very depths of my soul, I unleashed my fury upon the inanimate object that I held. The bottle, once a vessel of shared moments and cherished memories, was propelled from my grasp and met the rocky cave wall with a thunderous crack. It shattered upon impact, its fragments scattering like the myriad pieces of my broken heart, each shard a reflection of my inner turmoil.

The sound of the shattering bottle reverberated through the cavern, a symphony of my frustration and sorrow. The echoes served as a haunting reminder of what had transpired, of what we had become. In the wake of the silence that followed, a profound realisation settled over me, as palpable as the cold that enveloped my form. The finality of the act, the symbolic breaking of the bottle against the unyielding rock, mirrored the irrevocable breaking of us.

In that solemn, solitary moment, the truth crystallised within me, resonating with the icy air of Clivilius and the desolation of my surroundings. We were over. This conviction permeated my being, settling into my bones with a chill that surpassed the physical cold. It was a realisation that marked the end of an era, the closing of a chapter that I had hoped would tell a different story. The emptiness of the cave around me mirrored the emptiness I felt, a void where once there was hope, now filled only with the echoes of my despair.

4338.206

(25 July 2018)

SEPARATION

4338.206.1

"Whoa! What happened in here?" The cavernous expanse of the Portal Cave, with its ancient walls and the eerie silence that often filled its vastness, seemed to amplify Freya's voice as she stepped inside. Her words, tinged with concern and surprise, bounced off the stone surfaces, a stark contrast to the solitude I had been enveloped in since my return.

The hours since I had fled Gladys's house had stretched into an eternity of reflection and regret. Not a moment of rest had graced me; instead, I was haunted by the vivid replay of my actions, each recollection sending shivers of pain and guilt coursing through my veins. As I bent to retrieve another shard from the floor, the remnants of my outburst, I masked the turmoil with a veneer of indifference. "It's nothing," I stated, my tone striving for detachment.

Freya moved closer, her steps measured in the dim light, suggesting a blend of concern and wariness. "Come, sit," she urged, gesturing to the cold rock beside her, a makeshift seat in our austere surroundings.

I countered, my attention fixed on the task of cleaning up the dangerous debris scattered around us. "Someone's going to get hurt if I don't clean up this mess," I said, focusing on the tangible, perhaps as a means to anchor myself amidst the storm of emotions.

Freya's retort was swift, carrying an edge of insight that pierced my defences. "Hmph. I'd say someone's already a bit hurt." Her observation, simple yet profound, forced me to confront the depth of my own pain.

My response was almost reflexive, my gaze, red and swollen from the tears and turmoil, meeting hers. "I don't know what came over me," I confessed, the words heavy with the admission of my rage. My hand, a physical manifestation of my inner struggle, clenched and unclenched as I grappled with the emotions. "I was so angry."

"I can see that." Freya's acknowledgment of my anger, indicated by a gesture towards the collected shards, prompted a desperate clarification on my part. "No," I insisted, driven by a need to convey the depravity of the situation. "It's much worse."

Her prompt, "Worse? How so?" opened the door to a confession I had dreaded to voice.

The words that followed came from a place of deep vulnerability. "I almost kidnapped her, Freya." The admission hung heavy in the air, a haunting revelation of the darkness that had nearly consumed me.

Freya's reaction was immediate, a mix of shock and disbelief etched into her features. "You did—how—but why?" she stammered, her words a reflection of the tumultuous thoughts that surely raced through her mind.

"I panicked," I admitted, my hands slicing through the cold air of the cave in a gesture of sheer frustration. But even that word felt inadequate, too controlled for the maelstrom of emotion that had engulfed me. "No," I corrected myself almost immediately, seeking a term that truly encapsulated my despair. "I crumbled." Settling next to Freya, I felt the stark contrast between the frigid rock beneath us and the warmth of her presence. She offered her attention, a silent anchor in the tempest of my confession, as I poured out the dark tale of the previous night's events.

Her response was not one of judgment but of compassion. Freya reached out, her palm warm against the chill of my cheek, offering a touch that spoke volumes. "Don't give up hope on Gladys, father," she whispered, her voice a balm to my frayed nerves. Her faith in Gladys, in the love I harboured for her, and in her potential role in our lives, shone through her words. "If you love her and believe that she is right to be our Guardian, then don't give up hope."

The simplicity of her advice clashed with the turmoil within me. "But the two glasses. Two bottles," I countered, the evidence of Gladys's betrayal—or what I perceived as betrayal—fuelling the tension that knotted my insides.

Freya met my gaze head-on, her conviction unflinching. "It means she had company. It doesn't mean anything more happened between them," she asserted, her words fierce, as if willing me to believe, to see beyond my doubts.

"But that was my bottle!" The pain of the moment I discovered the bottle, the shattered plans it represented, spilled out. "We were going to share it while I told her about us," I confessed, seeking solace in Freya's eyes, a plea for understanding, for a way forward.

"Then maybe you should just ask her," Freya suggested, her solution deceptively simple.

"Ask her?" The idea seemed as foreign as the concept of peace in that moment.

"Yes. Ask her if she was with somebody last night. You'll know whether she is telling the truth." Freya's advice, rooted in honesty and directness, offered a path I hadn't considered, a way to confront the gnawing doubts head-on.

"And what if it is the truth? What if she doesn't join us? She's the leverage we need to get Luke to find us," I confided, the weight of our predicament, of the roles and expectations I had placed on Gladys, making my hands tremble. The enormity of what hung in the balance—not just my personal turmoil, but the fate of hundreds of lives—pressed down on me, a burden that felt both personal and profound.

Freya's expression shifted rapidly, her brows knitting together as a storm of anger brewed in her eyes. "Please tell me that's not why you want her — to separate two sisters for your own gain." Her words cut through me, a sharp reminder of the moral implications of my actions.

"It's for the greater good," I countered, my voice a blend of conviction and desperation. I tried to justify my plans with the noblest of intentions, hoping to paint my motives in a light that could, somehow, be understood and accepted. "It will give Luke a reason to come looking for us." The words felt hollow, even as they left my lips, a feeble attempt to cloak my actions with a veneer of necessity.

Freya rose, her movements animated by a surge of frustration. "If I had a wine bottle for myself, I'd be throwing it against the rocks right now," she declared, her anger palpable, her finger jabbing in the direction of the cave's cold, stone wall. Her challenge to me was clear: "Have you listened to yourself? Have you really thought about what you're proposing?" Her words echoed in the cavernous space, a stark reminder of the gravity of my contemplated actions.

My face fell from the internal turmoil her words ignited. The skin on my forehead gathered into deep furrows, markers of a life fraught with challenges and decisions that now seemed to loom larger than ever. The lines etched into my skin felt like the physical embodiment of my moral and ethical quandaries.

Freya's voice softened, her earlier anger giving way to a plea for reason. "Look, I get it. You're tired. You're lonely. But if Gladys is going to come here, let her know the truth. All of it. No tricks. No manipulation. And for the sake of Clivilius, no kidnapping!" The earnestness in her voice, coupled with the softening of her features, underscored the sincerity of her appeal.

A brief smile flickered across my face, a momentary light in the darkness of my thoughts. Freya's eloquence, her ability to articulate the heart of the matter with such clarity and passion, never ceased to amaze me.

"Gladys deserves better than that," she persisted, her conviction unwavering. "I deserve better than that." Her words, a testament to her own integrity and expectations, resonated with a profound truth.

Taking a deep breath, I allowed the weight of her words to settle over me, the reality of my actions—and their potential impact—coming into stark relief. "You're right," I conceded, the words escaping in a heavy exhale. "I am just an old, selfish man."

Freya's return to my side brought with it a sense of calm, her presence a soothing balm to the turmoil that had churned within me. "You have a good heart," she affirmed, her words echoing in the cool air of the cave. "You're just trying a little too hard. Be honest and transparent and let things work the way they will." Her advice, simple yet profound, resonated deeply, a reminder of the path I knew in my heart to be right but had strayed from in my desperation.

"I will tell her," I committed, the nod of my head reinforcing the promise I made to myself and to Freya. The weight of this decision settled on me, a mantle of responsibility I was determined to bear with integrity.

"When?" Freya's question, laced with skepticism, pierced the newfound resolve I felt. Her doubt was not of my intention, but of my timing, a reflection of the urgency she sensed in our predicament.

"Soon," I answered, the word hanging between us, laden with the complexities of the situation I faced.

Freya clasped my hands with a strength that belied her gentle nature, her grip a tangible manifestation of her support. "Until you're ready, if you truly believe that this Luke Smith is the one you've told me about for all these years —"

"I do," I interjected, cutting through her words with the certainty of my conviction. Luke Smith was not just a name, but a beacon of hope in the darkness that surrounded me.

"Then help him," she urged, her counsel clear and direct. "Help him in any way that you can. If he is the Guardian you say that he is, he will want to find us. Whether Gladys is here or not." Her words painted a picture of a future where our fates were not tethered to manipulations or schemes, but to the strength of our cause and the bonds of our shared destiny.

Looking into Freya's eyes, "You have the logic and wisdom of your mother," I acknowledged, my voice soft with emotion.

"And the kindness and gentleness of my father," Freya added, a gentle reminder of the balance of traits that she embodied, traits that I had admired in her mother and hoped to see in myself.

Squeezing Freya's hands in return, I felt a surge of determination. "Okay," I affirmed, the word carrying the weight of my renewed purpose. "I'll help Luke." The decision felt like a turning point, a step away from the shadowed paths of deceit and towards the light of honesty and action. Freya's faith in me, her belief in the goodness of our intentions, fortified my resolve.

❖

"I really need to activate a closer location," I grumbled under my breath, the words barely escaping my lips as I faced the final stretch of my ascent. Each step up the steep incline felt like a battle against gravity, my muscles protesting with every movement. The journey from the dilapidated shed, a structure that had served as my secret lookout over Gladys's house, had been a gruelling trek of over ninety minutes. That shed, standing alone on an otherwise vacant lot, had been more than just a vantage point—it was my haven, a place where I could watch over her unseen. Yet, the necessity of shifting my focus towards Luke had rendered my favoured hideaway in Hobart less than ideal.

Reaching the top of the driveway, I paused, hands resting on my hips as I fought to catch my breath. The physical exertion of the climb reminded me of the relentless demands of my life as a Guardian, a role that typically kept me in peak condition. Yet, this particular challenge had pushed my limits, a testament to the urgency and weight of my current mission.

My eyes immediately fixed on the small truck parked in the driveway, its presence signalling the day's early activities. *Luke's been busy this morning*, I observed silently, the truck standing as a testament to his industriousness.

As I edged closer to the vehicle, the abruptness of the command halted me in my tracks. "Speak to me, boy!" The voice, gruff and imposing, sliced through the morning's quiet like a knife through silence. It jolted me, sending a shiver down my spine that felt like an electric shock. Recognition dawned with a cold dread; it was Nelson Price, a name synonymous with danger and a moniker feared as a Portal Pirate of notorious repute.

"Where are they?" His voice, laden with a threat that needed no embellishment, dredged up memories I had long tried to bury. *Los Angeles...* The recollection of our last encounter flashed before my eyes, a moment so fraught with peril it had imprinted itself indelibly in my mind as the closest brush with death I had ever faced.

"Luke," the name escaped my lips in a whisper, strained and barely audible, laden with a sense of impending doom. The mere thought of what might be unfolding before me sent waves of apprehension crashing through my mind.

With a caution that bordered on the instinctual, I moved, my steps silent and measured, towards the front of the truck. Merging with the shadows, I became little more than a spectre in the morning light, pressing my back against the vehicle's cold, unyielding metal. The world around me seemed to sharpen, every detail pronounced under the weight of my heightened senses. The front door of Luke's house, slightly ajar, caught my attention—a detail that seemed at once an invitation and an ominous omen. *Shit!*

My gaze dropped to the ground, to the unmistakable sight of Nelson's well-worn black boots visible beneath the truck's rear door. That door, left carelessly open, offered no clues to his intentions, masking them as effectively as the darkest night. I watched, heart pounding, as those boots moved with a purpose toward the back gate, each step a silent testament to the threat they posed. Then, in a moment that felt both surreal and terrifying, they disappeared from view, swallowed by the swirling hues of Clivilius.

"Shit!" The word erupted from me, a whisper-sharp reflection of the adrenaline coursing through my veins. My pulse hammered against my temples, echoing the acute sense of danger that enveloped me. Portal Pirates, the very name a harbinger of peril, whispered among Guardians with a mix of respect and fear. Their reputation preceded them, a shadowy collective known more for their ruthlessness than for any ideological pursuit. While they didn't primarily hunt for kills, their willingness to eliminate those who stood in their way was well-documented. And yet, the life of a Guardian, especially one as pivotal as Luke Smith, represented an invaluable asset—leverage that could tip the scales in their nefarious dealings.

"Stand up!" The command, issued from Nelson's unseen accomplice, sliced through the tension, a venomous challenge that left no room for hesitation. The voice, laced with a threat as cold and sharp as a blade, emanated from the truck's shadowy recesses, turning the air thick with anticipation.

I tensed, every muscle coiled like a spring, as the scrape of shoes against metal underscored the immediacy of the threat. There was no time for deliberation; my response had to be both immediate and decisive. Edging closer to the precipice of action, I positioned myself at the truck's door, the metal's chill seeping into my palms, a stark reminder of the stakes at play.

The weight of the moment pressed down on me, a tangible force that demanded a reckoning. As a Guardian, my role was not only to protect but to confront the darkness that sought to disrupt the fragile balance of our realms. The thought of Nelson Price and his ilk laying hands on Luke, using him as a pawn in their twisted games, ignited a fire within me. They sought to wield power, to manipulate the very fabric of our existence for their own ends, and standing against them, I was acutely aware of the fine line that separated courage from recklessness.

In that breathless instant, with the threat looming just beyond the truck's door, I steeled myself for what was to come.

The distinct sound of a sharp blade slicing through flesh made me gasp. My heart plunged into my stomach, eyes bulging, while I heard the gurgling and coughing of someone drowning in their own blood. The body hit the bed of the truck with a loud thud. Anger surged through my entire body.

The door collided with a sickening thud as the man catapulted from the truck, gravity claiming him in a chaotic dance with the cold asphalt. Swift and unyielding, I closed the distance, boots crunching on the cement, only to find my adversary already on his feet, hunched in pain, nursing the wounded shoulder that bore the brunt of my door-induced assault.

"Ah, Cody Jennings," he sneered, his voice dripping with malice, a dark mirror to our shared history. *Griffin Langley*—a name that conjured memories of conflicts past, a ghost that had lingered in the periphery of my thoughts, now standing before me in flesh and blood.

"Griffin Langley, we meet again," I responded, my voice steady, my focus sharp. The air between us crackled with the tension of our gaze, two predators locked in a moment of recognition. "I see you've lost a few more teeth since we last spoke." The words were a barb, a reminder of our last encounter, the physical toll it had taken on him evident in his grimace.

"It's been a rough year," he shot back, his defiance manifesting in a spray of saliva and blood, a grotesque testament to his resilience. The act was both a challenge and a declaration, a sign that Griffin, despite his injuries, was far from defeated.

"Don't do it," I warned, my instincts flaring as I noticed the subtle shift in his posture, the telltale sign of a hand inching towards a concealed weapon. Griffin's reputation for unpredictability was well-earned; his movements, though pained, were laden with intent.

"I'm the one with the knife here," he boasted, the flash of the blade in the sunlight a foreboding warning. The weapon, though small, was a clear indication of his readiness to escalate the confrontation, its edge catching the light in a sinister promise of violence.

"Try it, and I'll cut you with that knife," I countered, my tone laced with the confidence of experience. Facing Griffin, I was acutely aware of his capabilities and his limitations. He was dangerous, undoubtedly, but his approach was raw, lacking the refinement that comes with disciplined training. My readiness to engage, to turn his own threat against him, was not just a physical stance but a psychological one, a battle of wills where every word, every gesture, was as potent as a strike.

In this standoff, beneath the unyielding gaze of the sun, the lines were drawn. Griffin Langley, with his brutish force and crude tactics, stood on one side; I, with the resolve borne of countless encounters and the wisdom to navigate them, stood on the other. The air hung heavy with the anticipation, a palpable tension that spoke of the inevitable clash. It was a dance as old as time, a test of mettle and mind, and I was prepared to see it through to its end.

With a swipe that carried all the venom of his intentions, Griffin lunged, the blade cutting through the air with a precision that spoke of his desperation. I moved with the agility borne of countless encounters, sidestepping his attack with a grace that felt almost like a dance with danger itself. The air around us was charged, thick with the tension of our silent battle, a clash of wills as palpable as the physical blows we traded.

"Do you know why we call you Portal Pawns?" I taunted, unable to resist the urge to needle him further, a smirk playing at the edges of my lips. The question hung between us, an added provocation aimed at unsettling him further.

Griffin's response was a silent, seething glare, his eyes narrowing with a mix of hatred and begrudging acknowledgment. He knew well the game of hunter and hunted we played, yet my words seemed to burrow under his skin, striking a chord.

"Because you're disposable," I finished for him, the declaration sharp, a verbal jab meant to undercut his resolve and remind him of his place in the grander scheme of things we were both entangled in.

The response was immediate—a low, guttural growl that vibrated from Griffin's throat, a sound that was both a warning and a clear indicator of the fury I had ignited within him. It was the sound of a cornered animal, desperate and dangerous.

Timing was everything. As Griffin prepared for another assault, I counted down internally, aligning my instincts with the imminent rush of action. *Three, two, one*—his body tensed, and he lunged, predictably falling into the trap I had mentally laid out for him. My movement was a blend of anticipation and precision, stepping aside just as he committed to his charge.

Seizing his arm, I felt the surge of adrenaline as I twisted it behind him, my grip ironclad. The snap of his wrist bones breaking under the pressure was a grim chorus to the dance we performed, a sound that was both shocking and satisfying in the context of our struggle. Griffin's cry of pain was immediate, a wail that cut through the standoff, and the knife falling from his grasp, marking the turning point of our confrontation.

With a swift kick, I sent the knife flying, its metallic glint winking out as it buried itself in the garden bed, rendered harmless. Pressing Griffin against the truck, I utilised every ounce of my strength to immobilise him, his body pinned by mine against the cold metal. "I did tell you," I whispered, my words a cold breath on his ear, a reminder of the warning he had chosen to ignore.

The lifeless gaze that met mine from the back of the truck sent a shiver down my spine, the stark emptiness of death laid bare in the dim light. The body, ensconced in its own crimson, offered a grim tableau. Yet, amidst the horror, a wave of relief washed over me—it wasn't Luke. This realisation, though cold comfort, steadied my resolve.

"Nelson will kill you for this," Griffin hissed between laboured breaths, each word laced with venom and pain. His threat, intended to intimidate, only drew a laugh from deep within me. "Not if he can't find me," I retorted, the confidence in my voice unshaken by his dire predictions.

Griffin's laughter, a deranged echo of his earlier defiance, cut through the tension. "You think we don't already have your location?" he taunted, his mirth tinged with madness. "We just... Don't... Like it," he spat, his words deliberate, intended to unnerve.

With a resolve hardened by countless conflicts, I moved. My action was swift—a calculated manoeuvre that brought Griffin's forehead crashing into the truck bed with a thud, his consciousness extinguished as quickly as it had flared. The weight of his body, now limp and unyielding, pressed against me.

My knees threatened to give way beneath the burden, a momentary weakness that belied the strength required to navigate the path I had chosen. The Portal, activated with a sense of urgency, shimmered against the side of the house, its swirling colours a gateway to safety, to secrecy.

Dragging Griffin's unconscious form was a task that taxed every fibre of my being. The concrete driveway scraped against us, the small garden bed of rocks and flax plants a minor obstacle in the path to the Portal. Each step was measured, a balance between haste and caution, as I moved us through the vibrant maelstrom of purple, blue, and green that marked the threshold between worlds.

The moment we crossed into the Portal, the familiar yet always unsettling sensation of transition enveloped us. The world behind us faded into darkness, the problems, threats, and the lifeless gaze in the truck relegated to a reality I had momentarily left behind. The immediate danger may have been averted, but the implications of Griffin's words lingered—a reminder of the ever-present threat Nelson and his ilk posed.

LUKE SMITH

4338.206.2

The sky, cloaked in a mantle of heavy clouds, seemed to reflect the turmoil churning within me as I made my way back toward Luke's house from the cover of the dilapidated shed. Each breath I expelled materialised into faint, ghostly puffs, dancing briefly in the cold air before dissipating, a silent testament to the chill that seemed to penetrate to the bone. My decision to avoid re-entering directly through Luke's brick wall was a tactical one, influenced by a deep-seated hesitation. It was a move that carried with it the weight of caution, a reluctance born from the desire not to reveal my presence or secrets before the right moment.

The time I had allocated to secure Griffin in the Portal Cave, a precaution to ensure his containment until I could interrogate him, and the council could decide his fate, now felt like both a necessary measure and a costly expenditure. With every step I took, urgency thrummed through my veins, a relentless drive that pushed me forward. The need to verify Luke's safety, to ensure that the shadows of my recent conflict with the Portal Pirates hadn't attracted unwanted attention, was paramount. The spectre of law enforcement, with its potential to unravel the fragile veil of secrecy we operated under, loomed large in my thoughts, a threat that could undermine everything we work to protect.

Ascending the incline that led to Luke's residence for the second time that day, my pace quickened despite the fatigue that clung to my limbs. A soft exclamation, "Oh no," slipped from between my lips, a spontaneous response to the sight that unfolded before me. The presence of Gladys's car, unexpected and potentially complicating, sparked a flurry of questions in my mind. *What was her role in this day's events, and how had Luke managed in the aftermath of my altercation with the Portal Pirates?* The uncertainty of her involvement added a new layer of complexity to an already intricate situation.

"Gladys," I called out, my voice slicing through the heavy, silent air like a knife, as I reached the end of the driveway. The world around me seemed to hold its breath, waiting for her response.

Silence greeted me back, the kind that prickles the back of your neck and sends your heart racing. My pulse kicked up a notch, a sense of foreboding crawling into the pit of my stomach, winding itself tight. "Gladys, everything okay here?" My question hung in the air, my steps towards the side of the truck measured and wary.

When Gladys peeked around the back, her smile was like a poorly fitted mask, one that didn't quite cover the tension etched deep in her features. "Cody!" Her voice was a jarring note of forced cheer, trying too hard to pierce the thick atmosphere of unease.

Shit! My mind raced, thoughts tumbling over each other. Something was off, terribly off. "Yeah, everything is great here," Gladys's voice broke through my spiralling thoughts, her words flat, as if she was trying to convince herself more than me.

Drawing closer, I took her in, from the anxious flicker in her eyes down to her feet. And that's when I saw it—crimson droplets, stark against the white of her sneakers. My heart skipped a beat. *Shit, what have you done, Gladys?* The question screamed in my head, louder than anything else. *Did you touch him?*

"Oh," she laughed, but the sound was brittle, like thin ice cracking underfoot. "That's just wine. I accidentally knocked my glass over." Her explanation hung between us, fragile and unconvincing.

I took a deep breath, trying to steady the turmoil inside me. "Doesn't surprise me, really." My words walked a tightrope between hope and skepticism, a reflection of the complex dance that was knowing Gladys. Her unpredictability was both a curse and a charm.

"How about I meet you back at home in an hour?" she suggested, her gaze darting nervously between me and the truck's rear, as if afraid of what might be seen.

What else can I do? The question was a heavy weight in my chest. *Anything more, and my cover will be blown.* With a sense of resignation, I started to walk away, each step heavy, my pace slow and deliberate. Inside, my mind was a storm, thoughts whirling chaotically. The distance between us grew with each step, but the unease, the questions, the fear—they clung to me, a cloak I couldn't shake off.

"Cody, wait!" Gladys's voice pierced the cold air, arresting my steps. At the end of the driveway, my body tensed, then relaxed ever so slightly, a glimmer of hope flickering across my face. *Could this be my chance to step in, to make things right?*

I turned, my heart pounding in my chest, waiting for Gladys to say more. But she only offered a small, uncertain shrug—a gesture that felt like a heavy door creaking open, inviting yet withholding. With a deep breath, I found my resolve and walked back, my steps heavy with the weight of uncertainty.

Bypassing Gladys, I approached the truck, bracing myself for what I might find. Then, the scene laid bare before me: a tableau so stark, so jarringly out of place in the quiet of Hobart. "What the fuck!" The words burst from me, a perfect blend of shock and disbelief, though my heart raced with the knowledge of the atrocity.

Luke, caught in the act over a body that spoke of untold stories, looked up, his face a canvas of surprise and fear. Nearby, Beatrix, Gladys's sister, stood frozen, her clothing a macabre tapestry of red. My gaze flickered between them, the sight igniting a flurry of questions in my mind.

"Who the fuck is that, Luke?" My voice climbed, a note of accusation threading through genuine concern. The sight of Beatrix, so close to the chaos, her clothes splattered with evidence, sent a shiver down my spine. *She hadn't touched the body... had she?*

Luke's response was a stutter, a stumble of words that betrayed his shock. "Wait. You know who I am?"

"Of course," I shot back, trying to maintain a veneer of control, to keep the upper hand in a situation rapidly slipping away. "We've been waiting for you." The words hung between us, loaded with meaning yet veiled in ambiguity.

"Waiting for me?" Luke's voice was a mix of bewilderment and fear.

Shit! The realisation hit me like a punch to the gut. I was teetering dangerously close to the edge, to revealing more than intended. I needed to steer this back, to regain control before it all plunged off another cliff. Dodging his question with the agility of a seasoned player, I pressed, "What happened to him?" as I climbed into the truck, my eyes never leaving the scene.

Shit," Luke's whisper cut through the tension, his eyes locking onto mine with a depth of recognition that sent a shiver down my spine. It was a look that unsettled me more than the sight of blood on Beatrix's clothing. "You were in my dream."

Focusing on the task at hand, I brushed aside Luke's cryptic statement. "Throat looks like it has been slit. Any idea who did this?" My voice was steady, despite the turmoil swirling inside me. Luke's mention of dreams was a distraction, one we couldn't afford, not here, not with the clock ticking against us.

"You were in my dream," Luke repeated, his voice softer this time, his gaze intense. "I recognise you now." His words were like a puzzle, pieces that didn't fit in the immediate crisis.

"We don't have time for this now, Luke," I pushed back, my tone firm, insistent. The urgency of the situation was mounting, the need to understand the unfolding mystery pressing. "I need to know who he is and what happened. We don't have much time." The words tumbled out, a rush of necessity. We were in the grip of something much larger than us, a shadowy dance with the Portal Pirate at its centre, awaiting a severe interrogation in Belkeep.

Luke faltered, words catching in his throat.

"His name is Joel," Beatrix cut in, her voice a beacon in the confusion. "He's Jamie's son." The information was a piece of the puzzle, a name to the face, a connection to the larger web we were caught in.

"Is he...?" My question trailed off as I nodded in Luke's direction, seeking a verification against the fear that Joel might be more deeply involved, perhaps even a Guardian.

"No, I don't think so," Beatrix responded, her words offering a sliver of relief.

"What happened?" My demand was more pressing, the need for clarity, for any shred of understanding in the madness that enveloped us.

Beatrix's shoulders lifted in a shrug, a gesture of uncertainty in a situation that demanded answers.

"I'm not sure," Luke admitted, his voice low. "He delivered a few tents here this morning. I took the opportunity to take them through the Portal while he was in the toilet. Then the boys accidentally ran through."

"The boys?" The question burst from me, a mix of confusion and urgency. *Who the hell are the boys?*

"Dogs," Beatrix clarified, her single word painting a clearer, yet still perplexing, picture of the events that had unfolded prior to my first arrival.

"And did he see?" My question cut through the heavy air, redirecting our focus back to Joel, the crux of our current dilemma.

"Yeah," Luke confirmed with a nod, his voice laced with a grim certainty. "I'm pretty sure he did. And when I returned, I found him like this."

"Shit," I whispered under my breath, my mind racing as I paced back and forth. *We need to get rid of the body.* The thought of persuading Luke to take him through the Portal nagged at me, a risky proposition that danced on the edge of desperation.

"Oh my god!" Gladys's exclamation cut through my thoughts, her voice tinged with panic and disbelief. "We've both seen the Portal too," she said, her hand wavering between herself and Beatrix. "Does this mean we are going to die too?"

I almost let out a chuckle, not at the gravity of our situation, but at the innocence wrapped in her fear. "Not today, Gladys. Not today," I reassured her, trying to infuse a sense of calm.

"I am really confused," Luke admitted, his confusion palpable as he rubbed his forehead. "Who are you again? And how do you know me? Did you have a dream too?"

The air was thick with questions and fear, a tangled web of reality and visions that seemed to ensnare us all. "I think Gladys and I had better finish making those deliveries,"

Beatrix interjected, her voice a beacon of pragmatism in the midst of our turmoil. "I'll call you later. When we're done."

Luke's nod was a silent agreement to her proposal, a temporary reprieve from the pressing matters at hand.

My eyebrows raised in realisation as the implications of Beatrix's words dawned on me. Making it look like the man made all the deliveries. It was a smart move, possibly clever enough to divert suspicion and buy us some time. *Perhaps I need to give Luke a little more credit,* I thought to myself, acknowledging the ingenuity.

"Be careful. Both of you," I warned the sisters, my voice heavy with concern. Relief washed over me at the thought of Gladys being removed from the immediate danger, yet the caution required of their next actions wasn't lost on me. The risks involved in making the deliveries were significant, and the consequences of being caught loomed large in my mind.

As the sisters' chatter and footsteps receded into the distance, situation settled back around Luke and me. His gaze found mine again, filled with questions, fear, and a hint of desperation. The silence between us was a chasm filled with unspoken words and the heavy weight of decisions yet to be made.

"I think you're in imminent danger, Luke," I said, holding his gaze with an intensity that I hoped would convey urgency. The thought of Nelson, trapped near Luke's new settlement, cast a long shadow over me. Everyone Luke had brought through to Clivilius could be in peril. Yet, a flicker of a cold, strategic thought crossed my mind—if Nelson were to eliminate Luke, he'd essentially be sealing his own fate as well, cutting off his only path back to Earth.

"Was he killed because of me?" Luke's voice broke through my contemplations, laden with guilt and fear. "Because I let him see the Portal?"

"No," I responded with a conviction I hoped would be contagious. "I don't think it was your fault at all." It was crucial he believed that; guilt could immobilise him when swift action was needed most.

Luke inhaled deeply, a silent struggle visible in the rise and fall of his shoulders as he grappled with the weight of the situation.

"We need to get rid of the body. You should take him to Clivilius," I suggested, offering a solution that, while grim, seemed the most practical under the circumstances.

"I can't. Jamie would kill me if he knew his son was dead because of me," Luke countered, the fear of reprisal evident in his voice. His concern for Jamie's reaction was understandable, yet it paled in comparison to the immediate dangers we faced.

"Luke!" I found myself gripping his shoulders, trying to anchor him. "It's not your fault." It was vital he understood this, that the blame lay not in his actions but in the dangerous world that he was now entangled with.

Luke's expression was a mix of frustration and desperation as he considered the options. "There has to be another way."

I began to pace, each step a measured beat as I turned over every possibility in my mind. The interior of the truck felt like a cage, confining my thoughts and options. After what felt like an eternity but was only a few moments, an idea struck me. "There is," I said, the words laced with a newfound resolve.

"Get out of the truck," I instructed Luke, not waiting for his response before jumping down myself. The cool air outside was a sharp contrast to the stifling atmosphere within, but it was here, in this space between confinement and freedom, that our next steps would unfold. My mind raced, plotting a course of action that could navigate us through the immediate labyrinth of danger and deception in which we found ourselves.

As Luke quickly obeyed, "I need the keys," I stated, extending my hand expectantly. It was a demand more than a request.

"Where are you taking him?" Luke's voice carried a mix of fear and curiosity as he placed the keys in my palm, his eyes searching mine for an answer I wasn't sure he was ready to know.

Without a word, I reached into my shirt pocket, the fabric brushing against my fingers as I retrieved my Portal Key. The small, unassuming device was inconspicuous to the untrained eye, but its power was immense, a direct line to realms beyond normal human reach.

Luke's intake of breath was sharp, a gasp that filled the silence between us.

With a practiced motion, I activated the device. A small ball of bright energy burst forth, darting through the air with precision and grace. It struck the large gate, a silent herald that awakened the portal. In an instant, the gate's surface came alive, swirling with radiant colours that danced across its expanse, a mesmerising display of light and energy.

"I'm taking him to Clivilius," I announced, the words heavy with the responsibility I was shouldering. It was a declaration that left no room for doubt or debate.

Luke moved aside, his actions automatic as he gave me space. His stare, filled with a complex blend of emotions, followed me—a silent observer to the unfolding scene.

Climbing into the cab of the truck, I felt the familiar weight of the keys in my hand. The engine roared to life under my touch, its rumble a steady companion in the stillness of the morning. With careful precision, I reversed the truck, guiding it towards the portal.

The moment of crossing was surreal, a sensation that never failed to stir a mix of exhilaration and trepidation within me. The truck, the lifeless form in the back, and I, we all vanished through the wall of colour.

❖

The brakes screeched to a halt, a jarring symphony that echoed through the cave as I jumped to the ground, my heart thundering against my ribs. The crisp air bit at my skin, a stark contrast to the tension that wrapped around me like a cloak. My gaze lifted to the small group assembled on the far side, their silhouettes casting long shadows against the rocky walls. The twins, Chief Lewydd, and his second-in-command, Brogyin Tillop, sat with a calm that belied the storm I felt brewing inside. *This can't be good*, the thought ran through my mind like a chilling premonition.

"It's good to see you back in one piece, son," I called out to Fryar, mustering a smile that felt as though it was carved from stone. The effort to sound casual, to inject a note of normalcy into the palpable tension, was a battle in itself.

Chief Lewydd rose with a deliberateness that seemed to draw the very light towards him, his presence commanding even in silence. He took several steps toward me, each one measured and heavy with an unspoken gravity. "Is this your idea of locking up a prisoner?" His voice was a low rumble, the words laden with a disapproval as cold and unforgiving as the cave walls. In his hand, he held up a rope, cut in pieces, a silent accusation that hung in the air between us.

A dry lump formed in my throat, my mind racing for an explanation, for any words that might diffuse the tension. "Where is Griffin?" I asked, my voice betraying the nervousness that gripped me.

The response was a collective silence, a wall of blank stares that offered no solace, no answers. Chief Lewyyd's shrug was callous, a gesture that seemed to dismiss my question, leaving a cold dread to settle in my stomach.

"Shit," I whispered under my breath, the word barely audible, yet carrying the weight of my realisation. The situation was unravelling faster than I could have anticipated, slipping through my fingers like grains of sand. With a heavy heart and a mind swirling with unanswered questions, I commanded the Portal closed.

As the reality of our predicament set in, the cave, with its cool shadows and ancient stones, felt more like a tomb than a sanctuary. *Further discussion with Luke would have to wait.*

THE TROUBLE WITH PIRATES

4338.206.3

Chief Lewyyd's voice sliced through the thick tension, sharp and commanding, echoing off the cavernous walls. "Who is he?" The question, loaded with expectation and authority, demanded not just a response but the truth. His eyes, intense and probing, seemed to bore into my very soul, seeking answers I was hesitant to give.

The air around us felt charged, every breath heavy with anticipation. I found myself momentarily caught in the Chief's gaze, the kind of look that compels truth even when silence seems the safer harbour. "His name is Griffin Langley," I admitted, the words tasting like ash in my mouth. My eyes darted briefly to the severed ropes in his grasp.

"And?" Chief Lewyyd's insistence was a palpable force, a clear indication that partial truths wouldn't suffice here.

I exhaled, a sigh heavy with resignation. The pride I had once felt at capturing a Portal Pirate was now overshadowed by the immediate peril his escape posed. "He's a Portal Pirate," I confessed, the title hanging between us, laden with the gravity of its implications.

A collective gasp cut through the group, a chorus of shock and disbelief that seemed to ripple through the cave. Yet, Chief Lewyyd's focus remained unflinchingly on me, as if our exchange had drawn him into a world apart from the reactions of those around us.

"Go home, Krid," Chief Lewyyd ordered, his voice a stern command that somehow didn't break our intense eye contact. At the mention of her name, I couldn't help but glance towards the cave's entrance. Krid's small, curious face was framed by the wild dance of her curly hair, caught in the wind's embrace. "Sorry, Cody," she called out, a note of genuine regret in her voice before she disappeared, her presence melting into the flurry of falling snowflakes.

A brief, involuntary smile flickered across my lips, despite the severity of our situation. Krid, with her boundless curiosity and fearless heart, had always had a knack for finding herself at the centre of intrigue. That she had been the one to alert the leadership was both entirely unsurprising and mildly amusing. Her spirit, a beacon of light in the often too-serious backdrop of our lives, reminded me of the stakes we were playing for—not just the safety of our community, but the preservation of the very qualities that made us human.

"Any idea where he might be?" My question was an attempt to steer the conversation towards actionable intelligence, a hope to claw back some semblance of control over the spiralling situation.

"No," Chief Lewyyd responded, his face a mask of stoicism, revealing nothing of his thoughts or concerns.

"Didn't you track his footprints through the snow?" I pressed, clinging to the hope that physical evidence might lead us to Griffin. The idea that we could simply follow his trail and resolve this crisis was a desperate one, but desperation had become a familiar companion.

"There weren't any," Fryar chimed in, his voice cutting through the silence. "Freya and I studied the snow carefully." His words, intended to be helpful, only deepened the mystery, casting a shadow of unease over the group. The absence of tracks was an unsettling development, one that hinted at skills or technologies far beyond our understanding.

The silence that followed was thick, a tangible presence that seemed to press down on us with the weight of unanswered questions. My mind, unbidden, drifted to fragments of conversations and theories discussed in quieter times, each memory flickering like a candle in the dark, illuminating possibilities but providing no warmth.

"That must mean he either knows how to fly or he's gone deeper into the cave," Chief declared, his voice cutting through the haze of my thoughts.

"He could have left through the Portal, couldn't he?" Freya ventured, her question laced with a mix of hope and fear.

"Maybe," I admitted, my response tempered with uncertainty. The mechanics of the Portal Pirate technology, their limitations and requirements, were still shrouded in mystery. "I'm not sure if they can without their partner, though."

"Where's his partner?" Brogyin asked, his quiet observation giving way to participation. His question was a piercing one, cutting to the heart of the matter.

"I assume he went through the Portal before..." My attempt to put forward a plausible scenario was abruptly interrupted by Chief's growing impatience.

"Assumptions aren't good enough, Cody!" His voice was a sharp rebuke, a clear indication that speculation was no substitute for action in his eyes.

"Let him continue," Freya's voice was a soothing balm, her intervention a beacon of support in the face of Chief's burgeoning frustration.

Swallowing the knot of anxiety that threatened to choke my words, I mustered what was meant to be an appreciative smile towards my daughter. The gesture, however, felt twisted by the tension gripping me, likely morphing into something that bore closer resemblance to a grimace. The oppressive weight of our predicament bore down on me, the search for the Portal Pirate looming large as we stood on the precipice of the unknown within the icy confines of the cave.

"I was going to say that I think he went through the Portal before Luke closed it," I managed to articulate, the words feeling heavy in the cold air.

"Luke Smith?" Freya's voice cut through the tension, her sudden movement from the rock where she sat a testament to her surprise and concern.

"Yeah," was all I could muster in reply.

"Damn," Fryar interjected. "Do you think they're safe?"

"Pirates are sneaky bastards, no doubt about that," I found myself saying, a bitter taste accompanying the words. *And this one has already killed Joel and I'm certain he wouldn't hesitate to kill again.* The rest of the thought lingered in my mind, a dark cloud I couldn't bring myself to voice out loud, the reality too grim to lay bare.

"Obviously," Chief's voice was laced with a hardness as he brandished the severed ropes once more, a visual reminder of the threat that had slipped through my grasp.

"I don't think we can assume he has left here yet," I ventured, voicing the gnawing fear that had taken root in my mind. The possibility that Griffin might still lurk nearby, or worse, return, was a scenario we couldn't afford to overlook.

Chief turned to Brogyin, decisiveness etching his features. "Have some of our sharpest people set up camp here. Keep watch night and day. If the bastard is still here, or returns, we'll catch him." His orders were a clear directive, a plan of action that brought a sliver of determination amidst the fear.

Brogyin's nod was swift, his understanding immediate. Without a word, he turned and strode towards the cave's entrance, bracing himself against the wintry blast that marked the transition from the cave's relative shelter to the harsh elements beyond. His departure was a silent promise of vigilance, a commitment to guard against the threat that had so suddenly and violently intruded upon our lives.

"Not good enough, Cody. You know our people are already in a fragile state of mind. They don't need this right now," Chief's words, laced with disappointment, struck me like a physical blow. Each syllable seemed to weigh heavily on my conscience.

"I know," I murmured, the admission barely escaping my lips. Internally, I berated myself for the oversight, for the lapse in vigilance. *There's no excuse for sloppy work.* The mantra echoed in my mind, a relentless critique of my actions —or, more accurately, my inactions. *I should have done better.*

As Chief disappeared into the swirling snow outside the cave, his figure momentarily outlined by his dark hood against the white landscape, I found my gaze drifting to the small truck parked inconspicuously to the side. The rest of the group, caught up in the urgency of the moment, seemed to have completely overlooked it. The decision to leave the truck untouched was made in silence, a quiet resolve settling over me. The presence of the lifeless body, hidden from view but heavy on my mind, was a secret I was not yet ready to reveal. The implications of sharing that grim discovery with the community, already teetering on the edge of panic, were too dire to contemplate. Until we had a clearer understanding of Griffin's fate, the shock and fear such a revelation would provoke were unnecessary burdens. Besides, I hadn't decided what to do with it yet. Bringing it to Belkeep was never my intention. *Maybe Freya would help...*

"Fryar and I will stay here until the guards arrive," Freya's voice, firm and decisive, snapped me back to the present.

Turning to face my daughter, I was struck by the sight of her long hair, whipped into a frenzied dance by the wind, framing her face with an almost wild grace. Her determination was palpable, a trait she and Fryar shared, a drive to put themselves in harm's way for a cause greater than their own safety. The instinct to protect them, to keep them safe from the dangers that lurked in shadows and secrets, was a fierce pulse within me. Yet, the realisation that any attempt to dissuade them from their chosen path would be futile was equally strong. Their courage, their willingness to face danger head-on, was not just typical of the twins; it was a fundamental part of who they were. A long time ago, I had come to understand that arguing with them, trying to curb their selfless instincts, would be an exercise in futility.

Fryar's methodical pacing at the cave's entrance was a silent testament to our shared tension, his steps measured and deliberate as if trying to map out our unseen adversary's potential moves. Freya, in contrast, found a semblance of calm by reclaiming her spot on her favoured rock, embodying a quiet strength that I've always admired in her.

"Be careful," I found myself warning them, the concern in my voice palpable even to my own ears. "He's armed enough to cut a rope. If he's still around, he won't hesitate to strike." The reality of our situation was grim; an armed foe, potentially still lurking in the shadows, was a threat that we couldn't afford to underestimate.

"That's unlike you to leave a man armed with a knife," Fryar remarked, his pacing coming to a brief halt. His observation stung, a pointed reminder of my oversight that had led us here.

"I don't think he's got a knife," I countered, my gaze drifting to Freya. Her expression, a mix of understanding and concern, silently affirmed my suspicions. The weapon used wasn't as simple or as benign as a knife, a fact we were both uncomfortably aware of.

"Then what?" Fryar's inquiry, laden with confusion and a hint of fear, momentarily anchored him in place once again.

As I sighed, the weight of the situation settled around us, the cave walls seemingly echoing the burden of our predicament. The remnants of a wine bottle, now scattered across the ground, served as a physical reminder what had unfolded, the dim light casting shadows that seemed to play out the night's events in a haunting reenactment.

"I'll fill you in," Freya interjected, her voice a beacon of clarity in the murky sea of our current crisis.

"Thank you," I responded, the gratitude in my voice tinged with the exhaustion of carrying a secret too heavy. Fryar, perhaps sensing the personal nature of what was to come, turned his gaze outward, towards the expanse beyond the cave's entrance. The frozen landscape, with its whispering winds, seemed to echo the uncertainty and fear that gripped us, a blustery reminder of the unknown dangers that lay in wait.

In that moment, the cave felt more like a refuge and a prison all at once, a sanctuary against the elements and the unknown, yet a place of confinement to our fears and the daunting task that lay ahead. The resolve to protect my family and community was a flame that burned brightly within me, yet the shadows cast by doubt and the weight of leadership threatened to engulf it.

"I need to go home," the words left my lips, hanging visibly in the frigid air as I frantically searched for my winter coat, a shield against the biting cold that awaited outside the cave.

"Shit!" The curse slipped out, a raw expression of my frustration and the mounting pressure. The realisation that the coat, likely pilfered by the very threat we were now mobilising against, was gone, felt like another setback in a day already fraught with too many.

"Here, take mine," Freya offered, her voice a warm contrast to the chill that enveloped me, as she began to shrug off her own coat in a gesture of selfless concern.

"No, you keep it. It's only a five-minute run from here," I countered quickly, refusing to let her sacrifice her comfort for mine.

I turned to Fryar, finding solace in the solidarity between us. "I'll be back as soon as I can. There's something I need to find first." The words were a promise, a vow to return not just with answers but hopefully with a solution to the peril that loomed over us.

"What is it?" Freya's curiosity was piqued as she moved closer, her silhouette framed by the cave's entrance, the backdrop lending her an ethereal quality.

"I'll let you know if I find it," I answered, cryptic not out of desire but necessity. The truth was, I wasn't entirely sure what I was looking for—only that it was vital, a missing piece in the puzzle of our current crisis.

With a final glance at my children, their faces etched with concern and the determination to stand guard, I steeled myself for the run. The chill seeped through my clothes, a harsh reminder of the environment's indifference to my plight. Rubbing my arms in a futile attempt to ward off the cold, I took a deep breath, the icy air sharpening my resolve as I prepared to dash into the wintry wilderness.

❖

"What are you looking for?" Krid's question, filled with the innate curiosity that seemed to guide much of her young life, floated towards me as I wrestled with the deep chest by the foot of my bed. Its weathered wood groaned in protest, like an old man being asked to stand too quickly, as I heaved open the lid. I began to extract several large blankets, letting them fall in a careless heap beside me, their fabric whispering softly to the floor.

Pausing, I looked up to find Krid's inquisitive eyes on me. She was perched on the edge of the bed, her small legs swinging with an energy I envied at the moment. The candlelight flickered across her face, casting her in a warm glow that belied the cold dread that had taken residence in my heart since returning from the Portal Cave. Krid had greeted me with a smile that could outshine the sun and an embrace full of apologies I didn't need. Her heart was in the right place, always.

"I'm looking for my old journals for information on the Portal Pirates," I found myself explaining as I dove back into the chest, the scent of must and memories rising to meet me. There was a certain comfort in the familiar smell, a reminder of days spent in pursuit of knowledge, of secrets unlocked within these very pages. Somewhere amidst these relics of the past lay the answers I sought about our current threat. Griffin's knowledge of Belkeep, his ability—or lack thereof—to navigate the Portals without Nelson, it was all a puzzle that needed solving.

As I continued my search, Krid's presence was a quiet constant, her curiosity now meshed with a sense of solemnity as she watched me unearth journal after journal. The leather-bound volumes, each a keeper of my past thoughts and adventures, felt heavy in my hands. I skimmed through pages filled with notes, sketches, and theories, the soft rustling sound accompanying my frantic search like a soundtrack to the urgency pulsing through my veins.

"I've heard Clivilius too," Krid's voice, unexpected and soft, momentarily halted the frantic pace of my search. The statement, so innocently delivered, drew my attention back to the present.

"You have?" My curiosity piqued, I looked up from the journal I was holding, my focus shifting entirely to her. "What did it say?"

"It told me to always smile," she replied simply.

I regarded her with renewed interest, puzzled by the straightforwardness of the message. "Is that all?" I probed, knowing that the depths of Clivilius's communications were seldom so shallow.

Krid shook her head, her movements quick and decisive. "I'm not allowed to tell you anymore." The firmness in her voice belied her years, and it brought a wave of concern over me. Clivilius, reaching out to Krid with a message she was forbidden to share fully? The implications were as unsettling as they were curious.

"Oh," I managed, my thoughts swirling with questions and theories. *What secrets did Clivilius hold that it chose to share with a child? And why the restriction on sharing?* "Maybe you should write it down somewhere? Keep it safe so you don't forget it." It was advice born out of my own practices, a way to hold onto the fleeting whispers of wisdom or warning that our strange world offered.

"Is that what you did?" Her question was innocent, yet it cut to the heart of my own endeavours.

"Yes," I answered, my voice softened by the glow of memory. I glanced down at the black, leather-bound journal in my hands, one among many that chronicled my thoughts, discoveries, and fears. "But I have so many now that I don't know which one contains the information I want."

"Can I read some?" Her interest was genuine, a mirror of my own thirst for knowledge and understanding in my early days.

"Of course you can. Start with this one," I suggested, handing her another journal from the pile. This one, its cover worn from handling, held the beginnings of my journey into the unknown. "This was my first one."

"Thank you," Krid accepted the journal with a reverence that warmed my heart. She opened it carefully, as if the pages were treasures to be unveiled. Her concentration was absolute, the candlelight illuminating her features, casting her in an aura of earnest curiosity.

In that quiet room, with only the rustle of pages and the crackle of the fireplace for company, a sense of camaraderie settled over us. It was a moment of peace amidst the storm, a shared connection through the written word that transcended our current predicaments. As she delved into the past recorded on those pages, I returned to my search, both of us seeking answers in our own way, bound by the quest for understanding in a world that often offered more questions than it did solutions.

Time seemed to evaporate, each moment blending seamlessly into the next as I thumbed through the pages filled with my past explorations, theories, and encounters.

"Aha!" The word burst from me, a beacon of success in the dimly lit room. I had found the entry I was searching for, a significant moment captured in ink that felt as fresh now as when it had first been penned.

Krid's attention snapped back from her own reading, her eyes alight with the spark of curiosity and wonder. "What does it say?" she inquired, her voice a mix of eagerness and excitement. She leaned forward, her youthful enthusiasm a stark contrast to the ancient whispers contained within the pages of my journal.

"Well, this portion is actually about a conversation that I had with Jeremiah in my early years as a Guardian," I began, the memory of the conversation already unfurling in my mind like a well-worn tapestry.

"Your Guardian Atum?" Krid interjected, her question slicing through the air for clarification.

"Yes. My Guardian Atum," I confirmed with a nod, acknowledging the unique bond shared between a Guardian and their Atum.

"About the Portal Pirates?" Her query was pointed, honing in on the heart of the matter with the precision of a seasoned investigator.

"Yes," I responded, meeting her gaze, which was now brimming with an unspoken plea for more. The anticipation in her eyes was palpable, a mirror to the thirst for knowledge that had driven much of my own journey. "Shall I read it to you?"

"Yes, please," Krid exclaimed, her excitement barely contained as she sat up straighter, embodying the essence of childlike curiosity that made moments like these truly special.

I shifted my position, giving my knees a brief respite from the unforgiving hardness of the wooden floor. Sitting back, I cleared my throat gently, preparing to dive into the narrative that had been etched into the journal so many years ago.

As I delved into the details of the journal, the weight of the history it contained seemed to press down on me, a tangible reminder of the gravity of our situation.

"From what we can tell, the Portal Pirates always travel in pairs. They have to. The device they use – unique technology developed over half a century ago by Italian Physicist, Ettore Majorana, has two distinct components. They need one part of the device on either side of the Portal – the Clivilius side and the Earth side. Very few understand the mechanics of Ettore's work, and it is well rumoured that he worked closely with his uncle, Quirino Majorana, an experimental physicist whose connections ran deep through the University of Rome, extending his realm of influence well into the highest echelons of government, providing Ettore with both the scientific and financial resources needed to achieve such a significant technological breakthrough.

With the two halves of the device, one on each side of the Portal, a signal composed of what has become known as Majorana particles, could be transmitted from Earth without the need for wire devices, and be received by the device in Clivilius. The result, the capability of recording both Earth and Clivilius locations with such precision and permanency that enable Portal Pirates to access any recorded Clivilius location from any recorded Earth location. The reverse is also believed to be true, that they can access any recorded Earth location from any recorded Clivilius location.

Over the years that have followed since the technologies development, it is believed that the Portal Pirates have amassed a large database of locations, which they exploit ruthlessly."

"But why?" Krid's question wasn't just a query; it was a challenge, a prod at the edges of known territory that beckoned me towards the unknown. Her inquisitive nature, always so vibrant and unyielding, pushed the boundaries of the conversation into realms I hadn't considered venturing into at this moment.

"Exploit? I don't know," I replied, my gaze lifting to meet that of my dedicated student. The journal, resting open in my hands, felt like a treasure chest whose contents had suddenly vanished, leaving us with more questions than answers. "That's where the journal entry stops." The finality in my voice was unintentional, a reflection of the frustration that came with hitting yet another dead end in our quest for understanding.

"Is there a way to find out?" Krid wasn't deterred; her voice, laced with determination and a hint of excitement, pressed on. Her eagerness to unravel the mysteries of the Portal Pirates was not just commendable—it was infectious.

"I'm not sure," I admitted, my thoughts a whirlwind of possibilities and dead ends. My mind raced, trying to keep pace with Krid's relentless curiosity. *Was there a piece of the puzzle we were overlooking? A clue hidden in plain sight that could lead us to the answers we sought?* The thought that there might be a way to unveil more secrets about the Portal Pirates and their exploits stirred a mix of excitement and apprehension within me.

"I think speaking with Jeremiah will be a good place to start," Krid suggested, her statement slicing through the contemplative silence that had enveloped us. Her solution was so straightforward, yet it held the promise of unlocking doors I hadn't even considered knocking on.

My eyes lit up at her suggestion, a spark of hope igniting in the sea of uncertainty. "Exactly! You are perfectly right there, Krid." The idea of consulting Jeremiah, someone who had been a part of my early years as a Guardian and who possessed a wealth of knowledge and insight, suddenly seemed like the missing piece of the puzzle. "I will speak with Jeremiah and see what more he knows. Somebody has to know more than this by now," I said, a newfound resolve strengthening my voice as I held up the now closed journal.

The serene atmosphere of scholarly pursuit was shattered in an instant by Freya's breathless entrance. "Father! The truck has gone!" Her voice, tinged with urgency and panic, sliced through the air, pulling me sharply back to the present dangers that lurked beyond our walls. She stood in the doorway, her silhouette framed by the dimming light, her expression etched with concern.

"What happened?" I found myself rising to my feet, propelled by a surge of adrenaline. The scholarly curiosity and contemplation of moments ago felt like a distant memory, replaced now by the immediate need to understand and react.

"Fryar and I were ambushed." The words fell heavy in the room.

"Ambushed? How?" My mind raced, trying to piece together how such a thing could happen under their watchful eyes.

"I'm not sure," Freya admitted, her brows furrowed in confusion and frustration. "We both blacked out." The admission sent a chill down my spine. The implications were dire, suggesting an enemy capable of striking swiftly and silently, leaving no trace behind.

"Shit," I muttered under my breath. "And Griffin?" My heart raced as I awaited her response, fearing the worst.

"We're pretty sure it was him. No idea how. There are no signs of any tracks beyond the cave, so we believe he's taken the truck through the Portal." Her words painted a clear picture of our vulnerability, of how precariously we balanced on the edge of safety and disaster.

"I guess that answers one question then, doesn't it, Krid," I said, attempting to mask my rising concern with a semblance of calm. I turned to the young child, who had been following our exchange with wide, understanding eyes. "Griffin had boasted that they had already recorded Belkeep's location. So that must mean once they have the location recorded, the requirement for the two halves of the device no longer holds true." The realisation dawned on me with chilling clarity, reshaping my understanding of the threat we faced.

"You speak wise logic," Krid replied, her grin offering a brief moment of levity in the midst of our troubled thoughts. Her ability to find a spark of positivity, even now, was a small beacon of hope.

"Do you think Belkeep is in any danger?" Freya's voice, laced with worry, brought the conversation back to the immediate concerns. Her question hung in the air, heavy with the weight of potential consequences.

"I don't think so. They've likely known of our location for years and if they haven't bothered us yet, the chance that they would start now, I believe, is very slim." I tried to sound more convinced than I felt, clinging to the logic as a shield against the fear. "Griffin told me himself, they don't like it here. Besides, I'm certain I interrupted the pair before they could record their intended location, which would mean that Nelson is trapped in Luke's settlement somewhere." This thought, at least, provided a small comfort, a silver lining in the cloud that hung over us.

Freya let out a loud sigh of relief, her shoulders dropping slightly as the tension began to ebb away, if only just a little.

"But talk with Chief. Tell him to have the people be extra vigilant. Just in case." My words were a reminder that vigilance was our best defence, a necessary precaution in a world where threats could materialise from thin air.

As Freya nodded, a silent agreement forged between us, I couldn't help but feel the weight of responsibility pressing down. The safety of our community, the protection of our secrets, and the constant battle against the unknown were burdens we bore together. In that moment, bound by duty and driven by a shared determination to safeguard our way of life, we were more than just a family; we were part of a legacy that transcended time and dimension.

SILENCE

4338.206.4

"Shit!" The word tore from my lips as a streak of grey fur darted past, a blur against the vibrant, swirling colours of the Portal. I had barely stepped through into Gladys's kitchen, my foot making contact with the cold floor, when the urgency of the situation hit me. Reacting instinctively, I pivoted on my heel, the motion rough and ungraceful, propelled by the singular desire to prevent any further mishaps. The colours of the Portal faded, closing off just in time to prevent another unintended journey.

Chloe, with an agility that only cats possess, had already found refuge atop the rocks lining the cave. There she was, perched like a queen surveying her domain, settled comfortably on my new heavy coat. Her meow, determined and commanding, broke through the silence as I approached, a sound that seemed to carry both a reprimand and a welcome.

With careful movements, born of a desire not to startle her further, I gathered both Chloe and the coat into my arms. Balancing her with one hand while attempting to manoeuvre my other arm into the sleeve of the coat was a juggling act that demanded more dexterity than I usually possessed. Finally, with Chloe securely nestled against me, I wrapped the coat around us both. Her head emerged from the gap at my neck, her soft purrs vibrating against my chest, a gentle reminder of the comfort found in unexpected companionship.

I couldn't help but smile, a genuine, warm expression that felt like a balm to the frayed edges of my nerves. Chloe, of all

Gladys's cats, had always been the elusive shadow, her presence more often sensed than seen. That she would seek solace with me, let alone display such affection, was a surprise that pierced the usual veil of concern and strategy that my mind was often shrouded in. For a moment, the weight of responsibilities, the constant vigilance against threats, seemed to lift, replaced by the simple, pure connection between human and animal.

Chloe's head retreated to the sanctuary of the coat's warmth as we ventured out of the cave, stepping into a world softly veiled by falling snowflakes. They landed with a silent grace, transforming the landscape into a serene tableau of winter's touch. I paused, the chill of the air biting at my cheeks, a stark contrast to the warmth emanating from the bundle I cradled. The realisation of Chloe's accidental journey to Clivilius weighed heavily on me, a knot of worry forming in the pit of my stomach. *How would I ever explain this to Freya?* The thought of concealing Chloe's presence, of weaving a tapestry of secrets in a place that had become a refuge from deception, troubled me deeply.

With my hands firmly wrapped around Chloe, ensuring her comfort and warmth beneath the coat, I ventured down the cobbled street that lay between Lake Gunlah and the quaint row of stone cottages. My steps were measured, my mind racing with the implications of my unintended companion. Shaun's presence on the street was a reminder of the normalcy that life in Clivilius usually offered. I managed a nod in his direction, a silent greeting exchanged between friends, grateful that he was absorbed in his own thoughts and did not seek conversation. My relief was palpable, a sigh escaping my lips as I passed, the tension in my shoulders easing slightly with each step.

Reaching the last cottage, a familiar structure that had become a symbol of safety and home, I hesitated at the door.

Taking a deep breath to steady my nerves, I stepped inside, the warmth of the interior embracing me like an old friend. The fire's crackle greeted me, its flames dancing with life, casting a glow that cut through the cold that clung to my skin.

Without bothering to remove my coat, I made my way to the small living area, the heart of our home where the fire burned brightest. The lively snaps and pops of the firewood were a comforting backdrop to the quiet that enveloped the room. Gently, I loosened the top button of my coat and peeled back the collar, revealing Chloe's curious gaze as her head emerged from the cocoon of warmth.

"Looks like it's just you and me," I whispered to her, a smile spreading across my face despite the whirlwind of emotions churning within. I stroked her head softly, her purring a gentle rumble that spoke of contentment and trust. In that moment, with the fire's warmth wrapping around us, the challenges that lay ahead seemed surmountable. Chloe, an unexpected companion in my world, symbolised more than just a secret to be kept; she represented the unforeseen connections that life often presents, the kind that enrich our stories in ways we could never predict.

The sudden cacophony in the kitchen shattered the tranquility of the moment like a stone through glass, sending Chloe into a panic. Her claws, sharp as the edge of a knife, found an anchor in my chest as she bolted, a streak of grey against the warm hues of the living room. Her destination: the sanctuary beneath the emerald armchair, a fortress in the far corner where shadows danced and the world seemed a little less frightening.

"Father! Are you alright?" Freya's voice, tinged with concern, cut through the aftermath of the disturbance. Krid, ever the silent shadow, appeared by her side, her eyes wide with the echo of my fright.

"Yeah," I managed, the sting from Chloe's claws quickly subsiding. I glanced at my arm, finding solace in the absence of blood, just a testament to a moment of fear etched lightly upon my skin.

Freya was at my side in an instant, her worry palpable. "What happened to your arm?" she inquired, her gaze fixed on the minor wound with an intensity that only served to amplify the situation.

"It's just a scratch. I'm fine."

"A scratch? From what?"

With a sigh, I shed my coat, draping it over the arm of the chair as if to mark the end of the ordeal. Kneeling before the chair, I peered into the shadowed recess beneath it, where Chloe had taken refuge. "It's okay, Chloe," I murmured, my voice a soft beacon in the dim light, hoping to coax her from her hiding place.

After a moment of whispered promises and gentle coaxing, Chloe's head tentatively emerged from her hideaway, her wide eyes scanning for danger. The sight of her, so small and frightened, elicited an unexpected reaction from Freya and Krid. High-pitched squeals of fear punctuated the air, their sudden alarm a shock to my calm.

"What the hell is that thing!?" Freya's voice, now laced with a mix of terror and disbelief, caused Chloe to withdraw once again into the safety of the shadows beneath the chair.

"There's no need to be scared," I reassured them, my words aimed at calming the storm of fear that had swept through the room. But Freya's protective instincts were already in overdrive, her sharp call to Krid an attempt to prevent her from venturing too close to the unknown.

Krid's cautious approach mirrored my own trepidation. As I lowered myself to the ground, my face just inches from the cool, wooden floor, I spoke with a gentleness I reserved for moments of delicate persuasion. Krid, emulating my posture, extended her hand with an innocence born of curiosity towards Chloe's shadowed refuge.

"Chloe," my voice was barely a whisper, a soft beckoning in the quiet of the room. "It's okay."

"Chloe," Krid echoed, her voice a tender mimicry of my own. Yet, the unfamiliarity of the gesture, perhaps too sudden or too strange for Chloe, elicited a defensive growl. Krid's hand snapped back, her reaction swift, a mixture of surprise and a touch of fear colouring her movements.

I fought back a chuckle, watching Krid's first encounter with a cat. "Why don't you sit on the chair and wait?" I suggested, hoping to ease her into a role of patient observer rather than direct participant.

Krid, though reluctant, complied, positioning herself on the chair's edge, her body language a mixture of disappointment and lingering curiosity. Her tiny legs dangled, twitching with the leftover adrenaline of the encounter.

After what felt like an eternity of coaxing met with steadfast refusal, I admitted defeat. The gap between the chair and the floor remained Chloe's chosen sanctuary. I joined Krid, balancing myself on the arm of the chair, a silent acknowledgment of our shared setback.

"What is it?" Krid's inquiry, laden with wonder, broke the silence.

"Chloe is a cat," Freya interjected, her voice tinged with a mix of exasperation and disappointment. My eyes met hers, pleading for patience, for understanding of the delicate balance I was navigating.

"Is she friendly?" Krid's question was laced with a hopeful innocence.

"Usually," I assured her. "Cats get scared easily. She just needs a bit of time to get used to her new home."

"Home?" Freya's repetition of the word carried a weight of concern, a silent dialogue of apprehension and caution passed between us. My glare, sharp and clear, was a silent command for discretion.

Encouraging patience, I suggested, "Why don't you sit here and wait patiently. If you're really quiet, she'll soon come out from hiding."

"Really?" Krid's voice was a blend of hope and eagerness, her wide eyes reflecting a world where anything was possible, where even a cat from another dimension could find friendship and acceptance.

"Yep," I affirmed, rising from my makeshift seat. "I need to have a quick chat with Freya and then I have some jobs to do. But I'll be back later, and I want you to introduce me to your new friend."

"Okay," Krid's response was a whisper of promise, a commitment to bridge the gap between fear and friendship.

I gave Krid a soft smile, a small token of affection. As I ruffled her curly hair, her innocence in this complicated world we lived in was starkly highlighted. The shift in atmosphere was palpable as Freya and I moved into the kitchen, the warmth of the fire replaced by a colder, more pragmatic air.

"What are you doing?" Freya's voice, laced with concern and frustration, cut through the silence. Her question wasn't just about the immediate situation but a reflection of the broader challenges we faced in Belkeep, a community clinging to survival in a world that offered little mercy.

"It was an accident," I admitted, the words feeling inadequate even as they left my lips. The arrival of Chloe into our lives, though unintended, had opened a Pandora's box of sorts, revealing desires and regulations long buried under the weight of daily survival.

"What are we going to do with it? You know Chief doesn't allow pets." Freya's reminder was a cold splash of reality. The rules were clear, born out of necessity in a place where resources were scarce and survival was the priority.

"Then you'd better not tell him about it," I responded, a half-hearted attempt to lighten the mood with a cheeky grin. But even as I spoke, the seriousness of our situation lingered at the back of my mind, a shadow that my humour could not dispel.

"This isn't funny, father. What do you think this will do to Krid when she gets attached to the creature and then Chief finds out and has the animal slaughtered?" The weight of Freya's words struck me with the force of a physical blow. The prospect of causing Krid pain, of snuffing out the flicker of joy that Chloe's presence had ignited in her, was unbearable.

The reality of Belkeep's harsh conditions, where even the simplest forms of companionship were governed by laws of survival, suddenly felt overwhelmingly oppressive. Krid's unfamiliarity with the concept of pets, her lack of experience with the unconditional loyalty and affection they offered, was a tragic reminder of all that our community had sacrificed.

"I think it's time some of our laws changed," I found myself saying, the words carrying a determination I hadn't known I possessed. It was a declaration not just of dissent but of hope, a belief that perhaps it was time for Belkeep to evolve, to rediscover some semblance of the humanity that survival had stripped from us.

"You're not seriously going to tell Chief, are you?" Freya's question was a tether, pulling me back from the brink of impulsive decisions. Her concern was valid; confrontation with Chief was not something to be taken lightly.

I paused, caught between the desire to fight for change and the immediate need to protect our new, unexpected companion. "No. I have other things I need to do," I conceded, my gaze drifting back to Krid. The sight of her, so engrossed in the simple act of petting Chloe, was a poignant reminder of the stakes involved. This moment of innocence and joy was a rare treasure in our harsh world, something to be safeguarded at all costs.

"I'll be back soon. Keep her safe," I instructed Freya, my voice carrying all the weight of my fears and hopes. Her response, "Of course, you know I will," was a beacon of trust in the constant storm that was our lives.

With one last look at my daughter, a sad smile playing on my lips, I stepped out into the blizzard, the door closing behind me with a finality that felt heavy with significance. As I ventured into the howling wind, my thoughts were a whirlwind of concern for Chloe, for Krid, and for the future of Belkeep. The laws that had once seemed so immutable now felt constricting, and my resolve to see them challenged, to bring about change, was solidifying with every step I took into the storm.

TO JOEL!

4338.206.5

Standing outside the front door of Luke's house, the crisp night air brushed against my skin, a small smile involuntarily playing on my lips. The new phone in my hand cast a soft glow, bathing my features in a pale light, creating a stark contrast with the darkness that enveloped everything else. I couldn't help but read, for the umpteenth time, the text message from Gladys about the farewell for Joel at eleven tonight. It felt surreal, this blend of digital connectivity and our tangled, real-world lives coming together for a moment that felt both ending and beginning.

With a sense of purpose, I had promptly replied, typing with a certain deliberation. "I'll be there," I typed out, confirming my presence at Luke's and promising to bring the whiskey—a bottle now cradled in my other hand, its glass cold and solid within the paper bag, a tangible promise of the night ahead. The whiskey, an old favourite, felt like a suitable companion for the evening, its presence a bridge between the past we were all parting with and the unknowns of the future.

The memory of Chloe's unexpected escape lingered in my mind, an unresolved chord in the symphony of Gladys' and my intertwined lives. Returning to Gladys's house after the fiasco, I had left behind a cryptic clue—a piece of me, in a way. The note, carefully placed on the label of a new bottle of shiraz in her pantry, was meant to guide her to the phone number of my first-ever phone. It was a breadcrumb trail back to a time when things were simpler, or at least seemed that way.

I sent a message to Jeremiah soon after, the words on the screen feeling like the closing of a circle. We agreed to meet at the usual place and time in two days. *Jeremiah was right*, I found myself reflecting, the realisation hitting me with a mix of relief and resignation. Guardian work was indeed so much easier with a phone. The digital age, with all its complexities, offered tools that made my clandestine activities more manageable, if not entirely straightforward.

Checking the time one last time, I slid the phone into my pocket, the action marking the transition from preparation to action. The night ahead loomed, filled with the promise of closure and the uncertainty of goodbyes.

Arriving early was a deliberate choice, fuelled by a sense of urgency that gnawed at my insides. The missing Portal Pirate—a puzzle piece lost in a vast, intricate game—weighed heavily on my mind. My steps were measured, each one taken with a purpose as I navigated the familiar path to Luke's front door. The possibility that the Portal Pirates might have recorded Luke's settlement location and added it to their database was a looming threat, one that could unravel everything Luke was working towards. The very thought tightened a noose of anxiety around my neck, my heart pounding against my ribcage as if trying to escape the impending doom.

I gave a solid knock on the front door, the sound echoing ominously in the quiet of the evening. My breath hitched, trapped in the limbo of anticipation and fear as the silence stretched, becoming a tangible entity that seemed to feed on my growing panic. A myriad of scenarios raced through my mind, each more dire than the last. *Has something happened to Luke?* The question pounded in my head, a drumbeat of dread.

Compelled by a mix of impatience and concern, my knuckles rapped against the door again, the action sharper, more insistent. The world seemed to hold its breath with me, waiting, until finally, light pierced the gloom. It spilled from behind the blinds, a beacon in the night, washing over the small porch in a warm glow that felt like a promise. The lightbulb overhead flickered to life, stuttering into a steady beam that cast long shadows and, for a moment, my heart found its rhythm again. I exhaled loudly, a gust of relief that felt like dispelling a ghost.

"Cody!" The surprise in Luke's voice was a balm, his silhouette framed in the doorway as he swung it open wide. The relief I felt was quickly tempered by the confusion etched on his face. "What are you doing here?" he asked, his expression a mix of surprise and mild annoyance, as if my presence was an unexpected variable in an already complex equation.

"Gladys invited me to come along," I managed, mustering a short smile that felt more like a grimace. The tension between us was palpable, a current of unspoken questions and half-answers.

"Oh," was all Luke replied, his features relaxing into resignation. "Come on in."

I stepped into the entryway, the unfamiliar space of Luke's home enveloping me. It was then that the large flat screen television in the living room halted me in my tracks, a beacon of modern luxury that seemed almost out of place. *It appears Luke isn't short on funds.* The thought flickered through my mind, unbidden but not unwelcome. *That'll be useful.* In the grand chessboard of Guardian endeavours, resources were as vital as strategy, and it seemed Luke had more aces up his sleeve than I had given him credit for.

"I've brought the whiskey," I announced, a hint of formality in my voice as I lifted the brown paper bag for him to see.

The sound of the paper crinkling seemed to echo in the quiet of Luke's kitchen, a small but significant herald to the evening's undertones of anticipation and nervousness. Holding the bag, I felt the weight of the bottle inside—a weight that seemed to embody so much more than just the liquor it contained. It was the weight of the evening ahead, of Joel's farewell, the unsettling mystery of the missing Portal Pirate, and the looming threat over Luke's mission. Each aspect felt magnified, as if the whiskey in my hand was a symbol of the complexities we were navigating.

"Whiskey?" Luke's response was one of genuine confusion, his eyebrows knitting together in a question mark. "What for?"

"For the farewell," I replied, simplicity in my tone. Yet, the concept seemed to hang in the air between us, unfamiliar territory for Luke.

He stared at me, the blankness of his expression revealing a gap in our shared understanding. "I've always toasted a shot of whiskey at memorials," I explained, a tinge of surprise in my voice that Luke wasn't acquainted with this tradition—a tradition that felt as natural to me as breathing.

"Why?" Luke's question was straightforward, but it struck me as odd in the moment.

Walking into the kitchen, I placed the whiskey bottle on the island bench, the sound of glass meeting stone a sharp contrast to the softness of our conversation. "You know," I began, reaching for the cupboard above the rangehood, my movements automatic in the ritual of preparation, "I don't have the foggiest idea." It was a moment of honesty, a confession that, despite the tradition, the origin of it was as unclear to me as the bottom of an empty glass.

"They're in the far cupboard. On the top shelf," Luke's voice guided me, a subtle indication of his acceptance to engage in the custom, despite his unfamiliarity with it.

"Thanks," I acknowledged, the cupboard swinging open under my touch. I retrieved the first two shot glasses, setting them down with a careful precision before reaching up again for another two, the movements fluid, a dance I had performed many times before.

"Where are Gladys and Beatrix?" Luke's inquiry came as I was unscrewing the cap of the whiskey bottle. "I'm surprised they didn't come with you."

"I prefer to travel alone," I found myself saying, a half-truth that danced on the edge of evasion. I avoided Luke's gaze, focusing instead on the task at hand, the twist of the cap, the pour of the whiskey. "I'm sure they're not far away," I added, a placation for any concern, as I filled each shot glass to the brim.

"So, you're a Guardian, then?" Luke's question cut through the air with an unvarnished directness that momentarily caught me off guard.

"Here," I found myself saying, an attempt to bridge the gap his question had created. I slid a shot glass across the polished stone surface of the island bench towards him, its journey a silent offering of camaraderie in the midst of our complex web of allegiances and secrets. Then, almost reflexively, I picked up a glass for myself, feeling the cool weight of it grounding me in the moment.

"You're not waiting for the others?" Luke's sideways glance was probing, hinting at a protocol or perhaps a courtesy I was bypassing. His question lingered in the air, adding another layer to the already thick atmosphere of anticipation and unspoken tension.

"It's been a tough week," I admitted, the words barely scratching the surface of the tumultuous sea churning inside me. Holding the shot glass, a fragile vessel of liquid courage, I felt the weight of the world pressing down. The truth was my heart was pounding in my chest and my mind had turned to a blended mess. I had come along to farewell a young man I never knew, and who had been slaughtered by a Portal Pirate who was now who knows where. I had almost kidnapped Gladys and instead had now inadvertently stolen Chloe, breaking the laws of Belkeep and placing my daughter in a precarious position of silence. And now, here I stood, about to cheers with the most important and powerful Guardian to have existed since the time of the Founders, and I was certain Luke didn't have any idea just how important he was.

"Indeed," Luke's response was soft, a word spoken with a depth of understanding that hinted at his own acquaintance with hardship and the weariness that comes with the duty of Guardianship.

"Oh, Luke, you have no idea. This is only the start," I said, a half-whispered confession that felt like a prelude to the myriad challenges he would face. The enormity of what lay ahead was a shadow that loomed large, a spectre of trials and tribulations yet to come.

"Well," Luke began, a note of resolve in his voice as he raised his glass, an acknowledgment of the unspoken pact between us. "Here's to tough weeks."

I nodded, a gesture of solidarity, and our glasses clinked—a sound that, for a fleeting moment, seemed to encapsulate the complexity of our journey, the bonds formed in the crucible of shared struggles. My eyes closed as I tipped the glass, the whiskey burning a trail down my throat. In that instant, the sharpness of the alcohol mirrored the sharpness of our reality—a world fraught with danger, alliances, and the perpetual fight for something greater than ourselves. The warmth of the whiskey spread through me, a fleeting comfort against the cold uncertainties of existence.

"Shit, that's one strong liquor." Luke's exclamation reverberated through the kitchen, a testament to the whiskey's potency. His reaction sparked a flicker of amusement in me, the corners of my mouth turning upwards in a grin that I couldn't suppress. The liquid fire that had just scorched our throats was indeed strong, but its intensity was a fitting metaphor for the life we led—harsh, sometimes overwhelming, but undeniably worth the struggle.

"But totally worth it," I affirmed, my grin broadening. I placed my glass on the bench, the sound of it touching down a crisp note in the quiet of Luke's home. The act of refilling my glass was deliberate, a physical punctuation to my statement of endorsement for the whiskey's fierce burn.

"Totally," Luke echoed my sentiment, a smile in his voice as he slid his glass across the bench towards me.

"Hey, you didn't answer my question," he pointed out, his tone lighthearted yet probing as I poured another round of whiskey into his glass. The liquid amber caught the light as it flowed, a golden stream that seemed to hold the promise of oblivion or perhaps clarity in its depths.

"Oh, didn't I?" My response was tinged with feigned innocence, my grin turning cheeky. I was fully aware of the sidestep I had taken from Luke's earlier inquiry about my Guardian status. It wasn't that I doubted my role or hesitated to claim it; it was more that the acknowledgment seemed redundant, superfluous even. My actions, my very presence here, should have served as confirmation enough. After all, the ability to open Portals wasn't a parlour trick but a mark of our shared calling.

"To Guardians!" Luke declared, a new fervour in his voice as he raised his glass once more.

"I'll drink to that," I concurred, my voice steady despite the whiskey's warmth spreading through my veins. Raising my glass, I touched it to Luke's with an almost clumsy clink. I wasn't accustomed to drinking much alcohol, and the first shot was already making its presence known, a buzz of warmth that seemed to lighten the weight on my mind, if only momentarily.

As the second shot passed my lips, a wave of anticipation mixed with apprehension washed over me. The effect of the alcohol was immediate, a gentle haze that threatened to cloud my senses. I was all too aware of its potential impact, a loosening of inhibitions and sharpening of emotions that could prove to be either a balm or a catalyst in the hours to come.

The front door's groan as it swung open was a jarring intrusion into the intimate bubble Luke and I had created around ourselves. The synchronised cheer, "Hey, Luke!" from two distinct voices, sliced through the air. Luke's reaction was immediate and unguarded; his glass clattered against the bench as if trying to escape the sudden shift in energy.

A hearty chuckle bubbled up from within me, an instinctive response to the scene unfolding. Yet, as I turned to face Gladys and Beatrix, my amusement was tinged with a hint of disappointment. Their arrival, though expected, felt untimely, cutting short the moment of connection I had been forging with Luke.

"You two couldn't even wait for us?" Gladys's scolding was a mix of mock indignation and genuine reproach, her words carrying the warmth of long-standing friendships. Beatrix's playful accusation, "How rude," added a layer of lightheartedness to the reprimand, yet beneath their banter lay my unspoken concern—the delicate topic of Portal Pirates and the looming threat they posed, now pushed further into the realm of the unaddressable.

"I was just cheering Luke up," I found myself saying, a defence mounted more out of a desire to preserve the night's remaining camaraderie than to explain our actions. My words were a veil over the underlying tension, the weight of conversations postponed and strategies unshared, knowing that convincing Gladys to join me now would be a Herculean task if she got wind of the existence of Portal Pirates.

"I'm sure," Gladys retorted, her skepticism a sharp note that cut through the conviviality.

Quickly, I refilled our glasses, attempting to steer the conversation away from dangerous waters. "So how..." Beatrix started, only to be cut off by Luke.

In an attempt to navigate the conversation away from the precipice of inquiry, I refilled our glasses, the action a physical diversion to match my verbal sidestepping. But even as I poured, Luke's interjection, "I don't really want to talk about it. I'm really tired," brought a halt to any further probing. His weariness was not just a mask for the evening's earlier tensions but a genuine reflection of the fatigue that our lives as Guardians, as keepers of secrets and balancers of worlds, often entailed.

"Or drunk," Gladys quipped, dropping her handbag onto the kitchen bench.

"Not yet," Luke replied, rubbing his brow.

As they settled into the kitchen, the space filled with the palpable presence of our collective experiences, I found myself teetering on the edge of inebriation. My thoughts, once sharp and focused, now swam in a sea of whiskey-induced haze. The earlier clarity with which I had navigated our conversation, the careful dance around truths too dangerous to voice, began to blur.

My gaze drifted to Gladys's handbag, an innocuous object that seemed to sag under the weight of its contents. Its bulging form, casually dropped onto the bench, piqued my curiosity. *What secrets did it hold?* The mystery of its contents, much like our evening, promised revelations and realisations yet to unfold, unravelling sooner than anticipated in the unpredictable ebb and flow of our shared destinies.

"We've brought the candles," Beatrix's announcement cut through the air, her voice a mixture of solemnity and readiness as she began to unload an eclectic assortment of candles from Gladys's seemingly bottomless bag. The array of colours and sizes she placed on the bench was a silent testament to the sombreness of the occasion, each candle a beacon for the remembrance we were about to undertake.

Luke, moving with a purpose that seemed to anchor him amidst the whirlwind of emotions, rifled through the kitchen drawers in search of a gas lighter. Beatrix snatched the lighter from him the moment it was found, her movements swift as she began to light the candles. The room was soon bathed in the soft, flickering glow of candlelight, transforming the space into a sanctum of remembrance and reflection.

"Are you sure you have enough candles?" I couldn't help but tease, a chuckle escaping me despite the solemnity of the moment.

Beatrix shot me a glare, her expression a mix of mock annoyance and focused intent. "Turn the lights off," she instructed, and with that simple command, the house plunged into darkness. The immediate transformation was striking—candlelight painted dancing shadows around the kitchen and living room, casting each of us in a soft, ethereal light. The four of us encircled the large island bench, a circle of light in the enveloping darkness, and I found myself distributing shot glasses, the dim glow accentuating the sense of shared camaraderie and purpose that bound us together.

"Do you have a picture of him?" Beatrix inquired, her voice soft, imbued with a mix of curiosity and compassion. It was a question that sought to bridge the gap between the known and the unknown, to bring a semblance of reality to the person we were gathered to farewell.

"No," Luke replied, his voice carrying a note of regret. "We only learnt about him a few months ago." His admission, simple yet heavy with unspoken narratives, underscored the complexity of our connections and the often fleeting nature of our interactions.

"Does... does Jamie know he's dead yet?" Gladys's question was delicate, her concern evident in the gentle timbre of her voice.

"No," Luke said again, the shake of his head visible even in the candlelit dimness. "And he won't ever find out. Cody took care of it," he added, his gaze finding mine across the flickering lights. The look he gave me was one of gratitude mixed with trust, a silent acknowledgment of the burden I had shouldered.

The whiskey bottle nearly slipped from my fingers at his words. "Yeah," I managed to respond, my voice barely above a whisper. I stared down into my shot glass, the amber liquid reflecting the flickering candlelight. I avoided eye contact with Luke, with all of them, as I finished the tale I had woven —a tale that now lay between us, a fabricated bridge over a chasm of unspeakable truths. "I took care of it," I repeated, the words a heavy cloak around my shoulders.

"It's so sad," Beatrix's voice cut through the dimly lit silence, each word heavy with genuine sorrow. Her empathy for the boy we never knew painted the room with a shade of melancholy that was both touching and profound. "He looked so young."

"He was," Luke's acknowledgment was soft, yet it carried the weight of undeniable truth. "He was only nineteen." His words felt like a cold gust of wind, reminding us of the fragility of life, especially in our line of work where youth offered no shield against the darkness we fought against.

"Tragic," Gladys murmured, her gesture of wiping her eye with her finger a silent testament to the raw emotions simmering just beneath the surface.

Luke seized his shot glass and raised it in the air, a silent clarion call to honour the departed. It was an impromptu memorial, yes, but no less poignant for its spontaneity. The gesture, a beacon of shared grief and respect, drew us together in a circle of flickering candlelight.

The sisters and I followed suit, the clink of our glasses a soft chime in the hush that enveloped the room. "What do we say?" Gladys's question, reflecting our collective uncertainty, hung in the air. It was a valid concern—how to commemorate someone whose life had brushed ours so lightly, yet left an indelible mark?

"You say whatever is in your heart to say," I found myself responding, the words coming from a place of instinctual wisdom. Surprised by my own counsel, I realised it was the truth. In moments like these, it was the sincerity of our sentiments that mattered most, not the eloquence of our words.

"I'll go first," Beatrix declared, her voice a mix of determination and vulnerability as she lifted her glass. "Joel," she began, her voice firm yet wavering with emotion, "We never had the chance to know you. But we love Jamie, and you are his blood." Her words, simple and heartfelt, struck a chord within me, igniting a surge of unexpected emotions. The compassion and love she expressed for Joel, a boy none of us had met but were connected to through the most unfortunate of circumstances, was a poignant reminder of the intricate web of actions and consequences that defined our existence.

The thought of the body, now potentially anywhere in the hands of a Portal Pirate, flashed through my mind, a dark cloud threatening to overshadow the moment. I fought to suppress the question, to focus on the here and now, on the act of remembrance we were engaged in.

"And so, we love you, too," Beatrix concluded, her voice echoing the sentiments of us all. I hastily wiped my eye, the gesture a futile attempt to stem the tide of emotions that Beatrix's words had unleashed.

"To Jamie's son," she proclaimed, her voice steady as she downed her shot in a single, fluid motion.

"To Jamie's son," we echoed, our voices merging into a single vow of remembrance.

Gladys took her turn, her hand steady as she reached for the glass I filled. "Joel. May your soul one day know your father, and know the good man that he is," she articulated, each word a testament to her depth of feeling. The brief pause to wipe her eye, a gesture so fleeting yet so laden with sorrow, echoed in the cavernous silence of our gathering.

"To Joel," Gladys said, raising her glass.

As I echoed, "To Joel," the whiskey's warmth clashed tumultuously with the surge of emotions within me, a maelstrom of grief and unresolved tension. My vision blurred, not just from the alcohol but from the swell of feelings that threatened to breach the walls I had meticulously erected.

My turn arrived like a spectre in the night, unexpected yet inevitable. Holding my empty glass before me, I found myself ensnared by its emptiness, a metaphor, perhaps, for the void left by Joel's untimely departure. "Joel. You met unfortunate circumstances, but..." The words lodged in my throat, each syllable a struggle as I grappled with the enormity of my actions, or rather, my missteps. My pause was laden with an unspoken apology to Luke, a silent plea for understanding amidst the chaos I feared I had wrought.

"But," I found the strength to continue, the word echoing in the charged air as I sought guidance from the ethereal whispers of Clivilius that threaded through my clouded thoughts. "Death is but a mere process, and when we learn to master that process, we will master death itself," I concluded, the words not fully my own but conveyed with a conviction that belied my inner turmoil. My gaze locked with Luke's, a silent transmission of a message that I barely understood yet felt compelled to deliver.

"To Joel," I announced, raising my empty glass in a salute to the unseen, to the mysteries that lay beyond our mortal grasp.

"To Joel," they echoed, their voices a harmonious blend of respect and remembrance. The mantra, *Death is but a mere process, and when we learn to master that process, we will master death itself*, reverberated within me, a cryptic puzzle left by Clivilius. Its true meaning eluded me, yet I sensed its importance, not just to me but to Luke, to all of us entwined in this complex tapestry of life and death.

And then, like a bolt from the blue, realisation struck. *Killerton Enterprises!* The name surged through my mind with the force of a tidal wave, breaking over me with revelations and implications that I had yet to fully unravel. The connection, previously obscured by the fog of grief and whiskey, now gleamed with a clarity that was both exhilarating and terrifying. The pieces of a larger puzzle began to align, a narrative unfolding that promised answers and, perhaps, a path forward through the labyrinth of secrets and shadows.

4338.207

(26 July 2018)

HUNTED

4338.207.1

"You really shouldn't be doing this now," I found myself whispering, the words barely escaping my lips as I trudged forward, each step a testament to my determination—or perhaps my folly. The dull throb in my head had blossomed into a relentless pounding, a rhythmic reminder of the whiskey's potency and the emotional weight of the evening's memorial. Yet, against the better judgment that the whiskey had dulled, I found myself on the precipice of infiltrating Killerton Enterprises, armed with nothing but an access card whose acquisition tread dangerously close to the line of legality.

The risk was palpable, a shadow that stretched long and ominous before me. Yet, it was the words of Clivilius, enigmatic and haunting, that propelled me forward. *Death is but a mere process, and when we learn to master that process, we will master death itself.* These words, though cryptic, resonated with a frequency that vibrated through my very core. They hinted at knowledge, at secrets that Killerton Enterprises might be harbouring—secrets that could unravel the mysteries we faced or perhaps entangle us further.

As I moved, the world around me seemed both vivid and distant. "Your coffee, sir," I overheard a young waitress chirp, her voice cutting through the fog of my thoughts. The sound of her voice, the clink of porcelain on wood, the rich aroma of freshly brewed coffee—it all beckoned with a siren's call, promising a brief respite from the storm that raged within me.

For a moment, I found myself rooted to the spot, caught between the urgency of my mission and the simple, human yearning for comfort. The allure of caffeine, of a moment's pause to gather my thoughts and steel my resolve, was a temptation that tugged at the edges of my resolve.

My eyes, bleary from the night's indulgences and the weight of the task ahead, lingered on the open coffee shop. The scene before me, so ordinary and yet so inviting, became a tableau of what I was momentarily forsaking—a chance to breathe, to recalibrate before diving into the unknown depths of Killerton Enterprises.

The cool breeze that caressed my face was a gentle reprieve, a natural contrast to the warm flush that the whiskey had painted across my cheeks. It was a moment of clarity, a whisper from the universe inviting me to contemplate the path I was about to take. The decision to move forward, to delve into the heart of Killerton Enterprises in search of answers, was mine to make. Yet, in that brief interlude, the world seemed to hold its breath, offering me a chance to reconsider, to weigh the cost of the knowledge I sought against the toll it might exact.

The path I chose, or perhaps the one that chose me, demanded sacrifices that cut deep into the fabric of my very existence. Telling my family about Clivilius or the Guardians was a line I could never cross, a forbidden revelation that could unravel the fragile balance I desperately clung to. And so, with a heart heavy with unspoken truths, I began the painful process of distancing myself from those I held dearest. After the death of my parents—a loss that tore through me like a storm—I reached out one last time, through letters that bore the weight of finality, before I receded into the shadows of their lives.

My youngest sister, her heart shattered by my sudden absence, respected my last request with a solemnity that only deepened my guilt. No missing person report was filed; she became the keeper of my secret, ensuring that my disappearance remained a mystery. Her dedication to my wish, even as it broke her, was a testament to our bond, one that I severed with a silent apology whispered to the stars. Over time, her efforts to find me waned until they ceased altogether, a reluctant acceptance of my vanishing act.

In my quest to become a ghost among men, I eradicated every trace of my existence in the tangible world. Bank accounts closed, digital footprints erased—I became an enigma, a shadow flitting through the bustling crowds, unseen and untraceable. This anonymity was my armour, a necessary shield against forces that would exploit any tether to my old life.

But survival in the shadows came at a cost, a relentless yearning for a connection I had sacrificed at the altar of duty. The thought of bringing my parents to Clivilius, to share with them the secret of my double life, was a temptation I battled with every fibre of my being. Yet, Jeremiah's warnings echoed in my mind, a chilling reminder of the consequences of such actions. The Guardians lived on the knife's edge, and to tip the balance by introducing those closest to us to our hidden world was to invite police scrutiny and potential catastrophe.

Jeremiah's stark declaration that our fate was sealed, that compliance to Clivilius was not a choice but a mandate, chilled me to the core. The entity we served, through whispered commands and veiled threats, wielded control with a cruelty that knew no bounds. Those who dared defy it faced not just their own destruction but the unimaginable suffering of those they loved. Clivilius's reach was far and merciless, a dark puppeteer pulling at the strings of our lives with sadistic pleasure.

In the company of Jeremiah and the few Guardians who shared my burden, we pondered the enigma of Clivilius, its origins shrouded in mystery, its motives unfathomable. Our existence was a constant battle, not just against the external threats that menaced our settlements, but against the existential dread that gnawed at our spirits. The question of who or what Clivilius was remained unanswered, lost in the cacophony of our daily struggles to keep death at bay for those under our protection.

The cycle of guardianship was a cruel loop, one that offered no reprieve, no moment of clarity or understanding. We were bound to it, not by chains forged of steel, but by the invisible bonds of duty and fear. And so, we continued, our questions unanswered, our doubts unvoiced, each day a testament to our silent, unending vigil. This was our reality, a world suspended between the shadows and the light, where survival was not a choice but a destiny we all bore.

The blaring horn of a passing car snapped me out of my daze, a harsh reminder that I was indeed not in some distant land governed by the rules of the Guardians and Clivilius, but rather in the bustling heart of San Francisco. I stumbled backward, narrowly avoiding a collision that would have been a disastrous end to my already tumultuous day. "Bloody Americans," I muttered under my breath, a knee-jerk reaction to the adrenaline coursing through me. It was easier to cast blame than to admit my own carelessness had almost led me into the path of an oncoming vehicle. I couldn't help but smirk at my own feigned annoyance with the American way of driving, a brief moment of levity in the midst of my spiralling thoughts.

As I stepped safely onto the sidewalk, the green glow of the crossing signal ushering me forward, I couldn't shake the feeling of being an outsider—not just in this country but in this world. The sight of the unassuming office building that housed Killerton Enterprises did little to ground me. Instead, my gaze drifted, catching a glimpse of a quarrelling couple in the distance. Their heated exchange, though muffled by the sounds of the city, was a stark reminder of the everyday human conflicts that continued unabated, oblivious to the hidden wars fought in the shadows.

The Guardian huntings—a phrase that sent a chill down my spine each time it crossed my mind—had once seemed a clear-cut narrative of us versus them, with Killerton Enterprises cast as the villain in a tale as old as time. Rumours had painted them as the architects of our demise, orchestrating the huntings with a cold efficiency that left little room for doubt about their intentions. Jeremiah's teachings had echoed this sentiment, framing the conflict in stark terms: Killerton's leaders believed that eliminating the Guardians would spell the end of Clivilius, severing the cycle of Portals and the transport of souls that fed its insatiable hunger.

The warning Jeremiah had imparted—that falling into the hands of Killerton Enterprises would mean certain death—had been etched into my mind, a constant beacon of caution in my interactions with the outside world. Yet, the truth, as I had come to learn, was far more complex. Killerton Enterprises, for all its outward appearance as a modest construction firm, harboured secrets within its walls. Branches of the organisation operated in the shadows, not as hunters but as protectors, tracking Guardians not to harm but to help.

This revelation had been a paradigm shift, challenging everything I thought I knew about the battle we were fighting. The notion that within the heart of what we believed to be our enemy lay allies working to safeguard our kind was both bewildering and heartening. As I stood there, on the streets of San Francisco, the stark façade of Killerton Enterprises looming before me, I couldn't help but feel the weight of the decisions that lay ahead.

The duality of my mission—to uncover the truths hidden within Killerton while navigating the treacherous waters of trust and betrayal—felt more daunting than ever. Yet, there was a glimmer of hope, a possibility that within this building, allies awaited, ready to join forces in the unseen war against Clivilius. The challenge was discerning friend from foe, truth from deception, in a world where appearances could be deceiving, and allies could be found in the most unexpected of places.

Crossing the small courtyard towards Killerton Enterprises, my pace quickened involuntarily, each step echoing my mounting apprehension. A lump formed in my throat, a tangible manifestation of the nervous energy coursing through me. As I neared the large glass doors, they swung open automatically, ushering me into the modest foyer beyond—a stark contrast to the grandeur I had imagined would house such a secretive operation.

Inside, I was immediately struck by the normalcy of the scene before me. The few occupants, clad in smart casual attire, went about their business with a sense of purpose that seemed at odds with the tumultuous thoughts racing through my mind. Construction workers, their rugged gear a testament to their trade, cast brief glances in my direction. Their scrutiny, however fleeting, amplified my self-consciousness. *I must look dishevelled*, I thought to myself, an outsider not just in mission but in appearance as well.

Compelled to maintain a semblance of normalcy, I kept my gaze forward, doing my best to blend into the environment. Yet, the inevitable happened. My path crossed with the piercing stare of the woman stationed behind the main reception counter—a beacon for guests and visitors, and now, an obstacle in my clandestine entry. Offering her a nod, I attempted to project a confidence I was far from feeling, continuing my march towards the secure door that promised entry to the heart of Killerton's secrets.

Reaching the door, I tried to exude calm as I retrieved the access card from my trouser pocket. Pressing the card against the validator, my heart sank as a red light flashed in denial of my entry. A cough escaped me, an awkward attempt to mask my surprise and growing panic. *Did anybody notice?* The question haunted me as I cast a casual glance over my shoulder, hoping my failed attempt had gone unseen.

With a feigned air of indifference, I tried the card again, only to be met with the same rebuffing red light. The situation was quickly unravelling, each failed attempt a blow to my composure. On the third try, as the card was rejected once more, the reality of my predicament settled in—a mixture of frustration and fear gripping me. My mind raced with potential explanations and contingencies, but in that moment, all I could do was to walk away casually, my palms now slick with sweat, which I tried to discreetly wipe on my thigh.

A firm grip on my shoulder spun me around, bringing me face to face with the source of the stern directive. "Excuse me, Sir. I'm going to need you to come with me."

Shit! My mind recoiled in panic, thoughts racing as I weighed my options. The instinct to flee battled with the realisation that any resistance could escalate the situation. "Of course, Sir," I managed to say, my voice steady despite the turmoil churning inside me. Cooperation seemed the only viable path forward, though it led into the unknown.

To my surprise, and perhaps relief, the security guard didn't drag me away or call for backup. Instead, he swiped an access card, the one tool I had failed to wield successfully, against the reader. The door responded with a welcoming flash of green light, swinging open to grant us passage. The guard motioned for me to enter first, a silent command I had no choice but to obey.

As we traversed the corridor, my mind was awhirl with questions and doubts. *It can't be this easy to get inside, can it?* I pondered, the simplicity of our entry doing nothing to ease my growing sense of unease. The deeper we ventured into the building, the more I felt like a mouse willingly walking into a trap, yet curiosity propelled me forward.

Unable to contain the questions bubbling up, I finally broke the silence. "Who are you?" My voice echoed slightly in the sterile corridor, the words hanging between us, unanswered. The guard's continued silence was a heavy shroud that offered no clues, only deepening the mystery of the moment.

We reached the end of the corridor, where the guard pressed the elevator's down button without a word. The arrival chime of the elevator broke the silence, its doors sliding open to reveal the next stage of our journey. "Step inside," he instructed, his voice devoid of any indication of what awaited us.

With a resigned sense of inevitability, I complied, stepping into the elevator's confined space. The guard followed, swiping his card once more. The doors sealed us in together, the finality of the act not lost on me. As the elevator began its descent below ground level, no buttons pressed to indicate our destination, a tangible anxiety settled over me. The silent descent was punctuated only by the hum of the elevator and the loud beat of my own heart.

Surely, nothing good could come from this? The thought was a whisper in my mind, a reflection of the fear and anticipation that coursed through me. The unspoken threat of descending into the unknown, guided by a silent sentinel whose intentions remained obscured, was a stark reminder of the precarious nature of my situation. Yet, despite the apprehension, a part of me was driven by the need to uncover the truth

"Step out," the guard's command was firm, his hand pressing into my shoulder blade with a force that left no room for misunderstanding. The subtle threat underlying his touch was clear—resistance would only complicate matters. Despite the whirlwind of thoughts and apprehensions swirling within me, I acquiesced, stepping out of the elevator into yet another sterile, impersonal part of Killerton Enterprises. The brightly lit corridors, devoid of any sign of life, stretched before us, leading us deeper into the bowels of the building.

As we navigated through the maze of empty corridors, each turn and doorway seemed indistinguishable from the last, adding to the growing sense of disorientation. The silence was oppressive, the only sound being the muffled echo of our footsteps against the polished floor. My mind raced, trying to piece together the puzzle of my current predicament and what awaited me at the end of this seemingly endless journey.

Finally, we arrived at a door marked "Briefing Room." The label, dull and unassuming, belied the surge of anxiety that coursed through me. *What sort of briefing could possibly require such secrecy and security?* The scenarios that played out in my mind ranged from interrogation to indoctrination, each more unsettling than the last.

Compelled by a mixture of curiosity and a desire to get this over with, I stepped into the room, my senses heightened to every detail of my surroundings. The room was austere, furnished with only the essentials—a small, rectangular desk and a few chairs. The starkness of the decor did little to ease the tension that knotted my stomach.

"Thank you, Percival," came a voice from the centre of the room, breaking the silence. The man seated at the desk rose to his feet, his demeanour calm and collected. His use of the guard's name, "Percival," momentarily caught me off guard. The formal acknowledgment and the swift, wordless exit of Percival, who closed the door with a definitive click, left me alone with the stranger.

The transition from the guarded escort of Percival to the solitude of the briefing room was jarring. The finality of the door's sharp click resonated within me. Here I was, standing in the heart of Killerton Enterprises, about to engage in a conversation whose content and consequences were entirely unknown to me.

"Cody Jennings," the man pronounced my name with a gravity that sent a shiver down my spine. His gaze, unwavering and penetrating, seemed to bore into the very essence of my being. *How could he possibly know who I am?* The question thundered silently in my mind, my pulse quickening in response. My fingers, acting of their own accord, fumbled for the Portal Key hidden in my pocket—a lifeline to another world, and possibly my only means of escape from this increasingly precarious situation.

As if sensing my inner turmoil, the man took several deliberate steps towards me. Each footfall seemed to echo in the sparse room, amplifying the sense of intimidation that his presence commanded. "My name is Eddie Hobson," he introduced himself, his hand extended towards me in a gesture of peace—or perhaps a calculated move to disarm me. "I'm the Chief Security Officer here at Killerton Enterprises." The title resonated in my head with a menacing ring. *Chief Security Officer*. The implications were clear: I was in the presence of someone with significant power and authority within the organisation, someone who could easily become my adversary.

"Please," Eddie insisted, his voice carrying a note of command masked as courtesy. He gestured towards the lone chair opposite his at the table, a silent order for me to take a seat and engage in this unexpected confrontation.

With a mind racing through scenarios of entrapment and betrayal, I weighed my options. The Portal Key, now a tangible reminder of the dual life I led, felt heavy in my pocket. Its presence was a comfort, a reminder of the world I was fighting to protect, but also a beacon of hope should things take a turn for the worse.

Reluctantly, I acquiesced to his request, pulling out the chair with a cautious deliberation. I chose to sit, yet positioned myself strategically, ensuring the desk remained between us—a physical barrier that offered a semblance of security in the face of unknown intentions. My decision to sit was not a submission but a tactical move, allowing me to keep Eddie and any potential threats within my line of sight.

Eddie positioned himself with a calculated casualness that belied the tension crackling in the air between us. The room, with its stark furnishings and the oppressive weight of silence, felt like a chessboard on which an intricate game was being played, with me as one of the pawns.

He leaned forward, the movement causing the dark straps of his braces to stretch taut against his chest, a demonstration of the control he wielded in this space. "Your stolen access card has been deactivated," he announced, a statement delivered with a blandness that contrasted sharply with the turmoil churning inside me. His hand, palm upturned, waited expectantly. Resigned to the futility of keeping the card, I handed it over, feeling a strange sense of surrender with the action.

The silence that reclaimed the room was stifling, a tangible force that seemed to compress the very air around us. Impatience gnawed at me, a growing restlessness that demanded answers. "What am I doing here?" The question erupted from me, a plea for some semblance of understanding.

Eddie's scoff, loud and mocking, was a jarring note in the quietude. "That's a very good question. What *are* you doing here?" His words, echoing my own, were a verbal mirror, throwing my question back at me with a challenge woven through the syllables. The frustration at his tactic, turning my demand for clarity into a rhetorical boomerang, simmered within me. I bit the inside of my cheek, a physical counter to the rising tide of irritation, reminding myself that silence might be my safest harbour in the uncertain waters of this interrogation.

As silence reclaimed its dominion over the room, my gaze wandered, taking in the sparse details of our surroundings. The simplicity of the setting—the lone table and two chairs—was not unexpected. Notably absent were cameras, an omission that sent a chill whispering down my spine. The realisation that there were no electronic eyes to witness this encounter, no silent guardians to record the proceedings, was both a relief and a source of acute anxiety. The thought, *Nobody will hear you scream,* hung in my mind like a spectre, a grim reminder of my vulnerability in this secluded space.

This awareness of isolation, of being cut off from any potential aid or witness, sharpened my senses, heightening my awareness of Eddie's every move and expression. The stakes of our silent standoff were clear, and the rules of engagement, though unspoken, were being drawn in this very room. My decision to withhold speech, to cloak myself in silence, was not just a defensive tactic but a choice to observe, to wait for the moment when the balance of power might shift, however slightly, in my favour.

"Has Belkeep gained any new Guardians recently?" Eddie's abrupt shift to questioning about Belkeep and its Guardians caught me off guard. His demeanour, previously cloaked in a veneer of professional detachment, now bore the marks of genuine concern—or was it suspicion? The sudden realisation of the earpiece, a detail I had embarrassingly overlooked until now, suggested a deeper level of communication and surveillance than I had initially assumed. This wasn't just a casual inquiry; it was a calculated probe for information, one that hinted at the complexity and reach of Killerton Enterprises' interest in Guardians.

"I know you've been tracking Guardians," I found myself saying, a statement that tread a fine line between accusation and acknowledgment. My admission was deliberate, a strategic play to acknowledge their surveillance without offering any concrete information that Eddie sought.

Eddie's reaction, a mix of curiosity and caution, was telling. His subsequent question, "What else do you know about us?" was an invitation—or perhaps a challenge—to reveal the extent of my knowledge. "Not a lot," I admitted, truthfully. My understanding of Killerton's operations and their interest in Guardians was fragmented at best, a puzzle whose pieces I was still struggling to assemble.

The conversation took an abrupt turn with Eddie's attention momentarily diverted by a voice only he could hear. The tension in the room thickened, a tangible presence that seemed to squeeze the air from my lungs, leaving me with a growing sense of unease.

Eddie's next question, delivered with a shadow of intensity crossing his face, was unexpected. "You've heard of Luke Smith?" The casualness of my response, "Hasn't everyone?" was a defence mechanism, an attempt to mask the sudden spike in my anxiety. Luke's name, a beacon in the tumultuous sea of Guardian affairs, was now a point of convergence between my world and Eddie's inquiries.

"You've crossed paths with him?"

I paused momentarily considering my response. *What if Jeremiah is right about Killerton?* the question nagged obnoxiously at my mind. "No," I said, suddenly unsure I could trust the motives of Killerton Enterprises.

The interrogation intensified, Eddie's demand for information about Luke Smith marking a turning point in our interaction. His fist slamming against the table was a physical manifestation of the frustration—or perhaps desperation—that underpinned his questions. The sound echoed in the room, a turbulent reminder of the stakes involved.

"Don't lie to me, Cody!" Eddie's command, underscored by the ringing left in my ears from his outburst, was a jarring call to reality. The intensity of his gaze, the authoritative stance as he rose to his full height, left no room for ambiguity. This was not a mere exchange of information; it was a critical juncture in the intricate dance of power and secrecy that defined the world of Guardians and those who sought to control or protect them.

"Tell me," he pressed, his tone laced with anger and an urgency that suggested the importance of Luke's whereabouts transcended mere curiosity. "Where's Luke?"

The abrupt descent into darkness was a disorienting shock, the sudden loss of power enveloping the room in an impenetrable cloak of blackness. The only sound breaking the silence was the grating scrape of Eddie's chair against the floor, a noise that seemed to amplify in the darkness, sending a fresh wave of chills cascading down my spine.

Instinctively, I saw my chance. With the room plunged into uncertainty, I reached for the one thing that offered a sliver of hope—the Portal Key. My fingers, slick with a mix of sweat and adrenaline, fumbled to activate it, desperately sliding across the button in the pitch black. "What the fuck!?" The words slipped out in a hiss, a mixture of frustration and disbelief, as my attempts to summon the portal met with failure.

Then, as if to mock my failed escape attempt, an emergency light flickered to life, its dim glow struggling against the overwhelming darkness. The light, feeble as it was, cast long shadows across the room, creating an eerie tableau that did little to reassure me.

With options dwindling, my next instinct was to flee through the conventional means—the door. My body coiled like a spring, I launched myself towards the only exit, only to find my path obstructed. The door flung open with a force that spoke of urgency from the other side, revealing a figure silhouetted against the dim light from the hallway.

Amber Styles! The name registered in my mind with a jolt of familiarity, a mix of relief and confusion flooding through me. Amber's unexpected presence in this critical juncture was a paradox, her familiar silhouette a beacon in the darkness, yet her arrival raised a multitude of questions. *How did she find me here? What was her role in this convoluted web that Killerton Enterprises seemed to be entangled in?*

The room, now partially illuminated by the weak emergency light, felt like a stage where the next act of an unfathomable drama was about to unfold. Amber's arrival had shifted the dynamics of the situation, introducing a new variable into the equation of my encounter with Eddie Hobson. As I stood there, momentarily frozen by the turn of events, I was acutely aware of the criticality of the coming moments. They held the potential to either unravel the mysteries surrounding Killerton Enterprises and their interest in Guardians or plunge me deeper into the labyrinth of intrigue and danger.

"We need to get Cody to a secure location," Eddie's voice, firm and resolute, broke through the tension, his grip on my arm an anchor in the swirling chaos. The urgency in his tone was unmistakable, yet it was met with immediate resistance.

"There's no time," Amber countered, her voice laced with an urgency that matched, if not surpassed, Eddie's. Her words, a stark reminder of the immediate danger posed by the power outage, hinted at layers of complexity within Killerton Enterprises that I had yet to fully comprehend. "We have more important things to deal with right now. A power outage is a major security threat. They'll become suspicious of us if you don't respond according to protocol." Her insistence on adherence to a seemingly mundane protocol in the midst of our crisis underscored the precariousness of our situation.

Eddie nodded silently, a concession to Amber's argument. The release of his grip felt like a temporary reprieve, a momentary pause in the relentless push and pull of allegiances and motives that surrounded me. His brief, inaudible exchange with Amber, a whisper of words lost in the shadows, was a mystery that added to the growing list of questions that tormented me.

Amber's fleeting glance, the frustration evident in her expression, was a silent acknowledgment of the complexity of our predicament. "Fine," she huffed, her voice a mix of resignation and determination. The grimace on her face, barely discernible in the dim emergency lighting, spoke volumes of the internal conflict she faced.

Driven by instinct, my fingers sought the familiar comfort of the Portal Key, sliding across the activation button in another futile gesture of hope. Eddie's disappearance into the darkness, a silent spectre retreating into the unknown, left me feeling more isolated than ever.

"That won't work here," Amber's words, cutting through the silence, brought a jarring halt to my escape attempts. "Killerton Enterprises has developed Portal blocking technology," Amber continued, looking directly into my eyes.

The revelation was a shock that sent ripples of disbelief through me. My mind raced, trying to reconcile this new piece of information with my existing knowledge of portal technology. The implications were staggering—trapped within the walls of an organisation that not only knew of our existence but had effectively neutralised our means of escape.

"Follow me," Amber's directive was not a suggestion but a command, her tone brooking no argument. "Stay close and you may just get out of here alive." The seriousness of her statement, the promise of survival tinged with an underlying threat, propelled me forward. My body moved almost of its own accord, following her into the darkened corridor, each step a leap of faith in the unknown.

The distant sound of alarms, a wailing symphony that punctuated the eerie silence, was a constant reminder of the escalating situation. The realisation that I was now relying on Amber, a figure from my distant past, shrouded in mystery and contradictions, to lead me to safety was both comforting and terrifying.

What the hell is going on!? The question echoed in my mind, a tumultuous storm of confusion and fear. The useless Portal Key, once a symbol of hope and freedom, now felt like a heavy weight in my hand, a token of my vulnerability in the face of an adversary that seemed to be perpetually one step ahead.

ESCAPE

1338.207.2

Amber and I were like shadows flitting through the underbelly of Killerton Enterprises, our sprint a desperate bid for freedom. The emergency lights, supposed beacons of safety, now felt like spotlights on a stage set for a tragedy, casting long, menacing shadows that seemed to chase us through the corridors. The shrill alarms slicing through the air served as a constant reminder of our precarious situation, a soundtrack to our escape that spurred us on with its urgency.

The sudden appearance of heavily armed security officers rounding the corner was a jolt of ice-cold fear. Their presence was an ominous sign, a physical manifestation of the danger we were trying to outrun. We pressed ourselves against the wall, our breaths shallow and rapid, as we tried to become one with the shadows. My heart hammered against my ribcage, each beat a drum of war in the quiet of my mind, adrenaline coursing through me with such intensity that it threatened to overwhelm my senses.

"Where are they going? What's happening?" I managed to whisper to Amber, my voice barely a breath, yet sharp with the need for answers. The sight of the guards, their purposeful stride and grim determination, sent a cascade of questions through my mind, each more alarming than the last.

Amber's face, illuminated intermittently by the flickering emergency lights, was a mask of concentration and concern. The deep lines that appeared on her forehead spoke of the weight of decisions resting on her shoulders, her gaze scanning our surroundings with a predator's focus. For a moment, she was silent, a statue carved from the very essence of determination, before the spell broke and she turned to me.

"We need to get out of here," she said, her voice a whisper that carried the weight of command. It was not just a suggestion; it was a necessity, spoken with the clarity of someone who understood the stakes better than anyone.

I nodded, my own resolve fortified by her certainty. Trusting Amber's instincts felt like the only logical course of action, a lifeline in the swirling maelstrom of danger that enveloped us. As the guards disappeared from view, their footsteps fading into the distance, we seized our chance, darting from our temporary haven with renewed purpose.

The sight of the elevator, a beacon of escape in the sprawling complex of Killerton Enterprises, momentarily filled me with a sense of relief, a brief respite in the storm of chaos. However, that fleeting comfort was quickly overshadowed by a surge of anxiety. My mind raced with the potential risks—*was it really wise to take the elevator, a likely monitored choke point, in our attempt to flee?*

Before I could voice my concerns, Amber's decisive action redirected our course. Her grip was firm, pulling me with an urgency that brooked no argument as she opened the heavy door to the stairwell. "Follow me," she commanded, her voice a mixture of command and resolve that I found impossible to resist.

Descending the stairs behind Amber, I felt the air grow progressively colder, an ominous chill that seemed to seep into my bones. Each step downward, away from the perceived safety of higher floors, intensified the sense of foreboding gnawing at my gut. "We're not going up?" The question slipped out in a hiss, my worry spilling over as we continued our descent into the building's depths.

Amber's brief pause, marked by a flash of determination in her eyes, offered a momentary halt in our relentless march into the unknown. "There's something I need to check first," she revealed, her words shrouded in mystery and leaving me adrift in a sea of speculation.

With a reluctant nod, I acquiesced to her lead, my trust in her judgment mingling with an undercurrent of apprehension. The stairwell, with its oppressive silence felt like a descent into the very heart of uncertainty. The echo of our footsteps was the only sound that punctuated the heavy silence, a reminder of our solitary journey through the bowels of Killerton Enterprises.

At last, the stairwell gave way to another series of corridors, each more foreboding than the last. The dim lighting cast long shadows, transforming the hallway into a labyrinth of half-seen shapes and lurking fears. Amber's sudden halt in front of an isolated, windowless door marked a striking contrast to the uniformity of the others we had passed. Her attention was fixed, her body tense with anticipation or perhaps apprehension.

Standing there, in the dimly lit corridor, facing the enigmatic door that Amber seemed drawn to, I was acutely aware of the precariousness of our situation. The isolation of the door, devoid of the small windows that offered a glimpse into the other rooms, set it apart—a silent sentinel guarding secrets that Amber felt compelled to uncover. My heart raced, caught between the desire to flee and the need to understand what lay behind that door, what piece of the puzzle Amber believed was crucial enough to warrant this detour into the unknown.

"This must be it," Amber's voice, barely more than a whisper, cut through the tension that clung to the air like a thick fog. Watching her hand retrieve an identification card from the depths of her jacket pocket felt like witnessing the final turn of a key in a long-locked chest. The swift motion as she swiped the card across the access panel, and the subsequent sliding open of the door, seemed almost ceremonial, an entry into a realm that defied my understanding of Killerton Enterprises.

The room that unfolded before us was a departure from the sterile, corporate corridors we had navigated. Stepping inside, I was immediately enveloped by an atmosphere that felt charged with an unspoken history, a place out of time. The air, thick with a metallic scent that tinged each breath, carried whispers of secrets long buried. Illuminated by a soft, bluish glow that seemed to emanate from the very walls themselves, the room cast us in an otherworldly light, transforming our surroundings into a scene from a dream—or perhaps a nightmare.

"What is this place?" The question escaped me as a whisper, a reflection of the awe and apprehension that battled within me. Standing beside Amber on a metallic grated platform, I felt like an intruder in a sacred space, the vast and mysterious chamber stretching out before us. The natural rock walls, rugged and untouched, spoke of the ancient origins of this hidden sanctuary, contrasting starkly with the technological marvels that Killerton Enterprises was known for. The ceiling soared high above, echoing the grandeur of a cathedral, yet here beneath the earth, it felt like a temple to an unknown deity.

Ornate pillars, shoulder-high and spaced evenly throughout the room, held large glass containers that demanded attention. Each container, bathed in the bluish light, cradled mysterious objects that teased the imagination, their true purpose and significance veiled by distance and shadow. The sight was mesmerising, each pillar a silent guardian of the mysteries that this room harboured.

The overwhelming sense of being privy to a hidden world, a place where the lines between science, history, and progress blurred, was both exhilarating and daunting. The awe-inspiring spectacle before me was a reminder of how much I had yet to understand about the forces that moved beneath the surface of our reality. This underground chamber, with its ancient walls and futuristic glow, was a paradox, a place where the past and the future seemed to converge in a silent pact.

Descending the metal stairs behind Amber, each step resonated with a metallic echo that seemed to underscore the gravity of what I was about to witness. As the ornate pillars came into view, each holding its sacred cargo, the realisation struck me with the force of a physical blow. "Portal Keys," I gasped, the words escaping unbidden as I took in the sight of the glass cases, each one a silent testament to the Guardians they represented.

The revelation that each set of five Portal Keys belonged to a distinct Guardian Group sent waves of awe through me. The meticulous arrangement of the cases, with many spots left vacant, hinted at a story of loss and anticipation. The names etched on the placards, some known and others marked as "Unknown," spoke volumes of the history and mystery enveloping these artefacts. The names of the settlements atop each case added another layer of connection, grounding these ethereal objects in the reality of the civilisations they linked to.

"There must be thousands of them," I murmured, almost to myself, as I lagged behind Amber. My gaze darted from case to case, driven by an insatiable curiosity to uncover the stories they held, the names and places that were part of a legacy far greater than I had imagined.

Amber's response to my awestruck observation was tinged with a blend of pride and reverence that caught my attention. "Yes," she confirmed, her voice a bridge to the unfathomable depths of history she alluded to. "The Gatekeepers have been collecting and protecting the devices for thousands of years."

"Gatekeepers? Thousands of years?" The repetition of these concepts aloud felt like trying to grasp the scale of eternity with mere words. Her brief pause, followed by a look that seemed to search the very essence of who I was, only deepened the mystery enveloping this revelation.

"Gatekeepers - key members of the Guardian Order," she elucidated, breaking the silence that had momentarily wrapped around us. Her explanation, although brief, hinted at a depth of history and purpose far beyond my understanding.

The admission that I was unaware of the Guardian Order's existence left me feeling unexpectedly vulnerable. My ignorance to the knowledge Amber possessed, was a jarring realisation. "Fuck," her muttered exclamation, more a reflex than a rebuke, underscored the weight of my oversight. "You've never heard of the Guardian Order?"

I shook my head, feeling a tinge of embarrassment. I had thought myself well-informed, but the existence of the Guardian Order had remained veiled in mystery.

As Amber's gaze softened, a bridge of understanding seemed to form between us. She invited me to walk with her, her steps measured, her voice now a conduit to the past. "The Guardian Order was formed over four thousand years ago by the First Guardians," she revealed, each word weaving a tapestry of legacy and duty. "Its primary purpose is to safeguard the knowledge, artefacts, and technologies of Earth, preserving them in Clivilius and ensuring the continuation of humanity's legacy."

"And Gatekeepers?" I prodded, eager to peel back the layers of this ancient order that I was only now beginning to learn of.

Amber's eyes sparkled like embers as she continued her explanation. "Gatekeepers play a key role in the structure of the Guardian Order. They specialise in managing the Portals. They regulate access and ensure the safety of both Guardians and the Order."

Her words painted a vivid picture in my mind. The Gatekeepers, the protectors of the gateways, held a crucial responsibility, balancing the preservation of knowledge with the safe exploration of other realms.

"Are you a member of the Order?" I asked, curious about the extent of Amber's involvement.

Amber's abrupt halt in front of a particularly imposing glass case marked a pivotal moment in our clandestine journey through the depths of this hidden chamber. Her eyes, alight with a complex blend of excitement and trepidation, gazed upon the enclosed Portal Keys. "Here it is," she announced, her voice imbued with a rich anticipation that seemed to resonate through the very air of the chamber.

The reverence in her tone as she uttered those words drew me closer, compelling me to peer into the glass case that had captured her attention so completely. The names etched on the placards beneath each of the five Portal Keys read like a roll call from the annals of history—Gilgamesh, Hammurabi, Hatshepsut, Nefekare, and Nefertiti. The realisation that I was standing in the presence of artefacts linked to such legendary figures was humbling, sending a shiver of awe down my spine.

"Who are they?" The question emerged from me in a whisper, a hushed reverence for the historical weight these names carried. Amber's response, delivered with a fervour that seemed to set her eyes ablaze, left no room for doubt.

"The First Guardians," she stated, her words heavy with the solemnity of their legacy.

The sight of Amber retrieving small picking instruments from her satchel sent a jolt of shock through me. The implications of her intentions, the audacity of the act she was about to commit, dawned on me with startling clarity. "You're going to steal them, aren't you?" The question, whispered in a blend of awe and apprehension, betrayed the tumult of emotions that her actions stirred within me.

Her hushed command for silence as she set to work on the glass case only heightened the tension that thrummed between us. I found myself torn between the desire to witness the unfolding of this audacious act and the fear of the consequences it might invite.

Driven by a restless curiosity, my gaze began to wander, drawn inexorably towards the other mysteries that lay enshrined within this sacred space. Amber's cautionary words, "Don't stray too far," reached me as a distant echo. I nodded, more out of instinct than any conscious decision to comply, my mind still reeling from the revelation of the First Guardians and the daring nature of Amber's plan.

Wandering amongst the labyrinth of glass cases, each step took me deeper into a silent narrative etched in history and mystery. The arrangement of the cases puzzled me, their order seemingly cryptic, defying immediate understanding. *Was there a hidden chronology, a story told in the sequence of these guardians of time and space?*

Then, like a beacon cutting through the fog of my curiosity, a name positioned prominently above a case snagged my attention. "Belkeep," the word slipped from my lips in a hushed reverence, propelling me forward with a rush of urgency. The connection to my home, to the very heart of my existence as a Guardian, drew me with a magnetic pull.

Peering into the case, a wave of emotions washed over me. The sight of the five Portal placards, placeholders for keys yet to be claimed by this sanctified archive, was both awe-inspiring and sobering. The absence of the Portal Keys was expected; Sylvie and Randal's keys were under my protection, hidden away in the safety of Belkeep. Yet, the declaration of Randal and Sylvie's demise on their name placards sent a shiver down my spine, a cold reminder of the cost of our struggle, the price paid in silence and shadow.

The revelation that I was listed as still alive brought a complex mix of relief and sorrow. Relief that my existence was acknowledged, that I had somehow managed to elude the fate that had claimed my comrades. And yet, the sorrow for those lost, for the emptiness their absence left was palpable.

The two unnamed placards, their blankness staring back at me, were a chilling harbinger. They stood as silent witnesses to the unknown, to futures unwritten and destinies yet to unfold. The ambiguity of their state, the absence of names, spoke volumes. It was a reminder that in the grand tapestry of the Guardian's saga, some threads were still loose, their patterns yet to be woven into the narrative.

Standing before the case marked "Belkeep," surrounded by the names of countless other Guardians, I felt a profound connection to the lineage I was part of. The realisation that my actions, my choices, were but echoes in the long corridor of time filled me with a sense of duty and determination. The names listed, the spaces left empty, were not just markers of what had been or what might be; they were a call to arms, a reminder of the ongoing battle we waged not just for the present, but for the continuity of the past and the hope of the future.

In this moment, amidst the eerie glow that bathed the underground chamber, I understood more deeply the weight of the legacy I carried. The knowledge that Randal and Sylvie's sacrifice was etched into the annals of our hidden history, and that my name stood amongst theirs, was both an honour and a burden. It solidified my resolve to continue the fight, to safeguard the keys entrusted to me, and to honour the memory of those we had lost. Here, in the presence of the Guardian Order's silent guardians, I renewed my vow to protect Belkeep and all it represented, to fill the empty spaces left by those gone and to shape the destiny that fate had yet to reveal.

The abrupt eruption of noise from the top of the stairs shattered the reverent silence that had enveloped me, snapping me back to the present with a jolt of adrenaline. Two young men, seemingly out of breath and charged with urgency, appeared at the edge of the platform, their sudden entrance marking an abrupt intrusion into the solemn atmosphere of the chamber.

"Amber, we've got the blueprints," one of the men announced, his voice booming through the chamber, the cylindrical canister he held aloft a visual testament to their mission's success. My gaze shifted to Amber, whose reaction mirrored the shock and surprise that rippled through me. The fear in her eyes, reminiscent of a deer caught in headlights, was a clear indicator of the importance of their discovery.

"We have to go, now!" The command from the second, taller man was laced with a desperation that sent my pulse racing. *What blueprints? And why did their retrieval spark such immediate alarm?* The questions cascaded through my mind, a torrent of confusion and curiosity mingling with the rising tide of apprehension.

Amber's response to the situation was a blend of determination and desperation. The force with which she attacked the glass casing she had been meticulously working on moments ago spoke volumes of the urgency now driving her actions. The glass cracked under the assault but held firm, a stubborn barrier to the treasures it protected.

"Now, Amber!" The taller man's urgent repetition, his gaze flicking around the chamber with palpable anxiety, underscored the imminent danger we faced. Yet, Amber's focus remained unshaken, her voice tight with tension as she pleaded for more time.

The final glance I cast toward the Belkeep case was a silent farewell to the moment of connection I had experienced. The urgency of our situation propelled me toward Amber, ready to assist or flee as the situation demanded.

The sound of the two men descending the stairs and racing toward us filled the chamber with a sense of impending chaos. "We don't have much time," the taller man reiterated upon reaching us.

Amber's switch in tactics, from brute force back to a more methodical attempt at prying the glass open, was a testament to her resolve to not leave empty-handed. Ignoring the warnings and the palpable tension that now filled the air, she focused solely on the task at hand.

Standing there, amidst the crescendo of urgency and the shadow of imminent threat, I was caught in the whirlwind of events unfolding around me. The knowledge that we were teetering on the brink of discovery, possibly confrontation, heightened every sense.

"It's fine, Josh," the calming voice of the first man sliced through the tension like a knife, his hand resting reassuringly on his companion's shoulder. "We have time for this." The optimism in his demeanour, marked by a glint of enthusiasm in his eyes, seemed to inject a momentary pause in the cascade of urgency enveloping us.

"I'm almost there," Amber's voice, a hiss of determination through clenched teeth, reverberated with the intensity of her focus. The palpable sense of nearing a critical breakthrough hung in the air, an electric anticipation that momentarily united us all in silent expectation.

Nathan, as I came to understand the first man's name through the brief exchange that followed, voiced his awe in a hushed, reverent tone. "I can't believe the rumours are true. This chamber actually exists." His words, imbued with wonder and disbelief, echoed my own initial shock upon entering this hidden sanctum. The realisation that we were standing in a place considered mythical, a whisper of legend brought to life, was both surreal and exhilarating.

"It's not on any of the floor plans," Josh's interjection, a mix of surprise and confusion, underscored the secrecy that shrouded this chamber.

"Most of the underground floors aren't on the maps," Nathan stated, as though such omissions were to be expected, a norm within the clandestine world we were navigating. His words painted a picture of a facility far more complex and secretive than its outward appearance suggested, a labyrinth of hidden depths and concealed truths.

Standing amidst this revelation, surrounded by individuals who each held pieces of a puzzle far greater than any I could have ever anticipated, I felt a mix of awe and unease. The acknowledgment of the chamber's existence, coupled with the understanding that it was but a fraction of Killerton's unseen architecture, expanded the scope of the enigma I now found myself entangled in.

Gunshots echoed through the corridor, a sinister symphony that sent a chilling tingle racing down my spine. It was a sound you never really got used to. The sudden entrance of a security guard, weapon drawn and ready, startled us all. A collective gasp, a shared moment of pure adrenaline and terror, escaped our lips as we found ourselves face-to-face with Percival, the very same man who had guided me with such calm assurance to the briefing room earlier. The irony of the situation was not lost on me.

The door slammed shut with a finality that echoed ominously through the room, sealing us away from the violence that lurked just beyond its metal confines. Percival, with urgency etched into every feature of his face, hurriedly spoke, "You need to get out of here." His voice was a mixture of fear and determination, a sharp contrast to the composed security guard I had met upon my arrival. He scrambled down the stairs, his actions spurred by the imminent danger that was all too real and closing in on us.

Josh couldn't contain his bewilderment. "Is your cover blown?" he asked Percival, his question hanging in the air, charged with a mix of hope and dread.

"No," replied Percival, pausing to catch his breath.

"Then why are they shooting at you?" Nathan chimed in, his voice tinged with tension and fear. The expression on his face was a reflection of the uncertainty that gripped each of us.

"It's not Killerton that's shooting at us," answered Percival, his words heavy with implications that widened our eyes and quickened our pulses.

"What!?" The word erupted from both Josh and Nathan simultaneously, their voices a perfect harmony of shock and disbelief.

Percival sighed heavily, the weight of the situation pressing down on him. "It appears that you aren't the only infiltrators of Killerton Enterprises today." His revelation was a bombshell, altering the landscape of my understanding and forcing me to reassess what I thought I was beginning to comprehend.

"Got it!" Amber's triumphant exclamation cut through the tension like a knife. With a motion both graceful and determined, she ripped open the glass case that had been her objective, sending it crashing to the floor with a sound that was alarmingly loud in the sudden silence that followed Percival's disclosure. Snatching the five Portal Keys, she wrapped them tightly in fabric, before placing them securely in her satchel.

Outside the room, the faint sound of gunshots grew louder, a menacing reminder of the danger that lurked just beyond our temporary haven. Then, with a resounding finality, heavy metal doors sealed the room shut, trapping us inside. The sound was like a death knell, signalling the end of one chapter and the ominous beginning of another. Trapped and isolated, I was left to ponder our next move, the weight of my decisions that had led me to this point, felt heavier than ever.

"Is there another way out of here?" Josh's voice cut through the tense silence, his eyes darting around the chamber, searching for a glimmer of hope amidst the enclosing walls of our confinement.

"Yes," Percival responded, a nod accompanying his words as if to punctuate the possibility of escape. He gestured for us to follow him towards the far end of the chamber, his movements imbued with a sense of purpose that reignited a spark of hope within me. "There's a special room through that doorway over there." His finger pointed towards a nondescript door, its existence previously unnoticed in the uniformity of the chamber's design. "It's lined with special material that mirrors the Portal blocking technology and will allow you to use your Portal Keys. It's the only place in the entire complex where you can."

Nathan commented wryly, "That's convenient." His dry humour, a light in the darkness of our situation, brought a momentary smile to my face, a brief respite from the weight of our circumstances.

"It's how the Gatekeepers have been coming and going for generations," Percival explained, his tone carrying a hint of pride.

As Percival stepped up to the access point on the wall next to the heavy, solid door, a moment of anticipation hung in the air. He paused, as if to ensure our undivided attention, before scanning his wrist across the pad. The door clicked open with a sound that signified the unlocking of possibilities, a portal to our salvation. "Come on in," Percival said, his voice a mixture of urgency and invitation as he ushered us inside before closing the door with a sense of finality behind us.

"Not much of a room," I couldn't help but comment, my eyes quickly taking in the utilitarian space that barely accommodated the five of us. The room was devoid of decoration, its walls a testament to its singular purpose.

"Its sole purpose is to act as an access point. Nothing more," Percival stated flatly, his voice echoing slightly off the bare walls. His words were a reminder of the room's function over form, a gateway designed for quick transitions rather than habitation.

Standing in that cramped space, I felt a mix of claustrophobia and awe. The technology and secrets this room represented were beyond my wildest imaginations, yet here we were, about to use it as our escape route.

Amber turned to me, her eyes holding a blend of resolve and regret. "I guess this is where we part ways," she said, her voice steady but tinged with an undercurrent of sadness. In her hand, the Portal Key seemed to come to life, pressing against the wall beside us. It lit up, painting the drab surroundings in a spectacle of colour that danced across the surface, casting our shadows in a fantastical display. The moment was surreal, like a scene from a dream where the laws of physics and reality were mere suggestions.

Adrenaline surged through my veins, a potent cocktail of excitement and apprehension. "But I have so many questions still," I blurted out, the words escaping my lips before I could corral them into something more coherent. There was so much I wanted to understand, so many threads of this complex tapestry that I needed to unravel.

Amber glanced at Nathan, who offered a subtle shake of his head, almost imperceptible but clear in its intention. Now was not the time for discussions or explanations. The urgency of our situation brooked no delay, and yet, my heart sank at the missed opportunity for answers.

"Sorry, Cody. Next time," Amber said, her voice softening as she offered me a brief embrace. It was a fleeting moment of connection, a small comfort amidst the tension. Her hand gave my shoulder a slight squeeze, a silent promise of future explanations, before she broke away.

"Wait!" The word tore from my throat as I reached out, desperate to hold onto the moment. My fingers brushed against the leather satchel, a tangible reminder of her mission. And then, as sudden as a flash of lightning, Amber was gone, disappeared into the portal she had opened, leaving behind a lingering echo of her presence.

Before I could turn to the two brothers, appeal to them for more time, more answers, they too activated their Portals. The room was briefly illuminated by the energy of their departure, and then they were gone, leaving a silence that was heavy, oppressive, like a smothering blanket over my thoughts and emotions.

"You'd better get going, too," Percival's voice cut through the haze of my thoughts, a gentle but firm reminder. He motioned for me to follow suit.

My mouth moved without sound, a silent testament to the whirlwind of thoughts racing through my brain. *How do I navigate this new reality? What dangers lie ahead?* And then, amidst the tumult of my thoughts, one in particular crystallised into clarity: *If I activate my Portal here, does that mean the location will also be registered and I can return here whenever I like?* The idea sparked a flicker of hope, a beacon in the fog of uncertainty.

With a final, acknowledging nod to Percival, I took a deep breath and set the wall ablaze with vibrant, colourful energy. The Portal Key in my hand felt alive, thrumming with potential as I activated it. Stepping into the cold Belkeep cavern, the air shifted around me, a tangible change in atmosphere that enveloped me in its icy embrace. The transition was instantaneous, a leap through space and perhaps even time. Yet, with that step, I carried with me the hope of return, of revisiting the path I had forged and the secrets I had uncovered. The adventure was far from over, and the questions that burned within me would find their answers, in time.

THE SAFE PLACE

4338.207.3

I entered my modest dwelling within Belkeep, the familiarity of its confines greeting me like an old friend, yet a friend whose presence was tinged with the sadness of what had been lost. The aged wooden floor beneath my feet creaked with each step, a symphony of nostalgia and trepidation that played with every movement I made across the room. It was as if the very planks remembered the weight of the days when laughter and plans for the future filled this space.

Reaching the far corner, my eyes fell upon an unassuming chest, its surface dulled by the passage of time, a silent guardian of memories from a bygone era. My heart clenched as I approached, the mix of anticipation and sorrow tightening its grip with each step. With trembling hands, I unlocked the chest, the lock yielding with a faint metallic click that seemed to echo louder in the silence of the room. Lifting the lid, the scent of aged wood and the whisper of old memories rose to greet me, enveloping me in a wave of reminiscence that was both comforting and heart-wrenching.

As the lid opened, a cascade of memories, each tied to the objects within, surged forth. Volumes of journals, keepsakes, mementos of adventures and escapades alongside comrades now lost to time. Wrapped delicately in handkerchiefs, as if to protect them from the ravages of time itself, lay the Portal Keys that once belonged to Randal and Sylvie. The sight of them, resting there as if waiting for their owners to return and claim them, struck a chord deep within me. It was astonishing, the weight of history and emotion these small objects could carry, how they could still resonate with the essence of those who had wielded them.

My fingers traced the cold, hard metal, a tangible link to Randal and Sylvie, to the days when our fates were intertwined in the dance of destiny.

Closing my eyes, I allowed the floodgates of memory to open, immersing myself in the past. Randal's infectious laughter echoed in my ears, a sound that had once filled these walls with joy. Sylvie's unwavering determination, her strength and courage that had inspired us all, enveloped me, a reminder of what we had fought for, of the sacrifices made in the name of protecting others.

They were more than just friends and fellow Guardians; they were a part of me, woven into the fabric of my being, their spirits etched into my soul. Though I refused to admit it to others, hiding behind a façade of composure, the truth was that when Randal and Sylvie perished, they took a part of me with them. A void was left in their wake, a chasm within my heart that no amount of time or distance could ever fill. Their loss was a wound that remained, a silent testament to the price of the paths we chose. In the quiet of my dwelling, surrounded by the ghosts of the past, I confronted the depth of my loss, the profound impact of their absence in my life, and the unending journey of carrying their legacy forward.

Sighing, the weight of responsibility settled on my shoulders like a heavy cloak, woven from threads of duty, loss, and unanswered questions. The Portal Keys, once vibrant tools in the hands of my fallen comrades, Randal and Sylvie, now lay before me, silent and inert. I had never considered their significance beyond the tragic ends of their guardians. Despite numerous attempts, both in Clivilius and Earth, to breathe life into these devices, they remained dormant, as seemingly lifeless as the friends I had lost. Since their passing, I had relegated these keys to the old chest, treating them as mere keepsakes, relics of a time when we dared to challenge the unknown with a blend of naivety and bravery.

Yet now, kneeling here in the quietude of my dwelling, a sanctuary filled with the echoes of the past, I was besieged by a profound sense of wonder and unease. *Why did Killerton Enterprises covet these seemingly useless pieces of metal? What hidden secrets did they hold? What knowledge did they possess that I, their current keeper, did not?* The notion that these Portal Keys might harbour significance far beyond the memories they represented gnawed at the edges of my mind, suggesting depths and mysteries I had yet to comprehend.

As I continued to gaze upon the keys, my thoughts drifted back to the recent encounter with Amber and the startling revelation of the Guardian Order. The legacy she hinted at, a lineage thousands of years in the making, safeguarded by Gatekeepers, was a revelation that had entirely blindsided me. This sprawling tapestry of history, knowledge, and artefacts, protected across the aeons, was a legacy I was now tangentially a part of, yet knew so little about. The realisation stirred a tumultuous mix of curiosity and anxiety within me. *Were these Portal Keys a fragment of this vast legacy?* Amber had left that question dangling, unanswered, sparking a cascade of further questions in my mind.

Could Amber herself be a Gatekeeper? The thought lingered, tantalising and elusive. *And what of Josh and Nathan?* I had initially assumed they were merely part of Amber's Guardian contingent, but the possibility that they, too, might be Gatekeepers added layers of complexity and intrigue to the puzzle. My mind spun, caught in a whirlwind of speculation, doubt, and the thrill of the unknown. The feeling that I was merely grazing the surface of a much deeper, more intricate mystery was inescapable.

"Hi Cody," the youthful timbre of Krid's voice sliced through the dense fabric of my thoughts, pulling me back to the present with an almost physical force. Surprised, I spun around, and in my abrupt movement, the chest lid fell shut with a solid, definitive thud. It was a sound that, for a moment, seemed to echo the closing of one chapter and the hesitant beginning of another.

"Hey, Krid," I managed, my voice a strained attempt at normalcy. I forced a smile to match hers, though I felt it waver at the edges, a poor mask for the swirl of emotions and questions roiling inside me.

Krid moved towards me with a serenity that belied her years, her steps measured and imbued with an almost ethereal grace. It was as if she tread on the very border between youthful innocence and ancient wisdom. "I see you're carrying a burden," she observed, her voice soft yet carrying a weight that suggested she saw much more than what the surface revealed. Her eyes, piercing yet gentle, seemed to look right through my hastily erected defences, resting on the Portal Keys I held tightly in my grasp.

I sighed, the sound heavy with the acknowledgment of my internal struggle. There was no concealing my emotions or the artefacts of my dilemma from Krid. "It's just..." I began, my voice trailing off as another sigh escaped me. *How much should I reveal to her? How much could she understand, or was it safer to shoulder this burden alone, away from her childhood optimism?*

Before I could articulate my thoughts further, Krid nodded, her expression suffused with understanding and empathy. "The weight of knowledge can be heavy, Cody, but remember that you are not alone in this journey," she said, her words weaving around me like a warm embrace. "The legacy of the Guardians runs through your veins too, and you have the strength to carry it forward." There was a depth to her words, an assurance that seemed to transcend her young age.

Compelled by her understanding, I unfurled my clenched fists, revealing the Portal Keys of Randal and Sylvie resting in my palms. "These aren't the remaining two Portal Keys, Krid. These are Randal and Sylvie's," I said, my voice imbued with a solemn reverence for the names I uttered, names that evoked memories of camaraderie and loss.

"I know," Krid responded, her tone simple yet layered with unspoken knowledge. A playful smile danced at the corners of her mouth, hinting at secrets and understandings far beyond what her childlike exterior suggested.

My eyes narrowed slightly, not in suspicion but in wonder and a dawning realisation of the depth of the person before me. *What else does Krid really know?* The question echoed in my mind, a mystery wrapped within the enigma of this seemingly young girl. *And how does she know the things she knows?* It was a puzzle, a new layer of intrigue in an already complex tapestry of events and revelations. Krid, with her cherubic face and ancient eyes, was a reminder that in this world of Guardians and Gatekeepers, appearances could be deceiving, and wisdom did not always wear the face of age.

Krid's touch was a balm to the turmoil churning within me, her small hand warm and reassuring against mine. "Start with your instincts," she advised, her voice a gentle nudge towards self-trust and discovery. "You have a connection to Clivilius, and it will guide you to the right path. Trust the voice, Cody." Her words, simple yet profound, seemed to carve out a space of calm within the storm of my thoughts.

Looking into Krid's eyes, I found myself peering into depths that belied her childlike appearance. Here was a being, I realised, who carried the weight of wisdom as if it were a feather. "You always seem to know just what to say, Krid," I acknowledged, my voice tinged with wonder and a deep sense of gratitude. Her presence, always so timely and insightful, felt like a guiding star in the darkest night.

She smiled then, a smile that seemed to hold secrets and understanding far beyond what one might expect. "I've lived in Belkeep my entire life, Cody, and I have learned many things." Her words floated between us, a testament to the mysteries she held.

"But you're only six, Krid," I found myself saying, a laugh bubbling up despite the seriousness of our conversation. It was a moment of lightness, a reminder of the absurdity and beauty that life could present, even in its most perplexing moments.

Krid's dismissal of my comment was both graceful and wise. "But it's not just me; it's the essence of Clivilius itself. We are all connected, and that connection brings wisdom and guidance when we need it most." Her conviction was a reminder of the unseen threads that wove us all together, a network of lives and destinies intertwined.

As if on cue, the clouds outside parted, allowing beams of sunlight to spill through the bedroom window, bathing us in a warmth that felt almost otherworldly. It was as though nature itself was conspiring to underscore Krid's words, lending a physical warmth to the emotional solace I had just been granted. In that moment, the weight I had been carrying felt lighter, as if Krid's assurance and the light's affirmation had conspired to lift some of the burden from my shoulders.

"Thank you, Krid," I found myself saying, the words heavy with sincerity. There was a profound sense of gratitude for her, for this moment of clarity and connection amidst the uncertainty of my journey.

Krid's response was a nod, her smile bright and unwavering, a beacon of positivity. "You're welcome, Cody. Now let's find a safe place for those Portal Keys." Her practical suggestion was a gentle nudge back to reality, a reminder of what needed to be done, yet her approach imbued even this mundane task with a sense of purpose and continuity.

❖

Nearing the outskirts of the small settlement of Belkeep, I followed Krid with unwavering trust, her youthful figure cutting through the harsh landscape with an ease that belied her years. The bitter winds around us seemed to gain strength with each step we took, a relentless force that tested the resolve of even the hardiest traveller. I found myself pulling my warm coat tighter around my body, its fabric rustling in protest against the symphony of nature's chill. The landscape, dusted with a fine layer of snow, unfolded before us like a canvas painted in muted hues of white and grey, a world asleep under the cold blanket of eternal winter.

"Cody, can I ask you something?" Krid's voice, gentle and melodic, cut through the cold, blending seamlessly with the soft whispers of the wind. It was a sound that, despite the harshness of our surroundings, carried warmth and curiosity.

"Of course, Krid. You can ask me anything," I replied, my voice carrying a continued sense of comfort in her presence. Despite the biting cold and the desolate landscape, her company provided a haven, a gentle reminder of the warmth of human connection amidst the elements.

Her eyes, a striking mix of innocence and wisdom, fixed on me as she asked, "Why were the Portal Keys kept in that old chest? It seemed like a less secure place compared to the other vaults in Belkeep." Her question was not accusatory but genuinely curious, a desire to understand the choices and actions of those who walked before her.

Krid's question gave me pause, a momentary halt in the rhythm of our journey. I took a moment to collect my thoughts, the clouds above us seeming to gather and swirl, as if to mirror the complexities and the churn of thoughts within my mind. "I don't fully understand the significance of these Portal Keys beyond their old connection to Randal and Sylvie," I began, my gaze drifting towards the distant caves, their shadows offering a glimmer of shelter to the snow-blanketed landscape. "They were part of my Guardian group, integral to our bond and our mission. After their passing, I kept their Portal Keys as a memento, a tangible link to the memories we shared, unaware of any other value they might hold."

Krid listened with a depth of understanding that seemed to transcend her years, her gaze locked onto mine as if she were peering into the very essence of my being. It felt as though she was gently sifting through my thoughts, uncovering layers I hadn't fully acknowledged even to myself. The realisation that the Portal Keys might harbour secrets far beyond my grasp seemed to hang silently between us, a shared understanding that was both comforting and disconcerting.

"Randal and Sylvie were incredible Guardians, skilled and devoted to their duty," I found myself continuing, the words laced with a nostalgia that felt both warm and achingly painful. "They were like family to me." The memories of our time together, and the laughter shared, flooded back with a clarity that made my heart ache. "Belkeep has suffered so much loss over the years, and when Randal and Sylvie were gone, I couldn't bear to part with the last remnants of their existence." It was a confession of sorts, an admission of my inability to let go of the past and move forward.

Krid's eyes seemed to glisten with a profound empathy, as if she were not just listening to my words but also feeling the weight of the emotions behind them. "There's more to it, isn't there?" she asked softly, her voice carrying a gentle yet insistent curiosity that urged me to delve deeper into the mysteries surrounding the Portal Keys.

I hesitated, a twinge of guilt knotting my stomach. Here was Krid, a child with an inexplicable wisdom, pushing me to confront truths I had barely admitted to myself. "I don't know," I finally admitted, the words heavy with the burden of my ignorance and confusion.

Her gaze intensified, cutting through the cold air between us. "The Guardian Order," she whispered, the name of the ancient order falling from her lips like a sacred incantation. "That's what they're connected to, isn't it?"

Gasping at Krid's revelation, I felt a mixture of astonishment and apprehension. "How do you know about the Guardian Order, Krid?" My voice was a mix of wonder and concern, marvelling at how this young girl could possess knowledge of a secret that had eluded even the most devoted Guardians.

Krid hesitated, a solemnity settling over her youthful features. Then, with a grace that belied her age, she extended her small hands towards the Portal Keys. "It's safer if I take them from here," she said softly, her voice imbued with a sense of purpose and an underlying strength that reassured and baffled me in equal measure.

As Krid's small, yet surprisingly firm hands took the Portal Keys from my grasp, a torrent of counter-arguments waged a fierce battle within my mind. Each argument clashed against the next, a tumultuous sea of doubts and fears. Yet, in the face of my internal storm, Krid's resolve was as unwavering as a lighthouse amidst tempestuous waves.

"I need to go alone," she stated, her gaze piercing through the fog of my confusion, anchoring me to the moment. Her eyes, so young yet filled with an ancient determination, held mine with an intensity that brooked no argument. "I know a safe place for them until we need them again." The simplicity and certainty in her voice clashed with the complexity of emotions swirling within me.

A thick fog seemed to envelop my brain, making it difficult to grasp the full implications of her departure. The weight of the Portal Keys, now in her possession, felt like a tangible loss, a part of me being severed and taken away.

Krid's expression, calm and assured, was a stark contrast to the turmoil I felt. "I may be young, Cody, but I understand the importance of what you carry. Clivilius depends on its Guardians, and you have the power to protect its legacy."

My confusion deepened, furrows etching themselves into my brow as I tried to decipher the layers of meaning in her words.

"Make Gladys a Guardian," Krid implored, her grip on my forearm tightening momentarily. Then, with no further explanation, she turned and made her way towards the caves. I stood there, rooted to the spot, watching her figure diminish against the backdrop of the wintery landscape, a lone sentinel marching towards an unknown destiny.

The wisdom in trusting Krid's advice was clear to me, yet I harboured reservations about Gladys's readiness to assume the mantle of Guardian. The doubts gnawed at me like a persistent whisper.

As Krid's silhouette merged with the distance, my thoughts shifted towards Luke and the tangled web of intrigue that enveloped Killerton Enterprises. *What did Luke know? Was he aware of the Guardian Order and its secrets?* The questions lingered like ghosts in the frigid air, haunting and unanswered.

BLOODY KISS

1338.207.1

The moment I stepped into Luke's downstairs living room, the air shifted subtly, as if the very house was bracing for the unknown. Gladys's voice, unmistakably hers, floated down like a melody infused with curiosity, gently disrupting the silence. "Luke?" she called out, her voice laced with a mix of confusion and concern.

Driven by an inexplicable urge to uncover the reason behind Gladys's presence, I began my ascent. Each step on the staircase felt like a note in a suspenseful symphony, the creaks and groans under my feet narrating my progress. The atmosphere thickened with anticipation, a tangible electricity in the air that hinted at the unforeseen.

Reaching the top, I paused at the threshold of the living room. "Cody?" Gladys's voice, tinged with surprise, greeted me. It was as if my appearance had disrupted a delicate balance, the surprise in her eyes mirroring my own. For a fleeting moment, time seemed to suspend, our mutual astonishment hanging in the air like a delicate mist. Yet, this ephemeral connection quickly gave way to a sharper emotion —a twinge of guilt—as I noticed the shadow of fear that had taken residence in her gaze. The room felt suddenly like a carefully set stage, awaiting the unfolding of an unexpected drama.

"What the hell are you doing with that knife?" I asked, my voice slicing through the tension, as sharp and direct as the blade she held. The question hung in the air, a challenge that demanded an answer.

Gladys seemed to shrink, her cheeks flushing a deep red as the knife lowered, its threat diminishing with her posture. "I... I thought... nothing, really," she stammered, her words tumbling out like leaves caught in a gust of wind. Her response, laced with hesitation and uncertainty, echoed in the room, filling the space between us with whispers of doubt.

The urgency of the situation hung heavy in the air, a palpable tension that seemed to quicken the pulse of the room. With Gladys's fear visibly escalating, a decision loomed over me like a storm cloud, dark and imminent. The truth about my real identity, a secret cloaked in shadows, now demanded the light. The risks were undeniable, the potential danger to her palpable, yet the haunting experience with Killerton Enterprises had laid bare a stark reality: silence harboured a far greater threat.

"I know you know what this is," I began, the words tumbling out with a mixture of resolve and apprehension. I extended my hand, the Portal Key nestled within my palm. Its surface shimmered, capturing fragments of ambient light and casting an ethereal glow, a beacon of truth in the dim room.

Gladys's expression shifted, a furrow carving its way across her brow as understanding dawned. "So, you are a Guardian?" Her voice carried a note of realisation, a bridge between suspicion and acceptance. It wasn't a question so much as an acknowledgment of a truth she had already sensed.

"Yes," I affirmed, the word heavy with the weight of my admission. It felt like acknowledging a part of myself long kept in the shadows, now laid bare in the soft light of vulnerability.

"I thought Luke was the only one," Gladys confessed, her eyes wide, a mirror to her inner turmoil—a blend of fascination at the unfolding mystery and trepidation at its implications.

"No," I responded, a simple negation that seemed to expand the boundaries of her world in an instant.

"How many of you are there?" Her question was a whisper in the vast expanse of secrets that lay between us.

I shrugged, a gesture of uncertainty and honesty intertwined. "Dozens, if not hundreds." It was a truth as vast and unknown as the stars themselves, a testament to the scale of our guardianship that even I struggled to fully comprehend.

Gladys's reaction was a silent gasp. It was as if the very air had been sucked out of the room, leaving behind a weighty silence that bore the magnitude of the revelation.

"I honestly don't know, Gladys," I admitted, my voice a soft echo in the charged atmosphere. Moving closer, I gently removed the knife from her grasp, an act of reassurance amidst the storm of revelations. The metal felt cold, opposing the warmth of human connection I sought to reestablish.

"Why didn't you tell me?" Her voice, tinged with a blend of hurt and curiosity, trailed off as she moved towards the kitchen. Her actions, opening cupboards in a methodical search for wine, spoke of a need to find solace. It was a typical Gladys reaction, an attempt to anchor herself to something tangible in the midst of upheaval.

Following Gladys into the kitchen felt like stepping into a different realm, one where the warmth of the room clashed with the cold reality of our conversation. I placed the knife on the bench. "It's a dangerous lifestyle. I wanted to protect you," I found myself saying, my voice a mix of defence and regret.

"Like you protected Joel?" Gladys's retort came swift and sharp, her words cutting through the air like the knife I had just set down. The accusation stung, a bolt of lightning that illuminated the storm brewing between us.

A scowl involuntarily crossed my face. "That's not fair, Gladys. I had nothing to do with Joel's death." My protest was earnest, a plea for understanding amidst the whirlwind of accusations and doubts.

Gladys's eyebrow arched, her silence speaking volumes. Her skepticism was a clear sign of the trust that had been eroded, a bridge we would now have to rebuild. "I didn't," I continued, the insistence in my voice betraying the desperation I felt to convince her, to maintain the fragile thread of belief that still connected us.

"Do you know who killed Joel?" she pressed on, her question slamming into the conversation with the finality of a door shutting. The absence of the wine she sought seemed to amplify the tension, each echo a reminder of the barriers growing between us.

I shook my head, a quick, almost reflexive action. "No, I don't," I lied, the falsehood a heavy cloak around my shoulders. The truth was a dangerous companion, one I was not yet ready to introduce to Gladys.

Desperate to steer us away from the precipice of too many truths revealed, I grasped at the first distraction I could find. "What are you doing here anyway?"

Gladys, momentarily distracted, pulled a notepad and pen from the drawer, her movements deliberate as she began to scribble. "Luke asked me to pick up some camping goods that he had purchased. It's all in the truck in the driveway." Her words, simple and mundane, offered a brief respite from the emotional intensity of our exchange.

"I see," I responded, a faint grin touching my lips despite the weariness that clung to me like a second skin. *It's good to see Luke took my advice.* The thought was a small comfort, a reminder of the connections and plans that still existed beyond the immediate turmoil. The brochure I had left for

Luke, now resulting in tangible actions, felt like a minor victory in a day filled with battles.

"Come help me unpack. I need to take the truck with me," Gladys instructed. Her request, simple yet grounding, prompted me without a word to stride towards the front door, each step a march towards a semblance of ordinary life. The early evening air greeted me like an old friend, its freshness a welcome contrast to the heavy atmosphere we'd left behind in the kitchen. Eager for this brief escape, I opened the back of the truck, my hands automatically reaching for the nearest box. The physicality of the task, the weight and solidity of the items we were unloading, served as a temporary anchor, pulling me back from the swirling thoughts that threatened to consume me.

"Come home with me," Gladys's voice, soft yet insistent, broke into my reverie. Her presence at my side, reaching into the truck for another item, felt like a tether in the storm. "I want to hear more about your Clivilius." Her words, an invitation to share more of my world, warmed me, offering a bridge between the tension of our current situation and the possibility of a moment's peace.

With arms laden, I paused, turning towards her. The act of kissing Gladys gently on the forehead was an instinct, a small gesture of affection and reassurance. "I can't right now," I admitted, my voice a mix of regret and necessity. The thought that Luke might be close, that my urgent need to speak with him still hung over me, was a reminder of the duties that I couldn't ignore. "But I will tell you more soon," I promised, the words a pledge I desperately hoped to keep.

"How soon?" The anticipation in Gladys's voice, mingled with a hint of uncertainty, underscored the importance of our connection, of the promises we made to each other in these turbulent moments.

"Hopefully later tonight."

"Do you want me to pick you up from somewhere?"

"No," I replied, allowing a cheeky grin to cross my face. "I've already activated my Portal in your kitchen and registered the location."

The moment my words hung in the air, I could see the shift in Gladys's demeanour. Her eyes, previously dimmed by the weight of our conversation, suddenly sparked to life, a vivid intensity burning within them. "Chloe! She's with you, isn't she?" The accusation in her voice, so fragile and desperate, pierced me more sharply than any physical blow could.

But reality, cruel and unyielding, forced my expression to change. The grin that had briefly played on my lips vanished, replaced by a grimace of regret. "I'm so sorry, Gladys. I never meant for that to happen." My apology, sincere as it was, felt hollow against the magnitude of her loss.

The transformation was immediate; the wildfire in Gladys's eyes gave way to a storm, tears gathering like dark clouds ready to burst. "I want her back." Her words, a simple demand, echoed with the unbearable pain of a mother separated from her fur child.

"I'm sorry, Gladys," I found myself repeating, each apology heavier than the last, a burden I bore with every intention to alleviate her pain, yet powerless to reverse the irreversible. "She can't come back." The finality of my statement, a sentence I had no right to decree, felt like pronouncing a verdict on our shared humanity.

"You bastard!" Her cry, a blend of anguish and betrayal, cut through the evening air as she lashed out. The impact of her fist against my shoulder, though physically mild, was emotionally devastating. It was the pain of loss, the agony of a wound too deep to mend, manifesting in her anger.

As I placed the box back onto the truck, turning to fully face the tempest of her grief, I moved instinctively to draw her close. My arms, though unsure, sought to provide a haven from the storm of emotions raging between us.

Her initial resistance, a push against the unfairness of reality, soon gave way to surrender. Gladys collapsed into my embrace, her body wracked with sobs. "You've taken my baby," she mourned, the words muffled against my chest, a lament for a loss too great to bear alone.

"I'm so sorry, Gladys," I whispered again, my own voice strained with emotion. Detaching myself from the moment, I reached for another box, a feeble attempt to resume some semblance of normalcy, to distract us both from the chasm of grief that I had opened up at our feet.

Working in silence, we moved between the truck and Luke's living room, unloading the camping goods. Each item we placed down felt like a testament to the ordinary lives we were struggling to maintain amidst the extraordinary circumstances that had entwined us. The mundane task, usually comforting in its simplicity, now served as an unwanted reminder of the complex web of emotions and responsibilities I navigated, a balance between the world as it was and the world as I wished it could be.

❖

Gladys's departure marked the end of an emotionally charged chapter, leaving me in the quiet aftermath of our turbulent exchange. Her emotions, complex and raw, reminded me once again of my ineptitude in navigating the intricate dance of human feelings—a fact Freya often pointed out with a mix of amusement and frustration. The brief, touch-less farewell with Gladys felt like a silent acknowledgment of the chasm that had widened between us, her swift exit a physical manifestation of the distance I had inadvertently created.

Her lingering resentment over Chloe's presence in Clivilius was palpable, and I knew I had my work cut out for me in mending that fractured connection.

Left alone with my thoughts, and an uneasy peace in Luke's seemingly abandoned house, I sought refuge in the mundane task of scavenging for food. The cupboards, however, offered little in the way of nourishment, their barren shelves a stark reminder of the transient nature of our existence. This emptiness, echoing the hollow feeling in the pit of my stomach, prompted a more thorough investigation of the house.

As I moved from room to room, the minimalistic state of Luke's belongings—or their conspicuous absence—spoke volumes. It seemed Luke had either embraced a spartan lifestyle or was in the process of transferring his life to Clivilius. This realisation brought a mix of admiration and concern. The deliberate stripping away of material attachments in favour of fortifying his settlement in Clivilius underscored the gravity of his situation. Guardians couldn't always shield those we cared about from the shadows that lurked just beyond the light.

The discovery of a whiskey bottle, hidden like a treasure behind the façade of emptiness, felt like stumbling upon a rare artefact in the desolation. "Whiskey," I whispered to myself, a small smile breaking through as I grasped the bottle. It was a modest comfort, a liquid companion to momentarily ease the weight of loneliness and the burden of responsibilities that lay ahead.

Holding the bottle, I contemplated the dual nature of my life—caught between the mundanity of human existence and the extraordinary demands of my role as a Guardian. The whiskey, with its promise of temporary solace, seemed a metaphor for the balance I sought to maintain: a moment of reprieve in the face of endless uncertainty.

As I gazed at the unopened bottle, the amber liquid catching the light in a warm glow, I allowed myself a moment of reflection. The task of mending the rift with Gladys, of navigating the complex web of relationships and duties, loomed large. Yet, in that quiet moment, with the whiskey offering its silent strength, I felt a renewed sense of determination.

"What the hell?" Luke's unexpected arrival, marked by the chaotic tumble of small kayaks, instantly shifted the atmosphere from one of solitary reflection to palpable tension. "Gladys," I found myself saying almost reflexively, emerging from the depths of my search in the cupboard with nothing more suitable than shot glasses for the whiskey. Placing one on the bench, I turned to face Luke, whose bewilderment was clear as day.

"What the hell happened?" His voice, sharp with concern and confusion, sliced through the air, demanding an explanation.

"It's the doing of Gladys," I responded, the calm in my voice belying the undercurrent of unease that Gladys's actions had stirred. Lifting the note she had left, I relayed the message to Luke with an attempt at nonchalance. "And she's left you a note. Shelving will be delivered tomorrow." Placing the note back on the bench, I sought refuge in the simplicity of the whiskey, letting the liquid courage wash away the remnants of the day's turmoil with a practiced ease.

"Ahh, this is great stuff you've got here, Luke. I had to open a new bottle. Hope you don't mind," I remarked, trying to steer the conversation towards less turbulent waters, appreciating the whiskey's fiery embrace as it offered a fleeting escape.

However, Luke's focus was elsewhere, his concern not with the disarray of camping equipment or the choice of drink, but with a matter far more grave. "I'm not talking about the camping shit. I'm talking about the fucking body!" His voice, now laced with a chilling intensity, brought a sudden clarity to the weight of his words.

"Body? What body?" I asked, my reaction a mixture of genuine surprise and a creeping sense of dread.

"Joel," Luke replied, his tone cold.

Shit, my mind raced, scrambling for footing in the quicksand of accusations and implications. Struggling to maintain a façade of ignorance, I shrugged lightly, a gesture meant to deflect, to obscure the truth that gnawed at the edges of my consciousness. "I'm not sure what you're talking about," I said, each word carefully measured, a thin veil over the turmoil that churned within.

The chaos of the living room, with its accidental obstacle course of kayaks and camping gear, seemed to fall away as Luke moved to join me in the kitchen. The simple act of him grabbing a glass and sliding it across the bench felt like a silent summons to share in the ritual of seeking solace in whiskey. As I obliged, pouring him a drink and sliding the glass back, a part of me sought justification for another round of liquid courage. *If Luke is drinking with me, I should pour myself another,* I reasoned, the whiskey momentarily offering a shared reprieve from the storm of revelations swirling around us.

"We found Joel's body," Luke said, the words landing with the weight of a verdict.

The shock of his statement hit me mid-swallow, causing me to cough violently, a spray of whiskey marking the bench as I struggled to regain composure. The harsh burn of the alcohol, now a traitor to my attempt at nonchalance, seemed to mirror the harsh reality Luke had just laid bare. "Yeah," Luke snapped, his response cutting through my feeble attempt to mask my surprise. "That's what I thought."

"I'm so sorry, Luke," I managed, the words feeling inadequate against the magnitude of the situation. My head shook, a vain attempt to dislodge the heavy burden of guilt that had settled over me. "I had no idea he'd get away." My admission, though true, felt hollow, an echo of the many apologies that had filled the air today.

"I hardly think he got away by himself." Luke's words were a cold splash of realisation, forcing me to confront a possibility I hadn't considered.

"Shit! I didn't think of that!" I exclaimed, the revelation hitting me like a sudden storm. The idea that Griffin's escape might not have been a solitary act sent a ripple of fear through me. The notion that he could have had help, that our adversary's reach might extend further than I feared, was a chilling prospect.

"So, you did know?"

"Yeah, I knew who he was, but I thought..." My attempt to explain, to unravel the tangled web of decisions and missteps, was abruptly severed.

"Then why the fuck did you pretend you'd never seen him before!?" Luke's interjection, fuelled by frustration and betrayal, felt like it should have been a physical blow. Yet, there was a confusion hanging between us that felt almost tangible, a dense fog that muddied understanding and intent. "Huh?" I asked, my mind scrambling to bridge the gap that had suddenly widened, the miscommunication casting shadows of doubt over our conversation.

"Joel. Why'd you act like you didn't know him?

"Ahh, shit!" The words escaped me as a sigh, frustration and realisation mingling in equal measure. My hand moved to my forehead, pressing against the skin as if to soothe the dull ache that throbbed beneath. It was clear that our lines of communication had not just faltered; they had collapsed, leaving me no choice but to reveal the existence of a threat I had hoped to keep shielded from Luke's immediate worries—Portal Pirates.

"What?" Luke's query, a mix of impatience and confusion, hung in the air, demanding clarity.

"I'm not talking about Joel." My clarification, though necessary, felt like peeling back a layer to reveal a deeper, more dangerous truth.

"Then who the fuck are you talking about?"

"Griffin Langley," I confessed, the name a heavy load to drop between us. Leaning against the kitchen's side bench, the cool stone beneath my palms offered a stark contrast to the heat of the moment, a physical grounding as I prepared to divulge further details.

Luke, his patience thinning, signalled for a refill of his glass—a silent yet potent reminder of the stress we were under. "And who the hell is Griffin La..." he trailed off.

"Langley," I supplied, the name hanging between us like a spectre.

"Yeah, him," Luke conceded, his action of throwing back the whiskey akin to a man bracing against a storm, seeking solace in the burn of the alcohol.

"He's a Portal Pirate." The words felt like casting light on shadows, revealing dangers hidden just beneath the surface of Luke's perceived security.

"A Portal Pirate?" Luke's response, a mix of disbelief and derision, was punctuated by a wild smirk. Yet, beneath the skepticism, a thread of curiosity lingered.

"Yes," I affirmed, the certainty in my voice a stark contrast to the incredulity of his. "And I believe his partner, Nelson Price, may be in your settlement." The possibility, a dangerous seed, was now planted, its implications far-reaching.

"Nobody's mentioned seeing anyone unfamiliar," Luke dismissed, the shrug accompanying his words attempting to convey indifference. His reach for the whiskey bottle, a gesture of both defiance and resignation, spoke volumes. "The people I do know are already struggling to survive. I doubt that anybody I don't know about could survive on their own for long. And besides, I really don't care right now."

The incredulity in Luke's demeanour was almost as palpable as the whiskey bottle I abruptly claimed from his grip. "Luke, this is serious. They're incredibly dangerous." My words, laden with urgency, sought to pierce the veil of his indifference.

"I don't understand," Luke countered, his attempt to reclaim the whiskey bottle a physical manifestation of his struggle to grasp the full scope of the situation. "How did he get into my settlement without me seeing him?"

"He may not have. But if he did, you'd never know it. They're sneaky bastards." The words left my mouth with a bitterness that matched the taste of the whiskey.

Luke's gaze drifted to his reflection in the kitchen window, a moment of introspection amidst the confusion. "Are they the ones who attacked Joel?" The concern in his voice, a suitable contrast to his earlier dismissiveness.

"I believe so," was my simple, yet heavy, acknowledgment.

"But even so, if you took Joel's body, how did it end up at our settlement?" Luke's question, logical and probing, demanded an explanation that I dreaded to give.

Sighing loudly, I braced myself for the confession, resentful of the circumstances that necessitated such a revelation. "I captured Griffin and was holding him captive at Belkeep. But somehow he managed to escape. He stole the truck with Joel's body." The words felt like admitting to a personal failure, a lapse in judgment and security that had led to unforeseen consequences.

"Can't you just follow his tracks?" Luke's suggestion, while logical, underestimated the capabilities of our adversaries.

"No!" The frustration that had been simmering beneath the surface finally erupted, my fist striking the bench with a force that mirrored the turmoil within. The sound of impact echoed through the kitchen, a testament to the futility and desperation that the situation engendered. "That's the thing with Pirates, once they have recorded a location, they can access any other recorded Earth or Clivilius location from it." The explanation, a grim outline of the Pirates' capabilities, underscored the complexity and danger of tracking them. Their ability to navigate and exploit the very portals we relied on rendered traditional methods of pursuit almost obsolete.

"Shit! There's more settlements in Clivilius?" Luke blurted incredulously.

"Yeah... uh... I think that's a conversation for another time," I hastily interjected, keen to steer our discussion away from the labyrinth of details that could further distract our already precarious situation. The last thing we needed was to dive into the intricacies of Clivilius' settlements, especially not when the immediate threat of Portal Pirates loomed over us.

"Shit," Luke mumbled.

I pressed on, eager to focus on our immediate concerns. "But wherever Griffin took Joel, it can't be too far from your settlement if you found Joel's body." The logic was sound, a beacon of clarity in the fog of uncertainty. "And if his partner is there, how do we find him?" Luke's question, a practical one, sought a strategy.

The possibility that Nelson could be hiding near Luke's settlement was a dangerous one, necessitating a cautious approach. "Not sure. If there are no signs of life around you, which I suspect is the case, then it is likely that he will not know where he is either." My speculation was grounded in the reality of our enemy's situation—lost, but dangerous.

"A pirate's instincts are for survival. He will happily steal whatever he needs, and he won't hesitate to use violence if he feels the situation needs it." The truth of my words painted a vivid picture of the threat we faced. "But in all likelihood, he will hang around the Portal for a few weeks, or as long as he can last, in the hope that another Pirate will come along and he can finish making the location connection." The strategy of waiting by the Portal, a beacon for any lost Pirate, was a double-edged sword. It offered us a potential advantage, a predictable pattern of behaviour that Luke could exploit.

"He will attempt to record the location at every chance he can get - but he needs the Portal to be active to do it. So expect him to remain close to your Portal." The tactical implications were clear, offering Luke a narrow window to act. "You could attempt to flush him out, but he is dangerous." The warning was a necessary one, underscoring the risk involved in confronting a Portal Pirate.

Luke's distress was palpable, his eyes a vivid testament to the toll our conversation—and perhaps the whiskey—had taken on him. His reaction left me questioning the wisdom of my approach. "You okay?" My concern was genuine, the touch on his shoulder meant as a pillar of support, yet I couldn't help but wonder if I had overstepped, pushing the information on him too far too fast.

His response, a shudder that seemed to echo the turmoil within, only deepened my worry. "Luke?" The repetition of his name, a bid for his attention, felt inadequate in the face of his evident distress.

Unexpectedly, Luke fell back against the cupboards, his knees wobbling and finally his body sliding down, his knees tucked in close as he reached the tiled floor. Tears burst from his swelling eyes.

Worried that his Guardian responsibilities were taking a heavy toll already, crouching in front of Luke, I gripped his shoulders firmly. "Luke, what's going on?" My voice, though steady, belied the concern that knotted my stomach.

"Just too much whiskey," he managed between sobs, a dismissive explanation that failed to mask the deeper currents of despair.

"Come on. Get up," I urged, extending a hand, a lifeline meant to pull him back from the brink. The physical act of helping him up, however, went awry as his grip, unsteady and desperate, resulted in both of us grappling with gravity. The unexpected force of his fall pulled me down, my knee meeting the hard floor with a painful thud.

"What the fuck did you do that for?" The words slipped out, a reflex reaction to the sudden pain and surprise, my tongue instinctively seeking out the source of a small but sharp pain on my lip.

"Sorry. I slipped. Way too much alcohol," Luke's apology, though mumbled, carried the weight of genuine remorse.

Allowing my features to relax, recognising the accident for what it was—a mishap fuelled by alcohol and high emotions—I wiped away another drop of blood. Sinking down beside Luke, I settled into a silent solidarity.

Luke's unexpected proximity, his shoulder pressing into mine, introduced a sexual tension I hadn't anticipated, a complexity that added layers to an already charged atmosphere. The air between us thickened, laden with an unspoken query that danced on the edge of my consciousness. Swallowing uncomfortably, I turned to face him, curiosity and an unnamable apprehension mingling within me.

As Luke mirrored my movement, our faces drew closer, the whispered taunts of Clivilius echoing in my mind—a seductive urging to embrace a connection I hadn't consciously acknowledged until this moment. *Accept him*, the voice, both a bane and a whisper of potential truths, seemed to find resonance within the depths of my being, challenging my perceptions of desire and connection.

Slowly, Luke's face inched closer to mine.

Accept him, the silent voice instructed again, as my head began a ridiculously slow retreat.

Luke's lips, rough yet insistent, pressed against mine in a moment that shattered any lingering denial of the attraction that simmered beneath the surface. My hands found his chest, a gesture that might have been intended to push him away, yet lacked the conviction of true resistance. The sensation of his tongue, tentative and exploring against the cut on my lip, sent a cascade of conflicting emotions and physical responses through me. Pleasure intertwined with concern, blurring the lines of our previously defined relationship.

As our tongues tentatively met, a door within me creaked open, revealing uncharted territories of desire and connection. My grip on his shoulders tightened, a silent acknowledgment of the tumultuous sea of feelings that threatened to engulf me. My rational mind clamoured for retreat, for the safety of familiar ground, yet the deeper, more primal part of me rebelled, yearning for the continuation of this unexpected intimacy.

Luke's actions, a blend of exploration and mumbled words, paused as he pulled back, his gaze piercing into mine with an intensity that seemed to seek answers to questions unasked. "Did you know?" His inquiry, loaded with implications, momentarily confused me.

"Know what?" My response was automatic, the confusion apparent as I tried to navigate the tumultuous waters of our interaction.

"So I am your first," he whispered, a revelation that, while true, caught me off guard. "Yeah. I've never been this close to a guy before," I admitted, the words tumbling out in a rush of honesty and vulnerability. "We should stop," I suggested, in a desperate bid for clarity and control over my emotions.

Luke's grin, wide and knowing, hinted at depths of understanding and experience beyond my own. "As sweet a sentiment as that is, that's not what I'm talking about." His words, playful yet profound, left me scrambling for comprehension.

"Then what are you talking about?" The question hung between us, a bridge spanning the gap of misunderstanding and unspoken truths.

Without warning, Luke's lips pushed against mine, his rough tongue gliding across my parched lips. Settling on the point of broken skin where the small drops of blood continued to seep, Luke paused and pressing his lips firmer against mine, he took a deep suck.

Pulling away, "I think you've been under too much pressure lately, not to mention the whiskey," I ventured, attempting to attribute Luke's uncharacteristic behaviour to the strain of our duties and the whiskey's influence. My efforts to distance myself from his advances, to regain some semblance of control over the situation, felt both necessary and oddly painful.

Luke's reaction, a vehement shake of his head accompanied by a soft denial, only deepened the mystery and my concern. "No," he said softly, "I see you now. Just as Clive sees us all." The mention of Clive, a name unfamiliar and yet spoken with a significance that seemed to hold weight, left me baffled and uneasy. *Who the hell is Clive?* The question echoed in my mind, a puzzle piece that didn't fit, adding layers to the enigma that was Luke in that moment.

Before I could voice my confusion, Luke's body gave in, slumping against the cupboards with an unsettling softness. The peaceful smile that graced his lips, in stark contrast to the turmoil that had preceded it, and his closed eyes painted a picture of serenity that felt out of place in the unexpectedness of our recent exchange. "Luke," I called out, my voice laced with concern as I shook his shoulders, seeking any sign of awareness. But there was none. His unresponsiveness, whether due to alcohol or something more sinister, spurred me into action, though a part of me recoiled at the thought of what the alternative to intoxication might be.

With a sense of urgency, I hoisted Luke into my arms, the weight of his body a tangible reminder of the responsibility I felt towards him. Dragging him to the bedroom, I was governed by a singular focus—to ensure his safety, to provide him the rest he so clearly needed. Placing him on the bed, the roughness of my actions belied the care and concern that motivated them.

Standing there, watching Luke lightly snore, a semblance of normalcy in his breathing, I was torn between relief and a lingering worry. The hope that he would retain even fragments of our conversation, that the morning would bring clarity and perhaps a bridge to mend the gap that had formed between us, was a slender thread I clung to.

Leaving Luke in the quiet of his room, I stepped out into the night, the cool air a balm to my unsettled thoughts.

4338.208

(27 July 2018)

A MIND MADE UP

1338.208.1

The serenity of the sunset, with its rich tapestry of colours, offered a striking contrast to the turmoil that churned within me. Standing at the edge of Glenelg Jetty, I found myself caught between the breathtaking beauty of the world and the complex web of emotions and duties that bound me. The tranquility of the scene before me, where the sky seemed to bleed into the sea in a symphony of colours, was a poignant reminder of the world's indifference to human strife and joy alike.

The soothing rhythm of the waves against the jetty served as a balm to my unsettled spirit, yet the peace offered by nature felt fleeting. The gentle caress of the breeze, carrying with it the salt and whispers of the sea, spoke to a part of me that longed for simplicity and clarity. Yet, the anticipation of Jeremiah's arrival, thick and palpable as the early evening mist, rendered me unable to fully surrender to the moment's peace.

As Jeremiah's voice broke through my contemplation, a mix of relief and tension coursed through me. Turning to face him, I was struck by the sight of his approach, his figure a dark silhouette against the dimming glow of the day. The weariness and resolve etched on his face spoke volumes, a reflection of the myriad challenges we faced, the decisions that lay heavily on our shoulders.

Our embrace was a moment of solace and strength. It was a silent acknowledgment of the burdens we bore, the choices we had made, and the uncertain path that lay ahead. In that embrace, the complexities of our situation seemed both magnified and momentarily alleviated, a paradox that underscored the depth of our Guardian connection.

"It's good to see you again," Jeremiah spoke, his deep voice carrying a touch of melancholy that echoed the struggles etched into the lines on his face. The setting sun cast long shadows across his worn features, highlighting the burdens of a life spent battling the encroaching darkness of our era.

"Likewise, Jeremiah," I replied, my voice steady yet tinged with a hint of apprehension. I studied his features for the subtle nuances that hinted at the toll our turbulent world had taken on him. The way his eyes seemed to carry a storm within them, the slight downturn of his mouth that spoke volumes of his internal battles. "How have you been?" I inquired, my gaze locked onto his, attempting to decipher the state of his mind beneath the façade.

He sighed wearily, a sound that seemed to carry the weight of Clivilius itself. "Surviving, Cody. That's all we can do in these troubled times," he said, his eyes scanning the horizon, as if seeking answers in the blur of fiery oranges and cool blues.

Nodding in shared understanding, I acknowledged the pervasive struggle that surrounded us. Clivilius was in turmoil. Even the remotest settlements, like my own Belkeep, were not immune to the upheaval that gripped the world. The sense of impending doom was palpable, a thick cloud that hung over us, tainting every breath with the taste of fear.

"Jeremiah, there's something I need to tell you," I began cautiously, my voice barely above a whisper. The air felt heavier, as if the very atmosphere was bracing itself for my confession. I was aware that my revelation might not sit well with my Guardian Atum, a man who had seen more of the world's darkness than I.

His eyes focused on mine, a mix of curiosity and concern swirling within them. "What is it, Cody?" he asked, his tone steady yet revealing an underlying tension.

Taking a deep breath, the words felt like lead on my tongue, but I knew they needed to be said. "I went to Killerton Enterprises again," I admitted, my voice steady yet filled with a hint of defiance. I watched for his reaction, the flicker of worry, the subtle tightening of his jaw.

Jeremiah's eyes narrowed, worry flickering across his face like shadows cast by an unseen flame. "You went there? Are you insane?" he asked, his voice laced with concern and a hint of incredulity. It wasn't just the words but the way he said them, a mixture of fear and frustration, as if he was battling his own demons while trying to shield me from mine.

"I had to, Jeremiah," I said, the conviction in my voice masking the turmoil that raged within me.

"And what of Luke? Did you find him? Did he go with you?" Jeremiah's questions cascaded, each one revealing the depth of his worry.

I shook my head, the movement slow. "No, I went alone," I confessed softly, my eyes diverting downward as I carried the weight of my choices. The admission felt like a betrayal, not just to Jeremiah but to myself. I had ventured into the lion's den completely alone.

"So you've not given the access card to Luke?" Jeremiah pressed for an explanation, his gaze piercing, searching for the truth beneath my words.

My face scrunched as I hesitated, the internal conflict evident. "No," I admitted softly. The word hung in the air between us, heavy and filled with implications.

"What else aren't you telling me, Cody?" Jeremiah urged for more information, his voice a mix of concern and demand for transparency. His intuition was sharp; he could sense there was more to my story, layers that I had yet to unveil.

"The access card got taken from me. I think they knew I was coming," I confessed in a hurried voice, the words tumbling out as I finally allowed myself to confront the reality of my situation. The realisation that my movements had been anticipated, possibly monitored, was a chilling thought.

Jeremiah's eyes widened in alarm. "I'm surprised they didn't execute you for it."

I chuckled softly at Jeremiah's dramatic leap, but my demeanour turned sombre quickly. "There's more you need to know," I said, my voice steady as I prepared to recount my recent experiences at the underground facility. The chamber of countless Portal Keys, the existence of the Guardian Order, portal blocking technology, and the secret solitary access room—it all poured out of me in a flood of words, a deluge of revelations that I had barely begun to process myself.

As I spoke, I observed the emotions playing across Jeremiah's face—surprise, disbelief, and finally, a deep sense of understanding settled in his eyes. It was like watching a storm brew over a once calm sea, the tranquility replaced by a tempest of realisation and unanswered questions.

Jeremiah's muttered disbelief hung in the air, the weight of the unspoken revelation settling between us like a shroud. The twilight around us seemed to deepen, casting long shadows that mirrored the darkening of Jeremiah's expression. "I can't believe it," he whispered, the words carrying the weight of years of unwavering trust. His voice, usually so firm and authoritative, now held a tremor of vulnerability. "All this time, and not once did Zenobias ever mention to me anything about the existence of a Guardian Order."

"To be honest, that does surprise me," I replied, the shock of the newfound knowledge reverberating through my thoughts. "I know the two of you are close."

"We were close," Jeremiah corrected, his voice barely above a whisper. A deep sadness etched lines across his once-stoic face, adding years to his appearance in mere moments. The fading light of day cast his features into relief, highlighting the grief that seemed to consume him.

"What do you mean, were?" I hesitated, the question hanging in the air, an unspoken fear lingering between us. The pause felt like an eternity, a chasm opening up that threatened to swallow us whole.

Jeremiah's eyes closed, a sigh escaping his lips. It was a sound of resignation, of a man coming to terms with a loss so profound it threatened to unmoor him. "She passed away a few days ago, not long after I met you." The words fell like stones into the stillness, each one a painful testament to the transient nature of our existence in this tumultuous world.

The news hit me like a physical blow, a wave of sorrow mingled with shock. Zenobias, the indomitable force, a beacon of wisdom and strength, gone? It seemed inconceivable. Jeremiah, the unshakeable Guardian Atum, now looked diminished, a figure of mourning shrouded in the twilight's gloom.

"What happened?" I asked, the words carrying the weight of an unspoken grief that settled in the caverns of my heart. There was a silence that seemed to stretch between us, a bridge over which the sombre truth would soon pass. Jeremiah's tales of Zenobias had painted her as an ethereal Guardian, a beacon of grace and intellect. Yet, our encounters had been scarce, leaving me with only fleeting glimpses of the profound aura that clung to her being, a presence so impactful yet so intangible, like the whisper of the wind through the leaves.

"Shrapnel wound from an explosion," Jeremiah answered, his voice a low rumble that seemed to resonate with the fading light around us. The words tore me from the reflections on the aged woman who had now departed from our world. The revelation struck like a bitter wind, leaving me frozen in disbelief. The demise of such a remarkable Guardian felt inconceivable, a harsh reminder of the brutal reality of a world engulfed in chaos. It was a blow, not just to the heart but to the very fabric of what I believed invincible.

"Come on, Cody, you know Syria is at war," Jeremiah interjected, his voice cutting through the fog of sorrow that clouded my thoughts. His words were a firm nudge back to reality, a reminder of the turmoil that ravaged lands far and near.

My brow softened, acknowledging the harsh truth laid bare. Syria, like much of the world, was a battleground, and the Guardians faced the perils of conflict head-on. The reality of Zenobias's fate, an acknowledgement to the dangers we all faced, settled heavily within me, a sombre note in the symphony of our existence.

Seeking refuge, I attempted to shift the conversation, yearning for a respite from the harsh truths that gripped us. "But now we do know there's a Guardian Order, it changes everything," I said, the words carrying a note of hope as I sought to redirect the dialogue to a more optimistic path. There was a lightness in my attempt to steer us away from the shadow of loss, an effort to find solace in the revelation that had shaken me. The existence of the Guardian Order, shrouded in secrecy, now promised a beacon of light in the enveloping darkness. It was a shift in perspective, a pivot towards the possibility that in the knowledge of this Order lay the potential to reshape our battle-scarred reality.

Jeremiah's gaze intensified, the gravity of his words hanging heavily in the air like a dense fog that refused to lift. "I think it's time that you complete your Guardian group, Cody," he declared, his resolve casting a firm shadow over my attempts to regain control over the discussion.

"I know," I admitted, a sense of urgency creeping into my voice. The words felt heavy on my tongue, laden with the realisation of the task ahead. "I'm working on preparing Gladys. But it's become a little complicated now that I know her involvement with Luke."

Jeremiah's brow furrowed in contemplation as he absorbed the complexity of the situation. "How so?" he inquired, his curiosity unwavering. The simplicity of his question belied the depth of understanding he sought.

"Luke's been asking her for help to gather supplies, and I've been encouraging her to assist him. We can't let Luke's settlement fail," I explained, the dilemma unfolding before Jeremiah like a delicate tapestry. Each thread represented a decision, a choice that could alter the fabric of our future.

"Agreed," Jeremiah nodded solemnly. "Any ideas for the second Guardian?"

"Not yet," I replied, uncertainty casting a shadow over my expression as I shook my head.

"Don't take too long," Jeremiah cautioned, his words echoing with the urgency of a ticking clock. The admonition, though gentle, was a clarion call to action, a reminder that time was a luxury I could ill afford.

I frowned, torn between the necessity of swift action and the unshakable feeling that Gladys wasn't fully prepared for the weight of Guardian responsibilities. The delicate balance of time and readiness lingered, casting a shadow over the path ahead.

"We can't stay hidden anymore. The Guardians are isolated and scattered, and I think it's time that changes," I insisted, my voice firm, resolute, echoing across the space between us like a manifesto against the darkness that sought to consume us. The distant hum of waves crashing against the shore provided an ominous underscore to our deliberations, a natural symphony that seemed to underscore the intensity of our conversation.

Jeremiah raised a hand, a gesture as if warding off the urgency of my proposition, his movements deliberate, measured. "Hold on a sec," he interjected. "I don't think we should rush into anything here. It's a precarious and dangerous situation." His voice was a calm counterpoint to my fervour, a reminder of the caution with which we must tread.

My gaze drifted to the distant horizon, the sea's expanse echoing the vastness of the challenges that lay before us. "I have a contact who can help us," I divulged, my words cutting through the ambient sounds of the evening, offering a sliver of hope amidst the enveloping gloom.

Frowning, Jeremiah reluctantly motioned for me to continue, his silhouette outlined against the backdrop of a darkening sky.

"Amber," I revealed, her name resonating like a whispered promise carried away by the ocean breeze. The mention of her name felt like casting a stone into still waters, the ripples yet unseen but inevitable.

Jeremiah's expression remained unchanged. "I've not heard of her."

"I first met her several years ago in London. She helped me to escape the ambush at Killerton Enterprises yesterday. She's a Guardian too. She was there with others in her group... Josh and Nathan, I think their names were. They said something about having stolen some blueprints."

"This is all new to me," Jeremiah admitted. "Do you have any idea what these blueprints are?"

"I've not got a clue," I confessed with a helpless shrug.

"Are you sure she will help us?" Jeremiah probed further, a thread of skepticism weaving through his cautious tone.

I hesitated, the rhythmic sound of waves crashing against the shore serving as a backdrop to my contemplation. "I don't actually know how to contact her," I admitted, laying bare the vulnerability in my plan.

"Some contact then," Jeremiah quipped, a soft chuckle breaking the serious undertones.

I scowled, the corners of my eyes narrowing at his straightforward assessment. Yet, deep down, I knew he was right. Amber's potential assistance held little value if I couldn't bridge the gap of communication. However, beneath the frustration and the fear, a spark of determination flickered to life. "But," I began, the word hanging in the air, pregnant with possibilities.

"I think you and I should meet with Luke first," Jeremiah suggested, redirecting the course of our conversation before it delved into deeper uncertainties.

"And tell him—" I started, the question trailing off as I attempted to grasp the extent of what we'd reveal to Luke. But Jeremiah cut me off abruptly, his interjection steering our dialogue down a path I hadn't anticipated.

"But there's someone else I need to meet with first. Someone that I hope can shed some more light on this Guardian Order." The seriousness with which he spoke, the weight of each word, hinted at the importance of this unnamed individual in the larger puzzle we were attempting to piece together.

Surprise etched my features. "Who's this mysterious contact?" I probed, the words echoing against the night's embrace.

"An old contact from many years ago," Jeremiah revealed, his voice carrying the weight of nostalgia, a hint of sorrow mingling with the resolve. "We haven't spoken for a long time, but I do know that she was quite close with Zenobias. I'll ask around about this Amber person of yours too."

A small scowl crept across my face, my features tightening with displeasure. Jeremiah taking the lead with my information irked me, stirring a mix of pride and annoyance within. Yet, I had learned, through grudging experience, that arguing with his resolute determination proved a futile endeavour. His methods, though sometimes abrasive, were born of a deep-seated commitment to Clivilius.

Suddenly, Jeremiah stood tall, a figure of resolve and unwavering purpose. His shoulders squared, he spoke decisively, a clear command cutting through the uncertainty that had begun to settle around us. "You've got two weeks to get Gladys and your second Guardian sorted. I'll gather intel, and we'll reconvene here to decide our next steps."

I nodded in acceptance, the weight of the situation settling over me like a heavy cloak. "That sounds reasonable enough. Two weeks it is."

Jeremiah gripped my forearms, squeezing tightly, a gesture that felt like an anchor in the tumultuous sea of uncertainties that surrounded us. The air seemed to hold its breath, a silent witness of the moment as he uttered a final plea. "Be careful, my friend," he urged, genuine concern gleaming in his eyes.

"You too, Jeremiah," I replied, my voice carrying through the breeze like a whispered oath, imbued with the weight of promises unspoken and the depth of our shared resolve. "Light the fire." The words felt symbolic, more than a mere farewell—a call to action, a reminder of the purpose that drove us, even in the face of overwhelming odds.

His face softened, a fleeting connection in the shadows, a momentary bridge between the worlds of light and darkness we navigated. "Share the light," he responded, his words a reverberation of our shared mission, an echo of the bond that united us. It was a reminder that, though our paths might diverge, our purpose remained intertwined.

As Jeremiah's figure melded into the dwindling crowd, moving towards the shore, a new plan began to crystallise in my mind. The ambient noise of the crowd, a distant murmur against the backdrop of the crashing waves, provided a soundtrack to my contemplations. Jeremiah was right about Gladys; she needed an extra layer of protection, a safeguard against the unpredictable tides of fate that threatened to engulf us.

The evening held its breath as I mulled over the risks and vulnerabilities, a complex tapestry unfolding in the recesses of my thoughts. The strategy that began to take shape was one of caution and foresight, a chess move in a game where the stakes were as high as the very fate of our worlds. At least it would offer Gladys an escape route from any situation, a lifeline in the tumultuous seas we navigated, as long as she stayed far from the looming shadows of Killerton Enterprises—a silent addition that echoed through the night, the recent events etched fresh in my memory.

GUARDIAN CYCLE

1338.208.2

The evening sky was a canvas, painted with strokes of purple and orange that seeped through the windows, bathing the living room in a warm, ethereal glow. Outside, the picturesque view of the Derwent River unfurled in the distance, a tranquil scene that under different circumstances, I might have found wholly relaxing. Yet, as I stood there, awaiting Gladys's arrival, a knot of anticipation tightened in my stomach. This wasn't just any meeting; the stakes were higher than they had ever been before, and the weight of that realisation made it impossible to fully appreciate the beauty sprawled before me.

Lost in a whirlwind of thoughts about what the evening might hold, the sudden thud from outside jerked me back to reality. The front door squeaked as I opened it, and what I saw next was both unexpected and slightly comical. Gladys, in her typically confident stride, had miscalculated her step and was now grappling with gravity, trying to reclaim her balance after tripping on the final cement step leading to the door.

"Gladys!" I exclaimed, my voice laced with surprise and concern as I hastened towards her. My heart raced, not just from the sudden burst of movement but from the worry that she might be hurt. Gladys was many things – formidable, determined, undeniably resilient – but seeing her in a moment of vulnerability struck a chord within me.

Despite her stumble, Gladys was a picture of resilience. She managed to break her fall with her palms, a small victory against the unforgiving cement. As she looked up at me, her cheeks painted with a flush of embarrassment and annoyance, I was momentarily captivated by her. Even in her clumsiness, there was a determination that I couldn't help but admire. My initial surprise quickly morphed into concern, especially as I noticed Snowflake attempting a daring escape past her.

"Snowflake!" Gladys's voice pierced the air, a mix of screech and command, as she leaped with surprising agility to intercept the little fur-ball. I watched, partly amused and partly in awe, as she expertly scooped Snowflake into her arms, thwarting the attempted escape with a grace that belied her earlier stumble.

With Snowflake securely in her grasp, Gladys's slight irritation at her pet's antics seemed to melt away as she glanced at me. Without missing a beat, she strode past me into the house, her presence as commanding as ever. I followed her, feeling slightly out of my element. Dressed in a clean black suit for the occasion, I couldn't shake the feeling that, despite the importance of this meeting, my attire made me seem like an actor playing a part, rather than a participant in a pivotal moment in our intertwined narratives.

"Why are you all dressed up?" Gladys queried, an eyebrow arching in a mix of amusement and curiosity as her gaze swept over my meticulously polished shoes and the formal lines of my suit. Her attire, in stark contrast, bore the casual, slightly ruffled signature of her unexpected encounter with the front step. Despite the dishevelled state, there was an inherent rugged charm about her that the mishap couldn't diminish.

Feeling a wave of relief wash over me that neither Gladys nor Snowflake had suffered any harm from their earlier tumble, I led her into the kitchen. The warmth of the space seemed to envelop us, shutting out the crisp evening air that lingered at our backs as the door clicked shut. "I want to make it up to you, Gladys," I confessed, my tone laden with a sincerity that I hoped would bridge the gap my previous actions had created, particularly those involving Chloe. Pouring her a glass of red wine, I offered it as both a peace offering and a symbol of my intentions.

"How?" The skepticism in her voice was palpable, mingling with a genuine curiosity as she accepted the wine. I noticed the way her eyes locked onto mine, searching, perhaps, for signs of the honesty behind my words. She took a tentative sip of the wine, her gaze still fixed on me, as if the answers she sought might be found in my expression.

"I'm cooking you dinner," I announced, gesturing towards the dining table I had meticulously prepared before her arrival. The table was set with care, each piece of cutlery placed with precision, a visual testament to the depth of my remorse and my desire to make amends. I hoped the gesture of a home-cooked meal, prepared by my own hands, would convey the sincerity of my apology, how deeply I regretted the rift my actions had caused.

Gladys turned, her attention captured by the dining setup, a look of genuine surprise crossing her features as if she hadn't noticed it upon entering. "How long do I have?" she inquired, an unexpected question that momentarily threw me off balance.

"What do you mean?" Confusion furrowed my brow, the shift from our previous conversation to this query leaving me momentarily adrift, unsure of the undercurrents at play.

"For a shower," she softly chuckled, her cheeks colouring a delicate shade of pink at the implication. The lightness of her laughter, tinged with a hint of embarrassment, cut through the tension, revealing a side of Gladys that was seldom seen — vulnerable, yet endearing.

"Of course," I stammered, the realisation dawning on me as my own face mirrored her blush. "Take as much time as you need." The words were out before I fully comprehended the intimacy of the moment, the offer extending far beyond the confines of hospitality to something more personal, more profound. It was an admission of my willingness to wait, to pause time if necessary, for the chance to mend what had been broken between us.

As Gladys set her wine glass gently on the kitchen bench, the moment seemed to pause, suspended in the warm glow that filled the room. She leaned in, closing the space between us with a tenderness that caught me completely off guard. Her lips met mine in a kiss that was both soft and deliberate, a gesture so unexpected that it took my breath away. The world outside the boundaries of that kiss seemed to blur into insignificance, leaving only the sensation of her lips on mine, a memory imprinted with a sweetness that lingered long after she pulled away. I felt the light touch of her hand on my back, a fleeting contact that left a trail of warmth and a tingling sensation that echoed the surprise and delight of the moment.

"I really should shower," she whispered, her voice a delicate blend of reluctance and underlying desire. It was a statement, but one that carried the weight of unspoken questions and possibilities.

"Okay," I managed to respond, my voice barely above a whisper, still lost in the aftermath of her kiss. "I'll have dinner prepared by the time you are finished," I promised, leaning in for one last peck on the lips, an attempt to capture and extend the fleeting connection we'd just shared.

"I don't take that long in the bathroom," Gladys teased, her words light but filled with an unspoken challenge. She punctuated her statement with a playful thump on my shoulder, a gesture that somehow managed to ground me back in the reality of the kitchen, of the impending dinner, and of the evening that lay ahead.

I gulped dryly, the sudden return to reality reminding me of my inexperience in these moments. "I guess I'm not very practiced at this," I confessed, the words slipping out in a mix of vulnerability and realisation. It had been years since I had found myself in a situation like this, years since I had cooked dinner with the intention of sharing it with someone other than myself. The confession was not just an acknowledgment of my culinary skills but a deeper admission of the solitude that had characterised much of my recent life.

Gladys, ever intuitive, seemed to sense my hesitation, my uncertainty. Moving toward the kitchen drawers with a grace that belied the earlier clumsiness of her entrance, she pulled out a handful of local restaurant brochures and vouchers. Spreading them across the benchtop, she offered an alternative, her voice playful yet considerate. "Maybe you should just order us something." It was a suggestion that carried with it an understanding, a kindness that sought to bridge my insecurities with a practical solution.

Then, with a final playful smile that seemed to light up the room, Gladys made her way toward the bathroom, leaving me standing in the kitchen, surrounded by restaurant options but feeling an unexpected sense of connection. In that moment, the kitchen transformed from a place of culinary challenge to a stage for a different kind of dance, one that involved playful exchanges, gentle touches, and the promise of shared moments to come.

As I watched her leave, I realised that the evening was unfolding in ways I could not have anticipated. The unexpected kiss and the playful banter—all of these elements wove together into a narrative that was new, exciting, and filled with potential.

Standing alone in the kitchen, the scent of red wine mingled with the anticipation in the air, creating a backdrop to my swirling thoughts. The dining table, meticulously set for two, seemed to mock my culinary ambitions, reminding me of the stakes of this evening. It wasn't just about a meal; it was about proving myself to Gladys, convincing her of my sincerity and my vision for our future as Guardians of Belkeep. The importance of this night weighed heavily on me, a reminder that failure wasn't an option.

Slipping into the apron I found in the pantry, a tangible symbol of my commitment to the task at hand, I felt a mix of nerves and excitement. The apron, a simple piece of fabric, somehow felt like armour, bolstering my resolve. I was determined to impress Gladys, to show her a side of me she hadn't seen before. My choice of dish, creamy garlic mashed potatoes, was more than just a recipe; it was a memory, a comfort, a piece of culinary warmth that Freya had shared with me on numerous occasions. It represented home, and tonight, I hoped it would bridge the gap between my intentions and Gladys's expectations.

As I began to prepare, I gathered the ingredients with a reverence that surprised even me. Potatoes, butter, garlic, cream, and the secret spices that Freya had once whispered to me with a conspiratorial smile. Each component was more than just a part of a recipe; they were the building blocks of a gesture, an attempt to weave magic into the mundane.

With a confidence that felt both foreign and exhilarating, I started peeling the potatoes. Each stroke of the peeler was deliberate, a rhythmic motion that seemed to sync with the beat of my heart. There was something meditative about the process, a focus required that momentarily pushed aside my anxieties about the evening. I found myself flicking the peels into the sink with a playful flourish, a small act of defiance against the insecurities of the night. It was a moment of lightness, a reminder that, despite the pressure, there was joy to be found in the creation, in the act of making something with my own hands.

As the pile of peeled potatoes grew, so did my anticipation. Each step of the recipe was a step closer to the moment Gladys would taste the fruits of my labour, a moment that held more significance than I cared to admit.

Moving on to the task of chopping garlic, a mischievous spark lit up my eyes. My appreciation for garlic was not just a culinary preference but a tribute to Freya's enduring belief in its almost mystical properties in cooking. "The more garlic, the better," I whispered to myself, echoing Freya's culinary mantra. I was aware that my generous hand with the garlic might not be to everyone's taste, but I was prepared to gamble on its charm, betting on its power to transform and elevate the humble mashed potatoes into something memorable.

With both the potatoes and garlic prepped and ready, I set the potatoes to boil until they yielded easily under the gentle press of a fork. As I poured the water out, the kitchen was enveloped in a cloud of steam, rich with the scent of garlic. "Smells amazing already," I couldn't help but remark aloud, a nod of approval to no one but myself as I anticipated the flavours that were starting to meld together.

The next step was where my kitchen theatrics took a comical turn. Eager to demonstrate a bit of prowess, even in solitude, I applied a robust force to the potato masher. My enthusiasm, however, betrayed me as it sent a spray of mashed potato vaulting onto the kitchen counter. The absurdity of the situation struck me, and laughter bubbled up uncontrollably. I imagined Gladys's amusement if she were here to see the spectacle, her laughter mingling with mine. Swiftly, I cleaned up the errant spuds, the incident adding a layer of humour and humanity to the evening's preparations.

The addition of the secret ingredients came next: a generous dollop of butter and a splash of cream were introduced into the mix. As I stirred, the potatoes transformed, becoming luxuriously creamy and rich in flavour. "This is where the magic happens," I muttered to myself, a grin playing on my lips, fully embracing the alchemy of cooking. The aroma that now filled the kitchen was nothing short of divine, a testament to the transformative power of simple, quality ingredients.

With the dish nearing completion, I turned my attention to presentation. Plating the mashed potatoes, I employed a touch of flair, sculpting a small, inviting mound on each plate. A sprinkle of chives added a burst of colour and a hint of freshness, the green vivid against the creamy white. "Time to impress," I murmured, a mix of anticipation and a flicker of nerves stirring within me.

While the mashed potatoes were destined to be the star of the evening, I knew a balanced meal required more than just a standout side. With the potatoes now ready and waiting to impress, I turned my attention to the chicken and vegetables, aiming to complement the creamy garlic richness without overshadowing it.

For the chicken, I chose to keep it simple yet flavourful, opting for a herb-crusted bake that would offer a crisp contrast to the smooth mash. I mixed together a blend of dried thyme, rosemary, and a hint of paprika for a bit of warmth, rubbing the mixture onto the chicken breasts along with a light drizzle of olive oil. As I placed the chicken in the oven, I felt a sense of calm. The sizzle as it began to cook was reassuring, a sound that promised a delicious outcome. Cooking, I realised, was not just about the end product but the process, the aromas, and the sounds that filled the kitchen with life.

Next, I focused on the vegetables. I wanted something colourful, something that would brighten the plate and add a crisp, fresh counterpoint to the meal. I settled on a medley of roasted carrots, green beans, and bell peppers. Each vegetable was chosen for its colour and texture, aiming to create a vibrant tableau on the plate. The carrots, sliced into thin batons, would offer a sweet, earthy note; the green beans, a snappy freshness; and the bell peppers, a slight char that would echo the warmth of the paprika on the chicken. Tossed in a light coating of olive oil, salt, and pepper, the vegetables were spread out on a baking sheet and placed in the oven alongside the chicken, where they would roast to perfection.

As the kitchen filled with the roasting aromas of the chicken and vegetables, I took a moment to step back and appreciate the symphony of scents and sounds. It was a culinary orchestra, each element playing its part, with the garlic mashed potatoes waiting in the wings for their moment to shine. I felt a swell of pride at the thought of presenting this meal to Gladys. It was more than just food; it was a gesture of reconciliation, of care, and of shared future ambitions.

The chicken emerged from the oven golden and fragrant, its herb crust a testament to the simplicity of quality ingredients well used. The vegetables, now tender and lightly caramelised at the edges, offered a burst of colour and texture that promised to delight the senses. As I plated the meal, arranging the chicken and vegetables around the creamy mound of garlic mashed potatoes, I felt a sense of completeness. This was a meal designed to impress, to comfort, and to express without words the depth of my feelings and the sincerity of my apologies.

"Time to impress," I repeated, this time with a renewed confidence. The table was set, the candles lit, and the wine ready to be poured. As I awaited Gladys's return, the kitchen stood as a testament to the effort and love poured into the evening's preparation. The stage was set for a night of healing, laughter, and, hopefully, a step forward together.

❖

Seated at the polished dining table opposite Gladys, the soft glow of the room's warm lighting enveloped us in a comforting ambiance. I paused, allowing myself a moment to appreciate the meticulous effort that had gone into preparing our dinner. The dishes laid out before us weren't just food; they were a testament to my hope for reconciliation, a carefully orchestrated attempt to bridge the gap that had formed between us.

Gladys's playful smile, a brief yet radiant expression, flickered across her face, momentarily lighting up the room. The amusement in her eyes as she surveyed the spread before her acted as a balm to my nerves, infusing me with a quiet optimism about the evening ahead. Her gaze, alight with a flicker of amusement, seemed to pierce through the layers of tension, offering a glimpse of the connection we once shared.

"If I didn't know any better, this could almost have passed as your own home-cooked meal," she teased, her voice carrying a lightness that was playful yet poignant, sparking a mixture of pride and wistfulness within me.

"Perhaps next time it will be Freya that cooks for you," I quipped back, eager to maintain the levity of our exchange. My words floated between us, a blend of jest and a veiled wish for a future where understanding bridged our differences.

"Who's Freya?" she asked, her curiosity breaking through as smoothly as the gravy she poured over her plate, the question punctuated by the comforting sounds of our dinner setting.

The question caught me slightly off guard, a momentary hitch in the seamless flow of our conversation. The soft clink of cutlery against porcelain filled the brief silence as I found myself momentarily preoccupied with the task of rearranging my food, a nervous diversion from the weight of her inquiry. "Freya is my daughter," I admitted, lifting my gaze to meet hers, a mix of vulnerability and earnestness in my admission.

Her response was a soft "Oh," a simple utterance that seemed to echo louder in the silence that followed. I watched as her eyes briefly shifted away, the change in her demeanour subtle yet unmistakable. It was a reaction that hinted at a cascade of unspoken thoughts, perhaps surprise or a hint of disappointment veiled beneath her initial curiosity.

In that moment, the dynamic of our dinner shifted palpably. The revelation about Freya wasn't just an addition to our conversation; it was a window into the complexities of my life, a piece of myself that I had not shared before. The silence that stretched between us was filled with a tension that spoke volumes, a reminder of the delicate balance between personal revelations and the shared understanding that I was aiming for.

Taking a deep breath, I steeled myself for the forthcoming conversation, my thoughts swirling like the delicate dance of the candle flames that lit our table. The mention of Freya had introduced a complexity to the evening that I hadn't fully anticipated, yet I recognised the necessity of navigating this new terrain with openness and honesty.

"Is she in Clivilius?" Gladys's inquiry sliced through the thickening tension. Her question, simple yet laden with implications, prompted a moment of introspection on the duality of my existence — the balance between the roles I juggled and the personal commitments that defined me.

"Yes," I found myself responding, the word emerging more as a confession than a mere fact. It was laden with the weight of countless memories, challenges, and the deep-seated joys of fatherhood. My admission hung in the air between us, a bridge made of words, inviting her into a segment of my life that had remained uncharted territory between us until now.

In the ensuing silence, we turned to our plates, a temporary retreat into the act of eating, perhaps in search of a reprieve from the intensity of our dialogue. The meal before us, once a mere backdrop to our conversation, became a focal point, offering a semblance of normalcy amid the unfolding layers of personal revelation.

Gladys mirrored my actions, her engagement in the meal seeming to reflect her processing of the information I had shared. The silence was contemplative rather than awkward, a mutual acknowledgment of the weight of the discussion and the need for a momentary pause.

After a few moments, filled with the clinking of cutlery and the soft sounds of our meal, I found the courage to delve back into the conversation. The initial plunge into the topic of Freya had been made; now it was time to navigate the waters I had stirred. It was clear that the evening had transitioned from a simple dinner to a significant moment of connection and vulnerability. The next words I chose would not only shape the course of our conversation but potentially the future of our relationship.

"Gladys?" I ventured, my gaze anchored to the plate before me as if it held the script to the confessions I was about to make. The clink of my fork against the porcelain sounded louder in the anticipation of baring parts of my life I had kept shielded.

"Mm?" Her response came, muffled by a mouthful of food, yet it was the casualness of it, the everyday tone, that somehow lent me the courage to proceed. The gravity of what I was about to share juxtaposed sharply with the simplicity of our dinner setting.

"I'd like to tell you more about me. Is that okay?" The vulnerability in my question was palpable, a rare admission of my desire to truly connect.

She paused, a moment of silence stretching as she finished her bite, a courtesy that allowed her to give me her full attention. Her nod was silent but significant, her eyes locking onto mine with an openness that was both an invitation and a brace for what was to come. As she took a delicate sip of her wine, perhaps in preparation for the weight of my words, I began to unravel the threads of my past, laying bare the tapestry of experiences that had shaped me.

I spoke of my childhood on a farm in Gawler, painting a picture of an existence that was as idyllic as it was mundane, a life far removed from the complexities I would later come to know. The narrative took a turn as I delved into the pivotal year of 1987, the year my life irrevocably changed with my initiation as a Guardian. The story unfolded further with the introduction of Grace, a chapter of my life marked by the blossoming of love, only to be followed by the sharp sting of loss as I recounted Grace's passing after giving birth to our twins, Freya and Fryar.

As I shared these fragments of my life, Gladys's expression transformed, her eyes becoming mirrors of the sorrow my story evoked. The empathy that flowed from her was a balm, her sadness a testament to the depth of her compassion. Yet, as we navigated this emotional landscape together, I couldn't help but notice a subtle shift, an undercurrent of relief that seemed to percolate beneath her empathetic façade. It was as if the revelations of my past, particularly the intricacies of my relationships and losses, had laid to rest any lingering uncertainties or unspoken questions about the nature of our connection.

As I delved into the narrative of Belkeep, I found myself painting a picture with my words, careful to tread the line between romanticising its rugged beauty and acknowledging the harsh realities it faced. Belkeep, for all its scenic vistas and untamed wilderness, was a statement of resilience in the face of adversity, a characteristic I felt deeply connected to. My role as a Guardian of such a place was not just a duty; it was a part of my identity, woven into the fabric of my being. I hoped to convey this dual nature without casting a shadow over the evening's lighter moments.

"I was the first in my Guardian group," I stated, pausing to allow the significance of that admission to settle in the air between us. It was a role that came with its burdens, a mantle I had accepted with a mix of pride and trepidation.

"Guardian group? What's that?" Gladys's question, punctuated by her pause in dining, mirrored her burgeoning interest. Her curiosity was a beacon, guiding me to share more, to invite her into the inner sanctum of my world.

"A complete Guardian group consists of five Guardians," I explained, allowing the intricacies of our unique calling to unfold in the delicate tapestry of my words.

"And your Guardian group is complete now?" she pressed, her inquiry cutting to the heart of a matter that was both personal and painful. Her eyes, alight with the intrigue of a story unfolding, sought to understand more.

"No," I found myself admitting, the word heavy with unspoken narratives. "There were Sylvie and Randal..." My voice tapered off, a sombre note to the melody of our conversation as the memories of Sylvie and Randal surfaced, their absence a void that still echoed after all this time.

Gladys leaned in, her gesture an unspoken encouragement for me to continue. It was a moment of connection, a bridge built on the mutual exchange of vulnerability and interest. Taking a measured breath, I bridged the gap between past and present, "Both Sylvie and Randal had long departed from our world." The simplicity of the statement belied the complexity of emotions it stirred within me, a mixture of sorrow, loss, and the unyielding grip of the past.

"What happened to them?" Gladys's question, filled with genuine concern, opened a door I had long kept closed. Her expression, etched with empathy, plunged me toward a descent into a chapter of my life marked by darkness and loss.

"The details aren't really important," I began, my voice laced with a hesitancy born from a protective instinct. I wanted to shield Gladys from the darker chapters of my past, fearing that the weight of these tragedies might overshadow the fragile connection we were nurturing. "The first Guardian in the group to activate their Portal Key opens a Portal in a new, random location in Clivilius. When I activated mine for the first time, I found myself in a dark, cold, empty place." Sharing this, I felt a resurgence of the isolation that had greeted me in those initial moments.

"Why?" Her question was simple, yet it unpacked layers of curiosity and concern, her engagement with my story undiminished by her continued enjoyment of the meal before us.

"Nobody seems to know the answer to that yet," I admitted, the mystery of our responsibilities as Guardians weaving an intricate tapestry that even I was still unravelling. "The next four Portals are close to this main one, each one appearing at random time intervals after the main Portal." In sharing this, I hoped to illuminate the unpredictable and often solitary nature of our path, a path that, despite its burdens, was also filled with a profound sense of purpose.

"How do you know that? Aren't there still only three Guardians in your group?" Her observation was astute, her quick mind piecing together the incomplete puzzle of my Guardian ensemble with the absence of two pivotal figures.

"Sylvie was using my Portal in Clivilius for about six weeks, and Randal was almost one year. Sharing a Portal in Clivilius poses plenty of challenges," I explained, a sombre note creeping into my voice.

Gladys, her brows knitting together in concentration, was clearly endeavouring to untangle the web of complexities that defined the life of a Guardian. "Like what?" she asked, her curiosity a beacon in the dimly lit room, seeking illumination on a subject that was as enigmatic as it was vital.

"For starters, only one Guardian can have the Portal active at a time," I explained, the words flowing from me with a mix of resignation and pride. "I'm surprised Luke hasn't discovered this already."

Her brow furrowed further in thought, confessing that she and Luke seldom delved into the nuances of Guardian life.

"When the fifth Guardian Portal Key has been activated, each Guardian receives another five devices that enable them to each repeat the cycle," I continued, each word carefully chosen to convey the magnitude and complexity of our existence. The cycles, the keys, and the portals were not just elements of our duty; they were the threads that wove the very tapestry of Clivilius and its guardianship.

"Sounds complicated," she remarked, her eyes widening as the layers of my reality unfolded before her.

"It is," I admitted, the complexities of our role settling heavily between us. "That's assuming all the Guardians are still alive when the fifth device is activated," I added, the harsh reality of our existence underscored by the acknowledgment that not all Guardians might survive to see the cycle renew.

"And if they're not all alive?" Her question was a whisper in the quiet of the room.

"The cycle ends," I confessed, the words heavy with unspoken implications. The finality of such an outcome was a shadow that loomed large over the life of every Guardian, a reminder of the precarious balance upon which our world was built.

"That still doesn't make any sense. Why would another five Portal Keys be given if they're only going to start a new location?" Gladys's question pierced the veil of complexities, her focus sharpening on the paradoxes that lay at the heart of guardianship.

Shrugging, I found myself at a loss, the mysteries of our existence often eluding even those who lived it. "I honestly don't know, Gladys."

As the conversation unfolded, I could see the wheels turning in Gladys's mind, her intellect grappling with the information I had laid bare. More questions hung in the air, each one a testament to the depth of her engagement and the breadth of her curiosity. However, sensing the weight of the revelations of the night, I gently steered our discussion towards lighter shores, aiming to offer her a reprieve from the burdens of Guardian life. In the warmth of our shared meal and the comfort of our conversation, I sought to remind us both of the beauty and simplicity that life could offer, even in the midst of its most profound mysteries.

❖

The soft glow of the television played in the background as Gladys and I sat on the couch, comfortably entwined. Her head rested against my chest, and I could feel the rhythm of her breathing against my skin. It was a serene moment, one that made my heart swell with affection for her.

As I relished the warmth of her body pressed against mine, I couldn't help but notice the gentle brush of her fingertips on my chest. It sent a jolt of unexpected desire through me, igniting a pulse of arousal. Her hand slipped under my shirt, and I could feel her fingers exploring the dark hairs on my abdomen.

"Sorry," she muttered, moving to pull her hand away.

I caught her hand, holding it gently but firmly against my chest. "It's okay. You don't need to stop," I reassured her, my voice soft and tender. I turned my head slightly, meeting her eyes, and there was a spark of desire in the air.

Her heartbeat quickened, and I could see a hint of nervousness in her eyes. I wrapped my arm around her, drawing her closer to me until our bodies were pressed tighter together. The sensation of her breasts against me sent a thrill through my body, and I could feel her responding to the intimacy between us.

Leaning in, I captured her lips with mine. The first kiss was slow and gentle, a delicate exploration of each other's lips. I could sense her hesitation, and I allowed her to follow my lead. My tongue traced her lips, and as she parted them, I deepened the kiss, savouring the taste of her.

Her thigh pressed against my lap, and I could feel her warmth. I shifted slightly, my own desire growing, but I wanted to take things slow, to savour every moment with her. Breaking the kiss, I looked into her eyes, silently asking if she was okay.

With a playful smile, she stood up, taking my hands in hers, inviting me to follow her. My heart raced with excitement as I got up from the couch, eager to see where she was leading me.

She led me to the bedroom, and I couldn't help but notice the electricity in the air. The door closed behind us, and I knew that we were both feeling the intensity of the moment.

I watched as she turned on the bedside lamp, her movements confident and alluring.

As I reached for her waist, she bent over, and I couldn't resist the opportunity to hold her close. My hands gripped her hips, pulling her closer to me. I could feel her body responding to my touch, her desire mirroring my own.

She straightened up, turning to face me, and I was met with the sight of a beautiful, bare-chested woman standing inches away from me. The desire in her eyes was evident, and it fuelled my own passion.

With steady hands, I guided her onto the bed, our bodies now fully entwined. A moan of pleasure escaped her lips, and it only heightened the intensity between us. In that moment, there were no words needed. We communicated our desires and feelings through our actions and gaze.

As the night unfolded, we surrendered to each other completely, finding a connection that was both passionate and intimate. It was a moment of pure bliss, and as we lay entwined in each other's arms, I felt a sense of contentment and love that persuaded me that Gladys was finally ready to become a Guardian.

❖

As Gladys nestled her head against my chest, the ambient sounds of the night enveloped us in a soft embrace, the distant murmur of the world beyond our secluded haven whispering secrets to the stars. In this moment, the relentless march of time and the burdens it carried seemed to pause, allowing us a reprieve from the complexities that had woven themselves into the fabric of our lives. Her presence, so close and so real, was a comforting balm to the frayed edges of my spirit, bringing with it a sense of solace that felt both profound and healing.

Instinctively, my arm found its way around her, drawing her closer into the warmth of my embrace. The night, with all its uncertainties and revelations, had unfolded in a way that exceeded my most hopeful expectations. Witnessing the contentment etched across Gladys's face, her smile a silent testament to the peace she felt, stirred something deep within me, a warmth that radiated from my very core.

"I know it really wasn't your fault," she whispered into the quiet of the night, her words floating between us like a gentle melody, soothing the remnants of tumultuous thoughts and fears. Her voice, soft yet laden with meaning, carried the weight of unspoken understandings.

"What wasn't?" I found myself whispering back, my fingers tracing gentle circles on her back in a silent language of comfort and reassurance. Each movement was a promise, a vow of presence and support that transcended the need for words.

"Chloe," she replied, her voice a quiet echo of sadness that seemed to fill the space around us. In that single word, I sensed the depth of Gladys's loss, the shadow of Chloe's absence that lingered like a silent spectre over her heart.

In the hush that followed, we lay together, the rhythm of our breathing a synchronised dance in the quiet night. Gladys's head moved gently with each breath I took, a physical connection that mirrored the emotional intimacy that had blossomed between us. It was a simple act, lying there with her, yet it invoked a sense of peace and tranquility that I had long forgotten was possible. In the embrace of the night, with Gladys by my side, I found a rare and precious calm, a momentary oasis in the tumultuous journey of life.

"Gladys," I ventured, breaking the tranquil silence that had enveloped us, feeling a shift in the air as I prepared to bridge our worlds even further. Lifting my head, I sought out her gaze, finding in her eyes a blend of curiosity and warmth that encouraged me to continue.

"Yes, Cody?" she responded, her voice a gentle prompt in the quiet of the night, her eyes shimmering with an affectionate light that seemed to chase away any lingering shadows.

"There's someone I want you to meet tomorrow," I found myself saying, the words tinged with an excitement I hadn't expected to feel. The thought of introducing her to Jeremiah, my Guardian Atum, ignited a flurry of anticipation within me, the significance of this meeting stirring a sense of importance in the air between us.

"Oh," she echoed, a simple utterance that belied the depth of her intrigue. Sitting up on one elbow, her posture spoke of keen interest, her gaze fixed on me in eager anticipation. "Who is it?"

I paused, the weight of the moment pressing down on me as I sought the right words to encapsulate Jeremiah's role in my life. "My Guardian Atum; the man who made me a Guardian," I finally shared, my voice imbued with reverence for the man who had so profoundly shaped my path. I hoped to convey not just the title, but the depth of the bond and the pivotal role Jeremiah had played in my journey.

Her reaction was immediate and heartening; her eyes lit up with genuine interest, a spark of excitement at the prospect of delving deeper into the world that had so defined my existence. Reaching out, she squeezed my hand, a gesture of support and connection that wrapped around me like a warm embrace. "I'd be honoured to meet him," she affirmed, her words buoying my spirits and reinforcing the bridge of understanding that had grown between us.

A smile broke through, a reflection of my deep appreciation for her openness and willingness to step into the intricate tapestry of my life. "Jeremiah is a wise and experienced Guardian. He's been my mentor since I first became a Guardian back in nineteen-eighty-seven. He's seen and experienced so much, and I owe a lot to his guidance," I explained.

The admiration I felt for Jeremiah seemed to resonate with Gladys, her expression one of anticipation and respect for the meeting to come. Sharing this part of my life with her, introducing her to someone as integral to my identity as Jeremiah, felt like a step into a future where our lives were more deeply intertwined.

"I'm looking forward to meeting him," she said, her sincerity striking a chord within me.

Pulling her closer, I enveloped her in an embrace. "I'm glad," I murmured, the words barely a whisper against the backdrop of the night, yet heavy with meaning. As the night wrapped us in its serene embrace, I felt a profound sense of peace and completeness, a feeling that, with Gladys by my side, the path ahead was one we were ready to navigate together, no matter the challenges or discoveries it might bring.

4338.209

(28 July 2018)

GLADYS, TAKE IT

1338.209.1

Parting with Gladys earlier that morning had set a storm of emotions whirling through me, a maelstrom of anticipation and excitement that was both exhilarating and daunting. The notion that she was on the brink of accepting the Portal Key, of stepping into the realm of Guardianship, lent a weight to my steps as I made my way to the Portal Cave. This wasn't just a transition; it was a passage, a sacred moment in the life of a Guardian, and although every fibre of my being ached to be the one to hand her the key, I knew in my heart that this was a moment she needed to experience through the official channels, through her Guardian Atum. It was a rite of passage, a ceremony that I wanted her to hold close and remember as a pivotal point in her life.

The path to the Portal Cave was familiar, yet today it felt different, as if charged with the significance of what was to come. My heart raced, a steady drumbeat against my ribcage, mirroring the tumult of my thoughts and the nervous energy that vibrated through my veins. The secret I had shared with Krid had now set the stage for this moment, and alongside Freya, they stood ready to play their parts in welcoming Gladys into our fold, into the intricate tapestry of Guardianship of Belkeep.

"Here," I found myself saying, a tremble in my voice as I handed Freya my heavy coat. My hands shook slightly, betraying the whirlwind of emotions that I struggled to contain. It was a small action, yet it felt monumental, laden with the symbolism of shedding layers, of moving towards something new and unknown.

Freya's gaze was perceptive, cutting through the veneer of my attempted composure. "Don't be so nervous. Everything is going to be fine," she said, her voice a soothing balm to my frayed nerves. Her smile, warm and comforting, was a beacon of reassurance, a reminder of the strength and support that surrounded me.

Krid chimed in with her own encouragement. Her smile was infectious, a wide beam that seemed to dispel the shadows of doubt. "Freya and I will be here when Gladys arrives," she promised, her words a solid ground amidst the shifting sands of my apprehension.

Taking that deep breath felt like drawing in the calm before the storm, an attempt to centre myself amidst the chaos of my thoughts, which mirrored the ferocity of the blizzard outside. It was a moment of introspection, a brief pause in the eye of an emotional hurricane that had swept me up in anticipation and nerves. Freya and Krid's presence, their unwavering support and encouragement, felt like a lifeline, grounding me in the reality of what I was about to do. With a final, affirming glance in their direction, I found the resolve I needed to step forward, crossing the threshold into the Portal's humming embrace.

The transition was immediate and all-encompassing. The Portal's energy enveloped me, a symphony of colours swirling around me in a vibrant dance. It was like stepping into a living kaleidoscope, where light and energy pulsed and flowed with a life of their own. I allowed myself a moment to close my eyes, not to shut out the experience but to fully immerse myself in it, to feel the energy of the Portal coursing through me, connecting me to Clivilius in a way that words could never fully capture.

This connection, this bridge between worlds, was a sensation I had become familiar with over the years, yet its magic never dulled. Each journey through the Portal was a reminder of the vastness of the universe, of the intricate web of energy that connected all things. It was a humbling experience, one that never failed to evoke a deep sense of awe and wonder within me.

❖

Stumbling through the door of Gladys's fridge, I found myself caught off guard by the sight of an unknown woman standing in the kitchen. This unexpected encounter threw me into a moment of surreal realisation, a stark reminder of the ordinary world's boundaries and the extraordinary elements of my own. The fridge, a mundane appliance, had momentarily become a portal, a bridge between the common and the incredible.

"Oh, hey," I managed, my voice a mixture of surprise and an attempt at normalcy as I steadied myself. The room felt charged with an awkward energy, the air thick with unspoken questions and confusion. Despite the absurdity of the situation, I strived to regain my balance, both physically and metaphorically, eager to smooth over the bizarre impression I must have made.

"I'm Cody," I introduced myself, extending my hand in a gesture of friendliness. My mind raced to piece together a coherent explanation for my unconventional entrance, but the immediacy of the moment demanded a simpler approach. The woman, taken aback, shook my hand with a grip that spoke of both bewilderment and a cautious curiosity.

"Abbey," she responded, her eyes flicking between me and Gladys, the wheels of comprehension turning as she tried to piece together the peculiar tableau before her. Her expression, a mix of surprise and intrigue, mirrored the countless reactions I had encountered in my life as a Guardian, yet each encounter never failed to stir a mixture of amusement and a twinge of discomfort within me.

Feeling a surge of responsibility to clarify the situation, I turned towards Gladys, hoping to offer Abbey some semblance of understanding. However, before words could form, the distinct knock on the front door sliced through the tension, redirecting our collective attention.

"That'll be Jeremiah," I announced, the name alone enough to convey the importance of the moment to Gladys, if not to Abbey. With a quick, apologetic glance towards Abbey, whose presence and confusion I could not properly address, I made my way to the door. The guilt of leaving her with more questions than answers gnawed at me, a silent promise forming in my mind to return to this conversation, to offer her the understanding she deserved.

Opening the door to Jeremiah, my voice carried a mix of urgency and restraint, a reflection of the tumultuous sea of concerns churning within me. "Jeremiah," I called out softly yet with a clear edge of urgency, drawing his attention as he stepped over the threshold into the haven that had suddenly become a stage for an unforeseen dilemma.

"What?" His response was sharp, a furrow of concern etching his brow as he closed the door behind him.

"We may have a problem," I began, the words tumbling out in a rush to articulate the gravity of the situation without alarming anyone beyond the walls of this conversation.

Jeremiah's sigh was a soft echo in the tense air, his shoulders tensing as if bracing against the weight of yet another challenge. The world of Guardianship was never devoid of its trials, but the intrusion of the unexpected was always a harbinger of complexity.

"Gladys has a visitor," I continued, watching closely for his reaction, hoping to convey the significance without sparking undue alarm.

His reaction, however, was underwhelming, marked by a nonchalance that belied the potential unravelling of the situation. "I'll come back later then," he offered with a dismissive shrug, misunderstanding the core of my concern.

"No!" My response was more forceful than I intended, a reflex born out of the need to underscore the urgency, the door slamming shut under the weight of my push. "She saw me come through the Portal," I added in a quieter tone, the admission heavy with the realisation of the risk now posed to Abbey.

Jeremiah's reaction was immediate, his features tightening as the full implications of my words settled in. "Gladys?" he queried, seeking clarification, his stance shifting as if preparing to address a threat.

"No. Abbey," I clarified, my stomach knotting as I acknowledged the inadvertent witness to our hidden world. The moment of my emergence through the fridge portal, a spectacle I had never intended for outsider eyes, now loomed large with consequences.

As Jeremiah moved towards the source of the voices from the kitchen, a silent signal for me to follow, my mind raced with scenarios, each more worrying than the last. "Do you think we should take her to Clivilius?" The question slipped out, a reflection of my spiralling concern for Abbey's safety amidst revelations she was never meant to encounter.

"She's probably better off with me," Jeremiah replied, his tone carrying a gravity that matched the seriousness of our predicament. His stride into the living room was purposeful, each step a testament to the weight of our guardianship duties.

"I could find Luke, or Beatrix?" I suggested, grappling for solutions, my desperation to protect Abbey from the unintended exposure to our world palpable in the tension that vibrated through my voice.

"I don't think we should-" Jeremiah's response was cut short, his thought interrupted by the approach of Gladys and Abbey, each holding fresh wine glasses, an odd contrast to the storm of worries besieging my thoughts.

Gladys's expression, etched with concern, oscillated rapidly between Jeremiah, Abbey, and myself, mirroring the tumultuous storm brewing in the room. The atmosphere was thick, charged with a palpable tension that seemed almost too dense to breathe through.

"I'm sorry," Jeremiah cut through the silence, his voice a solemn echo of regret. His eyes, dark and unwavering, were fixed on Abbey. "But you're a witness now. It's too dangerous for you to stay here." His words fell like stones into the quiet, stirring ripples of dread that lapped at the edges of my consciousness.

Gladys reached for my arm in a futile attempt to bridge the chasm that was rapidly opening between us. Her touch was light, yet it carried the weight of her concern—a silent plea for restraint. I understood her fear, felt the vibration of her worry through the slight pressure of her fingers. Yet, beneath that, I also recognised the necessity of guarding the secrets of Clivilius with a zeal that bordered on fanaticism.

Jeremiah and I, united in our cause yet divided in our methods, each grasped Abbey's arms in a show of solidarity that felt more like a betrayal. "You don't understand!" she cried out, her voice a mix of anger and fear, struggling against the inevitability of our grasp.

"I can't," Abbey's voice cracked, a fragile sound that splintered the moment her wine glass met its end against the hard floor. The shattering of glass, a sharp and sudden intrusion, seemed to punctuate her desperation, her refusal to be ensnared in a reality she had not chosen.

"Is this really necessary, Cody?" Gladys's voice, now tinged with an edge of desperation, sought to find a crack in the armour of our resolve. "I've seen the Portal and I'm still here." Her words, meant to soothe, instead felt like a challenge, a reminder of the delicate balance we navigated between secrecy and trust.

Jeremiah's gaze locked onto Gladys with an intensity that felt almost tangible. "For now," he uttered, his voice a harbinger of uncertain fates, sending a shiver down my spine

The gravity of the situation hung heavy in the air, the weight of impending choices palpable. Yet, before I could fully process it all, Abbey's frustration reached a breaking point, and she took matters into her own hands.

With a swift stomp on Jeremiah's foot, she freed herself from his grasp, delivering a sharp elbow to my gut that forced me to release her other arm.

Doubled over, the taste of bile rising in my throat, I was a portrait of vulnerability in the face of Abbey's fierce determination to escape. The room seemed to spin, the edges blurring as I struggled to catch my breath. In that moment, as the situation spun out of control, a part of me lamented our approach, wished for a path less fraught with conflict.

The moment unfolded with a kind of surreal clarity, as if time itself had slowed to allow me to absorb the passing of each second. Gladys's rush towards me was a blur of motion, her voice a beacon of concern. "Cody!" she cried, her distress painting the air, wine sloshing from her glass as if to mark the path of her urgency.

Jeremiah, ever the steadfast Guardian, moved with a purpose that spoke of years honed in the service of Clivilius. Yet, Abbey's authoritative stance, an immovable force of conviction, arrested his advance. I stood there, torn—a guardian of secrets and a protector of hearts, my own caught in the crossfire of duty and desire. The weight of my role pressed heavily upon me, a mantle that both elevated and ensnared.

"Stand down!" Abbey's command sliced through the tension, her voice a surprising crescendo of authority. The command, delivered with hands raised defiantly, brokered no room for disobedience. Jeremiah and I, bound by our oaths yet momentarily swayed by the force of her conviction, found ourselves acquiescing, a testament to the unexpected power she wielded.

Gladys's plea, eyes alight with a mixture of fear and hope, sought to bridge the chasm that yawned between understanding and secrecy. "Please!" she implored, her gaze piercing into mine, a silent entreaty for compromise. "If we explain the situation, I'm sure Abbey will understand the importance of secrecy." Her words echoed the sentiment that had begun to gnaw at the edges of my resolve, the belief that perhaps, in understanding, there lay a path to resolution.

Jeremiah's response, though, was a steel-clad reminder of the stakes at play. "I'm sorry, Gladys. It's a risk we can't afford to take right now." he intoned, a bastion of his sworn duty, his voice devoid of hesitation. The finality in his tone marked the boundaries of our predicament, a line drawn firmly in the sand.

Gladys's frustration, a palpable wave of emotion, crashed against the resolve that Jeremiah and I had built. Her exasperation, so vividly expressed, was a mirror to the turmoil that roiled within me. "Oh, come on!" she exclaimed, the essence of her dismay hanging between us, a tangible testament to the clash of ideals. "Surely–"

"It's okay, Gladys," Abbey said, her gaze a balm to the frayed edges of our confrontation. As she lowered her hands, a gesture of peace, the unfolding of her left fist revealed a twist that none of us had anticipated.

The device nestled in her palm, an emblem of our cause, spoke volumes in the silence that ensued. "I'm a Guardian too," Abbey declared, her words a revelation that reverberated through the very foundations of our understanding.

In that moment, as Jeremiah and I exchanged glances, a myriad of emotions played across our faces—surprise, disbelief, realisation. Abbey's disclosure, a bombshell that shattered the barriers of assumption, forced us to reconsider not just the situation at hand, but the very fabric of our alliance.

Gladys's reaction was immediate, her voice laced with incredulity, as if the words struggled to form amidst the whirlwind of revelations. "But how? When?" she stuttered, her questions hanging in the air like fragments of a puzzle we were all trying to piece together. The atmosphere was charged with a palpable sense of curiosity and disbelief.

Abbey's response was a gentle touch, a soft anchor in the tempest of our emotions. Her fingers brushed against Gladys's elbow, a simple gesture that seemed to carry the weight of reassurance and solidarity. "It's been a few years," she began, her voice a calm amidst the storm. "I'm the last member of my Guardian Group."

"What's your settlement?" Jeremiah seized upon the moment to gather intelligence.

"Enders Climb. It's near the Capital, Port Stower. Well, it was the capital," Abbey disclosed, her words sketching the outlines of a world both familiar and fraught with the shadows of change.

"Yeah, we know about the unfortunate fall of Port Stower," Jeremiah acknowledged.

As I opened my mouth to weave in more threads of understanding, to add my voice to the tapestry of our unfolding narrative, Gladys's hand rose in a silent command for silence. "And close that bloody Portal!" she demanded, her gaze piercing Jeremiah with a mixture of fear and authority. Her concern for Snowflake, who had been drawn to the mesmerising dance of colours within the Portal, underscored the personal stakes at play. "I can't afford to lose a second baby!" Her words cut through the air, a sharp reminder of the tangible dangers that our secrets harboured.

With a swiftness born of necessity, Gladys exited, leaving a brief void in her wake. The clatter of cat biscuits in a bowl from the kitchen filled the silence, a mundane sound that seemed almost alien amidst the complexity of our situation. When she returned, her movements were a study in domesticity, offering wine with a persistence that brooked no refusal.

"No, thank you," Jeremiah declined, waving his hands in front of him.

"Yes, thank you," Gladys insisted, forcing Jeremiah to accept the precious vessel.

I chuckled as I admired Gladys's determination to enforce the wine, even though it felt like we were navigating through a fog of uncertainty. Abbey, Jeremiah, and I re-engaged in heated conversation, while Gladys slumped against a chair and sipped her wine.

Jeremiah's words sliced through the charged air, a definitive line drawn in the sands of our tumultuous reality. "There is only so long you can remain a bystander, Gladys. Soon, you will need to make a choice on which role you want to play," he declared, his voice laden with a gravity that seemed to pull at the very fabric of the room. The firm squeeze on her shoulder was meant as reassurance, perhaps, or a silent plea for understanding, but it carried the weight of inevitable change. His statement, a harbinger of decisions that lay ahead, hovered between us, an unspoken ultimatum that demanded contemplation.

Gladys, ever the emblem of resilience wrapped in a veneer of casual indifference, met his proclamation with a quizzical arch of her brow. "Huh?" she responded, her voice a mix of confusion and defiance. It was a simple utterance, yet it spoke volumes of her internal turmoil, the clash of a present comfort against the tide of an uncertain future.

Jeremiah's insistence, unyielding and sharp, brooked no room for ambiguity. "Either you become a Guardian or a Clivilius citizen. Remaining on Earth is not an option for you, Gladys," he pressed on, his gaze unflinching, a mirror to his resolve. The intensity of his stare, unwavering and piercing, seemed to challenge her very essence, prompting a discomfort that writhed visibly beneath her skin. With a twist and a turn, she managed to escape his grip, a physical manifestation of her struggle to evade the impending choices that loomed over her existence.

His silent departure, marked by a stern glance cast in my direction, felt like a passing of the torch, a silent command for me to understand the ultimatum he had presented Gladys. The hallway, set ablaze with the mesmerising colours of his departure, seemed to echo the turmoil of my heart, painting my reality with the hues of uncertainty and the burden of choices that defined the paths ahead.

Abbey's voice, a soft yet firm echo of Jeremiah's resolve, pierced the lingering tension. "Sorry, Gladys, Jeremiah is right," she said, her sideways glance a silent acknowledgment of the shared burden of her options. "You need to make a choice. And soon." Her words, though spoken with a gentle firmness, carried an undercurrent of urgency, a reminder of the inexorable tide of decisions that awaited us all.

Gladys, a portrait of weariness and contemplation, rubbed her temple as if to soothe the ache of our intertwined fates. "Please go," she whispered, her voice a fragile thread in the fabric of our confrontation. The plea, devoid of her usual strength, was a testament to the overwhelming cascade of realities we had imposed upon her. Her inability to meet our gaze spoke of the internal chaos that our revelations had wrought, a storm of emotions and decisions that she was unprepared to navigate.

In that moment of hesitation, a silent goodbye lingered in the air, a pause filled with the unspoken words and the heavy burden of my next steps. Abbey's departure, a swift movement through her own portal, left a finality that hung heavily in the room.

Casting one last glance at Gladys, I grappled with a maelstrom of emotions. Guilt, for the upheaval I had brought to her doorstep; sorrow, for the innocence that had been irrevocably altered; and a deep, unyielding empathy for the choices that she, too, would have to make. With a heavy heart, I stepped back into the familiar yet now seemingly distant realm of Belkeep, leaving behind the echoes of a life that, for Gladys, would never be the same. The portal closed behind me, a door to one chapter ending as another, fraught with uncertainty and the weight of newfound responsibilities, beckoned.

❖

As I stepped into the Portal Cave, the transition was like moving from one world to another, the vibrant kaleidoscope of the previous destination fading into the dim, earthy hues of our cavernous hideaway. The warm colours that danced across the walls as I selected my new destination couldn't quite pierce the veil of melancholy that had begun to drape itself around me. The contrast between the lively colours and my sombre mood was stark, as if the cave itself was trying to lift my spirit that felt tethered to the ground.

"Cody!" Krid's voice, filled with unguarded enthusiasm, momentarily cut through the fog of my thoughts. Her eyes, wide with the anticipation of my return, searched mine for signs of Belkeep's newest Guardian. The absence of Gladys, however, hung in the air like a silent spectre, its presence palpable even in the dim light of the cavern.

"Where's Gladys?" Freya's inquiry, laced with a concern, felt like a gentle nudge towards a reality I was reluctant to face. "Gladys isn't coming," I confessed, the heaviness in my voice a mirror to the burden I felt, a mixture of disappointment and the sharp sting of reality biting at the edges of my hope.

Krid's young face, a reflection of innocence and budding strength, drooped visibly at the news. Her reaction, so raw and genuine, prompted me to grasp at the threads of hope that still lingered within me. "Not today, anyway," I found myself saying, the words more a balm for my own disappointment than anything else. The possibility of Gladys joining us, of standing beside me as we navigated the complexities of our existence, was a beacon of hope I wasn't ready to extinguish. Perhaps, in my heart, I was holding on to that future more tightly than I cared to admit.

Freya, ever the pillar of strength and understanding, seemed to sense the turmoil swirling within me. Her hand, warm and steady on my shoulder, was a tangible reminder of the support that surrounded me, even in moments of doubt. "It's okay, Cody," she assured me, her smile a small yet significant gesture of empathy. "She'll come around when she's ready." Her words, meant to console, did offer a measure of comfort, though the shadow of uncertainty lingered, a silent companion to my hopes.

I nodded, appreciating my daughter's support, but still feeling a twinge of disappointment. "I hope so," I replied, my voice revealing the uncertainty.

Krid's voice, chiming in with her own brand of wisdom, surprised me. "Gladys is strong-willed, but she's also curious. She'll come to us when she's ready to embrace her destiny." The certainty in her tone, the unshakeable belief in the path that lay ahead for all of us, was both baffling and heartening. *How could this young soul, so new to our world and yet so insightful, understand the complexities of a heart she had never encountered?*

"Thanks," I responded, managing a smile that, though strained, was genuine in its gratitude for their presence, their faith.

The silence that enveloped us was a tangible thing, thick with the myriad emotions that churned beneath the surface. It was a moment of shared understanding, of collective anticipation and uncertainty, where words seemed superfluous, unable to encapsulate the depth of our connection or the complexity of our situation. Then, Krid's voice, a beacon of resilience in the quiet, pierced the stillness, her suggestion to return to Belkeep a gentle nudge towards normalcy. "Come on," she urged, her hand reaching for mine in a gesture of solidarity, "Let's head back to Belkeep. Maybe some fresh air will do you good."

I found myself momentarily caught in the warmth of her intent, her concern a balm to the unease that had settled within me. Yet, even as her fingers closed around mine, a sense of duty, a reminder of the obligations that lay beyond the immediate comfort of companionship, urged me to gently pull away. "I appreciate the gesture, but I have somewhere else I need to be," I confessed, the words heavy with the weight of responsibilities unseen yet deeply felt.

Freya's response was immediate, her curiosity piqued, halting her movements as if my words had physically drawn her back. "Oh? What's so urgent?" she probed, her tone laced with a mix of intrigue and concern.

The pause that followed was mine, a moment of internal debate over how much to share, how much of my burdens to lay bare before the eyes of youth and hope. "Other Guardian business," I settled on, a response shrouded in the vagueness of necessity, a shield against the complexities that were unfolding.

Freya's lips pursed, a silent but eloquent expression of her frustration with my evasion. It was a familiar dance between us, this balancing act of protection and honesty, and her unimpressed demeanour was a testament to her growing impatience with the half-truths that often coloured our exchanges.

Thankfully, Krid's intervention was timely, her gentle tone a contrast to the tension that had begun to weave its way through our conversation. "Cody," she began, her voice a soothing presence, "It's going to be alright. Whatever happens, we'll face it together." Her assurance, so simply stated, was a powerful reminder of the strength found in unity.

Turning to face them, the gratitude I felt was profound, a deep-seated acknowledgment of their significance in my life. "Thank you," I expressed, my words imbued with the sincerity of my appreciation. "I don't know what I'd do without you both." It was a truth, raw and unadorned, a recognition of their roles not just as companions or family, but as pillars upon which I leaned more heavily than I often admitted.

Krid's smile, warm and affirming, was a light in the shadow of our uncertainties. "We're family, Cody. We'll always be here for you," she stated, her hand squeezing mine in a gesture of unwavering support.

With their reassurance bolstering my spirits, a renewed sense of purpose coursed through me. The path ahead, though fraught with challenges and shadowed by the unknown, seemed less daunting with the knowledge that Krid and Freya stood beside me. And somewhere, in the quiet hope that flickered like a distant star, I harboured the belief that Gladys, too, would find her way to us. Until that day, the relentless march of Guardian work awaited, a constant reminder of the duty that defined me, of the legacy I sought to protect and the future I aimed to secure.

ULTIMATUM

4338.209.2

As I emerged through the Portal into Glenelg, I found myself in the familiar surroundings of a secluded alcove. It wasn't the most elegant entrance; I had to pull myself out from the smooth flat rock, but this spot was perfect for my secure access point, shielded from prying eyes and conveniently close to the Glenelg jetty where I usually met Jeremiah.

The lush greenery surrounding the alcove provided excellent cover, making it nearly impossible for any passerby to notice my arrival. The crashing waves on the nearby shore masked any noise my entry might produce, adding an extra layer of secrecy. In all of the places that I had registered a Portal location, this one had become my favourite. It was a place of tranquility, a moment of respite before immersing myself in the hectic world of Earth and my Guardian responsibilities. This spot had become a sanctuary for me, a hidden gateway between Clivilius and Earth. Over time, it had grown to symbolise the trust and camaraderie among Guardians. We safeguarded our access points, ensuring the veil between our worlds remained intact. It was a responsibility we took seriously, knowing the delicate balance we had to maintain.

Taking a deep breath, I centred myself, preparing for what lay ahead. As I emerged from the alcove and set foot on the soft sand, I cast a final glance back at the smooth, flat rock. It was more than just an access point; it embodied the essence of being a Guardian. The worlds of Clivilius and Earth were intertwined in ways that I still didn't understand, and I knew that I was one thread connecting them. The lines between my two worlds were blurred, and I had to navigate the complexities with care.

The salty tang of the sea air was almost overwhelming as I followed the footpath that snaked its way toward the Glenelg jetty, a concrete finger stretching out into the embrace of the ocean. The jetty, a vibrant tapestry of life, was alive with the hum of activity. Tourists snapped photos, their laughter mingling with the cries of seagulls, while locals strolled leisurely, soaking in the warmth of the sun. Amid this idyllic scene, my mind was a tempest of concern and urgency, the light-hearted joy of the scene around me in stark contrast to the gravity of my thoughts.

Abbey's sudden emergence and her revelations had thrown me into uncharted waters. The fact that she, too, was a Guardian wasn't what unsettled me the most. It was her inexplicable visit to Gladys and the mysterious connection between them that gnawed at me. The implications were vast and unsettling. My steps quickened with my racing thoughts. If I didn't act swiftly, I risked losing a critical advantage, a chance that was rightfully mine to seize.

As I reached the terminus of the jetty, I paused, letting my gaze drift over the expanse of the ocean. The waves crashed against the pillars with relentless energy, mirroring the turmoil that surged within me. The situation with Abbey, Gladys, and now the uncertain future, demanded immediate attention. I needed Jeremiah's insight more than ever. The thought of our hasty exit from Gladys's house replayed in my mind, fuelling my resolve. This spot, where the land reached out to touch the sea, had always been our rendezvous point, a place of beginnings and, sometimes, of endings.

Standing there, amidst the ebb and flow of strangers, I felt a solitary figure caught in the grip of unfolding events beyond my control. The possibility of losing Gladys loomed over me like a dark cloud. The very thought was suffocating. Yet, deep down, I recognised the truth that Gladys's path was hers to choose, not mine to dictate. Whether she embraced her potential as a Guardian or forged her own destiny in Belkeep or elsewhere, I would stand by her decision.

But it was the hope that Jeremiah would see the necessity of keeping Gladys within our circle that preoccupied me as I waited. Her connection to us, regardless of her decision regarding the Portal Key, was a bond I believed was worth preserving. I could only hope that Jeremiah would share my perspective, understanding the delicate balance between guiding and allowing freedom to choose. As the sea breeze tousled my hair, I braced myself for the conversation ahead, ready to navigate the delicate intricacies of our situation. The fate of our relationships, the future of our missions, all hinged on the outcomes of discussions yet to be had.

Waiting at the end of the pier for Jeremiah, I frowned momentarily as the brief thought crossed my mind, *if not Gladys, then who would I give the Portal Key to? And there's still two of them!* the unwelcome reminder echoed through my mind.

My uncertainty manifested in a relentless pacing back and forth on the weathered wood of the jetty, the minutes stretching into what seemed like an eternity. The anticipation of Jeremiah's arrival only served to amplify my anxiety, each step I took a testament to the unease that gripped me. And then, at last, a familiar figure emerged from the crowd, his presence a beacon amidst the sea of faces.

"Cody," he greeted, his voice tinged with concern.

"Jeremiah," I responded, our exchange brief but laden with an unspoken understanding. The air between us was charged with tension, a residue of conversations paused but not concluded, of questions asked but not answered.

Breaking the silence, I delved into the heart of the matter, my voice betraying a familiarity with Abbey that belied the truth of our non-acquaintance. "So, Abbey is a Guardian too," I stated, the simplicity of the words belying the complexity of the implications. "And she knows about Port Stower," I added, the significance of this knowledge not lost on either of us.

Jeremiah nodded, his expression serious. "Yes, it appears that way. Enders Climb, near the former capital, Port Stower, was her settlement."

"I've never heard of Ender's Climb," I admitted, rubbing the back of my neck. "I can't believe I didn't know about her," I murmured, wondering how I could miss a critical close influence of Gladys.

"Clivilius is vast, Cody," Jeremiah replied. "There are so many settlements, and most of them are isolated from any other settlement. Abbey's group likely operated independently, away from the main network."

"I know," I replied, the words heavy with the weight of my oversight. I berated myself silently for not being more vigilant, for allowing the existence of a Guardian with potential ties to Gladys—and possibly to broader concerns like Killerton Enterprises or the Guardian Order—to slip beneath my radar. The implications of Abbey's knowledge and her proximity to our network gnawed at me, sparking a flurry of questions and fears about the depth of her understanding and her intentions.

"Do you think she knows more about our world and the current situation?" I ventured, breaking the silence that had fallen between us. Jeremiah's thoughtful pause was telling, his contemplation a mirror to my own. "It's possible," he conceded, his response opening the door to a myriad of possibilities. "We should try to find her again and see if she's willing to share any information. She might know things that could be valuable to us."

"But what about the risk?" I asked.

Jeremiah's gaze grew distant for a moment. "Being a Guardian is inherently dangerous," he said. "And having a witness from Earth who knows about Clivilius seems to be attracting unwanted attention. We'll have to be careful."

I sighed inwardly as I accepted Jeremiah's assessment of Gladys's position. My mind raced with the newfound knowledge, and I couldn't help but feel overwhelmed. "I never imagined all of this when I first became a Guardian," I admitted. "It's so much more complicated than I ever thought."

"We all had to learn the hard way," Jeremiah said, his tone empathetic. "But it's our duty to protect both worlds, and sometimes that means dealing with difficult situations."

"Yeah, I guess you're right," I replied, a mix of determination and anxiety swirling inside me.

Jeremiah placed a hand on my shoulder, offering reassurance. "You're doing a great job, Cody. We just have to keep moving forward and do what we can to make a difference."

I nodded, grateful for his support. "Thanks, Jeremiah. I try my best."

"Now, let's talk about Gladys," Jeremiah said, suddenly shifting the focus back to the pressing matter at hand. "How did it go with her after Abbey left?"

"She appeared rather overwhelmed by it all. It's clear she's conflicted," I replied.

"That's understandable," Jeremiah said with a heavy sigh.

"I'll find a way to make her see how important she could be," I said, frustration tingeing my voice.

"I hope you know what you're doing," Jeremiah said, preparing me for the possibility that Gladys might not accept the device. "If she doesn't accept the Portal Key, maybe it's time to consider other options."

"What do you mean?" I asked, already suspecting where he was heading, but not yet ready to accept any other option.

"I'm saying that maybe Gladys isn't cut out to be a Guardian," Jeremiah suggested. "Perhaps I should just bring her through my Portal and keep her safe in Clivilius."

Anger surged through me, and I couldn't believe what I was hearing. *It was one thing for me to bring Gladys to Belkeep as a Clivilian. Hell, or even if she joined Luke's settlement. But for Jeremiah to even think about suggesting that he take her...* The thought made my blood boil. "You can't be serious," I retorted, clenching my fists. "Gladys is not some pawn you can just move around at your whim!"

"Cody, calm down," Jeremiah said, holding his hands up in a placating gesture.

But I couldn't calm down. The idea of taking Gladys away from her life, from Earth, and forcing her into a world she might not be ready for was infuriating. She deserved the choice, just like any other Guardian.

In a moment of heated frustration, I swung my fist, landing a punch squarely on Jeremiah's jaw. He staggered back, looking at me with a mixture of surprise and betrayal.

"You don't get to decide her fate," I snapped, my voice shaking with emotion.

Jeremiah touched his jaw, his expression softening. "I'm sorry, Cody. I didn't mean to suggest forcing her. But we can't afford to wait forever. The situation in Clivilius is dire, and we need all the help we can get."

"I know that," I replied, my anger subsiding slightly. "But pressuring her like this won't help. We need to give her time to process everything."

Jeremiah sighed, his gaze drifting to the horizon. "You have three days, Cody," he said firmly. "If she hasn't activated the Portal Key by the end of the third day, I'm taking the device off her and finding someone else. And you won't have a choice about it."

My heart sank at the ultimatum, but I knew Jeremiah was right about one thing – *time is running out. Especially now that Luke is active, Clivilius needs every Guardian it can get, and Gladys has the potential to be a powerful ally. I have to find a way to convince her to accept the responsibility.*

With a heavy heart, I nodded. "I'll do my best," I said, my voice barely above a whisper.

Jeremiah placed a reassuring hand on my shoulder. "I know you will," he said, his tone softening. "And if anyone can make her see the importance of this, it's you."

Before I could respond, "Light the fire," Jeremiah said, offering me a small smile as he pushed the Portal Key into the palm of my hand.

"Share the light," came the instinctive reply, my mind already racing with how to approach the situation with Gladys.

As Jeremiah quickly turned and vanished into the crowds, I was left standing alone at the end of the jetty, the weight of the ultimatum heavy on my shoulders. I had three days to convince Gladys to become a Guardian, or I would almost inevitably lose her forever. It was a daunting task, but I was determined to give it everything I had. My worlds depended on it.

4338.210

(29 July 2018)

THE VANISHING

1338.210.1

The room was bathed in the warm, flickering glow of the fireplace, the delicate dance of flames casting intricate shadows on the walls like ethereal dancers in a silent ballet. The crackling embers whispered tales of forgotten warmth, offering a momentary respite from the weight of my Guardian duties. Freya, cocooned in a blanket of cozy light, found solace in the pages of her book, the gentle rustle of paper creating a soothing melody that underscored the quiet of our small home.

The sudden knock jolted me from my reverie, a sharp reminder of the world beyond our door, a world where duty and danger often intertwined. My body reacted before my mind fully grasped the situation, muscle memory guiding me towards the unknown waiting on our doorstep. "I'll get it," my voice, steady yet tinged with an undercurrent of apprehension, broke the silence, offering Freya a nod to stay her curiosity. She nodded back, a silent understanding passing between us, her eyes briefly meeting mine with a mixture of concern and trust.

As the door swung open, the chill of the afternoon invaded our warm haven. Sam Tawny, a familiar face within the community and a harbinger of news, stood before me, his features etched with urgency. "Guardian Cody, sir," his voice, usually confident, now held a tremor of unease, "Krid's gone missing. There's trouble at the Portal Cave." His words hung between us, a cloud of impending doom.

The impact of his news was immediate and visceral. A storm of emotions raged within me, a whirlwind of concern, duty, and an unbidden fear for what this meant for Krid and our community. Freya's gasp, sharp and laden with worry, was quickly followed by the sound of her book hitting the floor, a thud in the quiet room.

My heart skipped a beat, and without a second thought, I reached for my heavy winter jacket, its familiar weight a grounding force in the face of impending turmoil.

The chill in the air bit at my skin as I stepped beyond the threshold of warmth and safety, only to be met by an unexpected force—Freya, her hand gripping my arm with an urgency that mirrored the tumult within my heart. Her eyes, wide and resolute, locked onto mine, an unspoken vow of solidarity in their depths. "I'm coming with you," she declared, her voice determined. The resolve in her gaze sparked a mix of emotions within me; pride intertwined with a gnawing fear for her safety.

Without a word, I nodded, the silent exchange cementing our shared resolve. A protective instinct, fierce and unwavering, coursed through me, tempered only by the knowledge that Freya possessed a strength all her own.

The journey through the snow-covered paths of Belkeep felt like a race against time, each step echoing with the urgency of the unknown.

"Do you know what happened?" Freya's voice, laden with concern, cut through the biting wind that swept across our path.

Despite his young age of thirteen, Sam's demeanour remained calm and controlled, a stoic reflection of a childhood that had vanished into adulthood too soon—a normal occurrence in Belkeep, where harsh conditions and isolation forced children to grow into adults prematurely.

"I'm not really sure," replied Sam, his breath visible in the frigid air. "Chief sent me to get you as soon as he heard the news. He's already on his way to the Portal Cave."

A sense of fear and urgency gripped my chest, and I looked over to Freya. "Where's Fryar?" I asked, feeling the sudden need to have both of my children close.

"He's already at the Portal Cave," replied Freya, pointing into the distance where the figure of Fryar could be seen approaching the entrance to the cave.

The icy wind cut through the air as we neared the entrance of the Portal Cave, a place where the fabric between worlds seemed thin and fragile. The cold seeped deep into my bones, matching the growing unease in my heart.

Chief Drikarsus stood near the entrance, his gaze fixed on the ominous darkness within. "Cody," he greeted solemnly, acknowledging our arrival. "This is a dire situation," added Brogyin, who had been standing nearby.

I nodded in agreement, my eyes scanning the surroundings for any clues. "What do we know so far?" I asked, my voice cutting through the eerie silence of the cave.

"Not a lot," answered Prim, stepping out from the cave's shadows.

My eyes narrowed curiously. "It was Prim's daughter who raised the alarm," Sam explained.

"Yes," Prim confirmed with a nod. "Laura and Krid had come here to wait for you."

"Wait for me? What for?" I asked, my confusion dissipating as I realised Krid's affinity for this place. It had always been her favourite spot, and aside from greeting me on my constant comings and goings, I couldn't fathom why.

Prim had a specific reply. "Laura wanted to ask you if you could get her one of these," she said, her hand unfurling to reveal a small magnet of Tasmania—the same one I had given Krid recently. A sinking feeling gripped my chest. "She wouldn't leave this behind willingly," I murmured, my mind racing to make sense of the puzzle.

"So, if Laura was with Krid, does she know what happened?" Freya's frustration with the lack of details showed in her tone. The cave's shadows seemed to close in, holding secrets that eluded our understanding, intensifying the urgency of the unravelling mystery.

Brogyin interrupted, gesturing towards a dark crimson stain on the floor. "There's evidence of a struggle here," he said, his weathered finger pointing to the ominous mark.

Forgetting the unanswered question, the small group huddled, their breaths visible in the cold air, as they examined the finding in more detail. The dark crimson stain seemed to seep into the very fabric of the cave floor, a sinister testament to an unsettling event.

"That looks like blood," said Fryar, his voice hushed with a mix of realisation and dread.

Freya gripped my arm tightly, her fingers pressing into my jacket, her face a mix of worry and determination. "We need to find her, Dad. Krid's just a child."

I placed a reassuring hand on Freya's shoulder, the touch an anchor in the midst of uncertainty. "We will, sweetheart."

"We need to piece together what happened here first," Fryar chimed in, his analytical gaze scanning the surroundings for any additional clues.

Chief, his expression grave, spoke up. "We've sent word around town. Everyone will be wanting to assist in the search."

"Are you sure that is wise?" Fryar asked, his concern etched across his brow. "We're not sure what happened yet. We could be putting others in danger."

"Time is of the essence," Chief replied, his determination cutting through the cave's heavy atmosphere.

Turning my attention back to Prim and my unresolved question, "I would like to speak with Laura," I told her firmly, my voice steady amidst the rising tension.

Worry burned behind Prim's eyes, and she nodded hesitantly. "I'll take you," she said, somewhat tentatively.

"Is Laura wounded?" Chief asked, a sensible question given the discovery of the fresh blood.

"No," answered Prim, her voice a mixture of relief and concern. "She's just a bit shaken up."

The sudden arrival of running feet caught our attention, and we all turned towards the cave's entrance. Peter had arrived, panting as he spoke. "Chief," he said, his breath visible in the cold air. "Krid's jacket has been found in the snow on the outskirts of town."

"Are you certain it's hers?" Chief inquired, his voice a sturdy lighthouse beam cutting through the fog of uncertainty.

"Yes," panted Peter. "It's that dark blue woollen one that she always wears." His face turned a darker shade of worry.

Sensing the unspoken as much as I had, Chief prompted for more details. Peter hesitated briefly. "There's traces of blood on it."

Freya gasped, her hand flying to her mouth in shock.

"Let's go," I said, rushing out of the cave, a storm of emotions churning within. "Take us to where her jacket was found," I commanded Peter, urgency propelling our steps into the bitter cold.

SAY THAT AGAIN

4338.210.2

The biting cold was merciless, slicing through the layers of my jacket as if they were mere whispers against the wind. Each step along the snow-covered paths felt heavier than the last, the crunch of snow underfoot a constant reminder of the relentless march of time and the urgency of our quest. Peter, a beacon in the gloom, guided us with unwavering certainty toward the location where Krid's jacket had been discovered. The encroaching snowstorm, with its howling winds and swirling flurries, seemed to deepen the shadows that clung to my restless thoughts, whispering doubts and fears with every gust.

Beside me, Freya walked with a purpose that belied the chill, her breath forming misty clouds in the chilly air, each one dissipating as quickly as it appeared. Her determination was palpable, a mirrored reflection of the worry etched across her face, visible even in the dimming light of the darkening skies. Prim kept pace beside Freya, her steps steady and unwavering, a silent sentinel in our midst.

It was Freya who broke the silence, her voice cutting through the cold with a clarity that pulled us all to a halt. "Father," she said, her voice laced with a mixture of determination and uncertainty. She hesitated, gathering her thoughts before voicing her concern. "Prim and I will return to town and speak with Laura. We might get more information about what happened." Her resolve in the face of the unknown, her willingness to step back into the labyrinth of our small town's whispers and secrets, struck a chord in my heart.

"Be careful, Freya," I found myself saying, my voice carrying a weight of fatherly concern mingled with a silent plea for answers, for anything that could lead us to Krid.

Freya's response was immediate, her hand finding Prim's in a gesture that spoke volumes, giving it a reassuring squeeze. "We'll be fine," she replied, her tone imbued with a strength that I admired yet feared. She looked back at Prim, her gaze firm and resolute. "We need answers," she stated, a declaration that echoed in the silence left by their departure.

With Freya and Prim's figures retreating into the distance, anticipation gnawed at me, a relentless companion in the uncertainty of our journey. Peter's silent figure beckoned us forward, a reminder that our journey was far from over.

❖

"Krid's jacket was here," Peter's voice, steady and sombre, cut through the silence, anchoring us to the spot with a gravity that seemed to pull the very air tight around us.

My eyes widened, the immediate shock sparking a surge of adrenaline that coursed through me. The snow, undisturbed except for the three sets of footprints that etched a path further away from town, seemed to mock us with its pristine calm. "Are those yours?" The question tumbled out, a reflex born of hope and desperation. Even as the words left my mouth, I realised the folly of the thought—a single person could not forge three distinct paths.

"No," Peter's reply was curt, a confirmation of my dawning realisation and a deepening of the mystery.

"Do you know whose they are?" Chief's voice, always authoritative, now carried an edge of urgency.

Crouching to examine the tracks closer, Fryar interjected with a note of surprise, "These look like a child's feet." His observation, so innocuous yet so chilling, sent a shiver down my spine that had nothing to do with the cold.

The urge to follow the tracks, to throw myself into the search for Krid with reckless abandon, was almost overwhelming. The clawing need to act, to do something—anything—to find her, was a physical ache in my chest.

"Caution, Cody," Chief's voice, firm and commanding, halted me in my tracks, his hand gripping my arm with a strength that spoke volumes. "We need to approach this carefully," he warned, his words grounding, a reminder of the perils that likely lay ahead.

As the first flakes of fresh snow began to fall, their delicate dance in the air was both beautiful and cruel. Each flake, a unique crystal, seemed to mock us with its serenity, a ticking clock threatening to erase the only lead we had. I clenched my fists, feeling the weight of responsibility heavy on my shoulders, a mantle I bore with both pride and fear.

"We can't afford to lose the trail," my voice broke through, edged with a desperation and urgency that mirrored the turmoil within. The tracks in the snow were our only guide, a fragile thread in the vast tapestry of the wilderness that threatened to be snatched away at any moment by the capricious wind and snow.

Chief met my gaze, his eyes steady, a bastion of calm in the storm of my emotions. "I understand, but rushing blindly could lead to more harm than good. We need a plan," he counselled, wisdom and experience lending weight to his words.

The falling snow intensified. My eyes darted between the vanishing tracks and the gathering storm, a battle raging between the impetuous desire to act and the rational, methodical approach Chief advocated. In that moment, the snowfall was not just a weather phenomenon; it was a metaphor for the race against time we faced, each flake a second lost, each moment a step further from Krid. The urgency was palpable, a tangible force that pushed against the barriers of caution and deliberation, demanding action, demanding resolution.

The air was thick, laden with a palpable sense of anticipation, as Chief, with a decisive nod, dispatched Brogyin to rally more men. The depth of his command, "armed and prepared for whatever lay ahead," echoed ominously through the stillness, underscoring the urgency and the potential peril we were about to confront. This was no ordinary search; it was a mission teetering on the brink of danger, demanding not just bravery but readiness for the unforeseeable.

Fryar seemed to sense the magnitude of the impending danger even more acutely. He turned toward me, and in that moment, the determination in his eyes was as clear and sharp as the edge of the knife he bore. "Dad," he said, his voice a steady beacon in the tumult of our emotions, "we need to be ready for anything." His words, simple yet profound, reverberated with the weight of our shared resolve.

From his hip, Fryar unclasped a sheathed knife. Its worn handle spoke volumes of the countless adventures and trials it had weathered at sea, a silent testament to the resilience and preparedness that had been instilled in him from a young age. With a swift, practiced motion, he unsheathed the blade, its gleam cutting through the dim light—a tangible representation of the readiness we needed to embody.

"Take this," Fryar urged, extending the knife toward me. Our eyes locked in a moment of silent understanding, a mutual recognition of the gravity of the gesture. The weight of the blade in my hand was a potent reminder of the dual nature of our quest—protection and threat entwined. It felt both familiar and foreign in my grasp, an emblem of the precarious balance between safety and danger we were navigating.

Next, Fryar revealed a smaller blade, strapped to his ankle, drawing a nod of approval from Chief. This act, simple yet significant, underscored our collective resolve to face whatever awaited us with every resource at our disposal.

As the snow began to fall more heavily, cloaking our surroundings in a serene white blanket, a deceptive calm settled over the landscape. This tranquility, however beautiful, stood in contrast to the urgency pulsing through our veins, a reminder of the duality of nature—peaceful yet perilous.

The wind, now carrying whispers of uncertainty, seemed to echo the tumultuous thoughts swirling within me. We stood on the threshold of the unknown, prepared to embark on the trail left by those who had taken Krid. The tension in the air was almost tangible, a manifestation of the risks and uncertainties that lay ahead.

In that moment, as Fryar and I exchanged glances, a silent vow was forged between father and son. It was a pledge of mutual support, a promise to face whatever dangers lay ahead with courage and determination. This unspoken agreement, fortified by the weight of the knife in my hand, was a testament to our shared resolve to bring Krid home, no matter the cost.

Chief's command, sharp and authoritative, sliced through the silence of the gathering gloom like a beacon in the night. "Stay vigilant. We follow the tracks but be cautious—the new snow could obscure them quickly." His voice, imbued with the weight of experience, served as a reminder of the myriad challenges we faced, not least of which were the capricious whims of nature herself. The elements, indifferent to our desperation, threatened to erase the very clues we sought to follow.

As the intensity of the snowfall increased, each flake seemed to land with a silent significance, echoing the tumult of emotions whirling within me. Beside me, Fryar stood resolute, his grip on the hilt of his knife unyielding.

"Let's move," Chief's voice, once more cutting through the silence, was both a command and a rallying cry. His gaze, ever vigilant, swept the horizon as if to challenge the very storm that sought to thwart us. We fell into formation behind him, each of us overcoming our individual fears to form a united front, driven by a collective determination that felt almost tangible in the heavy air.

With every step, the snow beneath our boots whispered solemn warnings, its crisp sound a constant reminder of the uncertainty of our path. It felt as though the very ground beneath us spoke of the precariousness of our venture, urging caution with every muted crunch.

The tracks led us through a landscape transformed by the snowfall, the quiet rocky terrain now shrouded in a blanket of white that muffled our steps and lent an otherworldly hush to our surroundings. This silence, however, was not comforting; it was the calm before a storm, a deceptive peace that masked the tension simmering just beneath the surface.

As we advanced, the scene that awaited us broke the eerie silence, shattering the illusion of tranquility. The tension, previously an undercurrent, now enveloped us completely, clinging to the air with an intensity that was almost palpable. The quiet had been a prelude, and what lay before us was a sharp contrast to the hushed anticipation of our journey thus far.

❖

As we edged closer, the world around us seemed to shift, the landscape blurring into a tableau where reality and the ethereal mingled. Shadows, elongated and distorted by the dimming light, danced on the periphery of my vision, heralding the approach of something—or someone— emerging from the snowy veil that enveloped the world. The scene that unfolded before us was almost surreal, bathed in an otherworldly glow that seemed to cast everything in a dreamlike quality. Yet, the danger was palpable, a sharp contrast to the serene beauty of our surroundings.

There, in the heart of this frozen tableau, was Krid, a figure of vulnerability amidst the harshness. The sight of her, held hostage by one of the men, ignited a fierce, protective surge within me. The captor, with several bruises marring his face and a small trail of blood trickling from a gash above his brow, stood as a stark reminder of the stakes of our endeavour. Beside him, a more seriously wounded man stood, his pain etched into every line of his body, a blood-soaked hand clutching at his side—a vivid testament to a violent encounter.

My instincts kicked in, urging me forward, a protective surge for the girl who had become a beacon of innocence in my tumultuous life. Fryar, mirroring my urgency, matched my pace, our unspoken vow echoing in the crisp air.

The tension spiked as the man holding Krid tightened his grip, a clear sign of his growing desperation. His eyes, wide with a mix of fear and defiance, darted nervously between us. "Ostanovis'!" he barked, the command sharp and authoritative, slicing through the frozen silence with the precision of a knife. His use of Russian, unexpected and jarring, added another layer of complexity to the already tense standoff.

Fryar and I halted, the sudden command freezing us in place as effectively as the icy landscape that surrounded us.

Our eyes, filled with uncertainty, flicked between each other and the men before us, trying to gauge the depth of the danger we faced.

"We're not here to hurt you," I found myself saying, my voice a steady calm in the storm of fear and tension that tightened my chest. The words, though spoken with conviction, carried the weight of our precarious situation, a delicate balance of threat and reassurance.

Beside me, Fryar's grip on his knife was a silent testament to our readiness to defend, to protect. The metal, cold and unyielding in his grasp, understood the potential violence that hovered on the edge of this encounter. The wounded man, his gaze flitting between us, wore an expression that teetered between pain, fear, and a curious sort of intrigue, as if our presence was as baffling to him as his was to us.

Edging cautiously closer, the connection between Krid and myself grew more intense, her eyes locking onto mine with a clarity that pierced through the tension of the moment. Within those depths, I found a silent plea, a call for help that needed no words to be understood. It was a moment of profound communication, bridging the gap between desperation and hope.

As Fryar's gaze sought mine once more, there was an unspoken exchange, a communion of souls that transcended the spoken word. His eyes, mirrors of my own turmoil, reflected a shared understanding of the complexity of our situation. "Don't do it," I found myself whispering, not just to him but to the part of myself that was teetering on the edge of action. "Not until we've got Krid safe." It was a plea for restraint, a reminder of the delicate balance we had to maintain between action and patience.

The tension was palpable as the man, his voice thick with an accent unfamiliar yet demanding, cut through the silent standoff. "Who are you?" he demanded, his gaze piercing through the falling snow and the uncertainty that cloaked us.

Chief, ever the bastion of calm and authority, stepped forward, his hands raised in a universal gesture of peace. "I'm Chief Lewyyd Drikarsus," he declared, his voice steady and clear, a beacon in the swirling uncertainty.

"Where am I?" The question from the man was loaded with confusion, a disorientation that seemed to go beyond our immediate surroundings.

"You're in Belkeep," Chief replied, his voice a grounding force in the midst of the swirling snow and emotions.

The man's confusion deepened, his vehement shake of the head betraying a profound disorientation. "Gde nakhoditsya Klivilius?" he asked, the name Klivilius slicing through the air with a weight that resonated deep within me. It was a name wrapped in knowing, a word that everyone who has traversed the Portal hears—a whispered voice that calls them by name, welcoming them to Clivilius.

Meeting Chief's gaze, I found a silent prompt, an unspoken command to bridge the gap between worlds. With a sweeping motion, encompassing the snow-covered landscape that enveloped us, I declared, "Here is Clivilius." It was an acknowledgment of his confusion, an attempt to guide him through the fog of dislocation he was experiencing.

"I don't understand," the man stuttered, his confusion a tangible presence that mingled with the cold air.

A sudden realisation dawned upon me, a spark of understanding in the midst of the swirling uncertainty. My blade began to lower, a gesture of cautious optimism as I grasped the true nature of the situation. This was more than a mere confrontation; it was a collision of worlds, of realities that had somehow intertwined.

"Father, be careful," Fryar's warning cut through my thoughts, a sharp reminder of the danger that still lurked within this delicate moment of revelation. The tension between us was a living thing, a palpable force that spoke of the risks I was taking with every breath, every decision. Yet, within that tension, there was also a glimmer of hope, a possibility of understanding and resolution that had not been there before.

The softly spoken words that rasped from Krid's mouth, "ty teper' Strazh," carved through the tension like a knife through the cold air, leaving a trail of bewilderment in their wake. Fryar and Chief exchanged glances, their expressions a mix of confusion and surprise, as if the world had shifted beneath their feet.

"When did Krid learn Russian," Fryar's voice was tinged with perplexity, his question hanging between us like a puzzle waiting to be solved.

A brief chuckle escaped me, a momentary release of tension in the midst of the unfolding drama. "Krid has many surprises," I said, the dry humour a thin veneer over the deep well of pride I felt for her resilience and adaptability.

"Osvobodi menya, i my smozhem predlozhit' tebe zashchitu," Krid continued, her words a bridge between desperation and hope.

The man's response, "How?" was laced with a vulnerability that seemed to soften his stance, his grip on Krid easing as if her words had reached a part of him that was still capable of trust.

Krid offered the reply, "Vy slyshite myagkiy golos vnutri sebya. Poslushay eto."

"Krid, in English, please," I prompted, gently steering her back to a common ground that we could all understand.

Slowly, the man lowered his weapon and released Krid, a gesture that seemed to carry the weight of a thousand unspoken words. As Krid approached us, I knelt and wrapped my arms around her, the relief of having her safe in my embrace a sharp contrast to the cold bite of the air. "Are you alright, Krid?" My question was a whisper, a soft inquiry amidst the storm of emotions.

I could feel Krid's nod against my cheek. "Yes," she said softly. Pulling herself back, she looked into my eyes. "He is our new Guardian," she said, her words a revelation that hung in the frigid air like a suspended breath.

The gasps of confusion from Fryar and Chief echoed my own internal turmoil. Krid's words, so clear and yet so laden with implications, reverberated through my mind. Relief at her safety battled with the shock of her revelation. The realisation that Jeremiah had granted another Portal Key unfolded with a weight that felt heavy in the air, a reminder of the ultimatum that loomed over me.

Fryar's gaze found mine, a mirror reflecting a storm of unspoken thoughts and questions. In that silent communion, a myriad of emotions passed between us—uncertainty, determination, a shared resolve. The wounded man seemed to pick up on this subtle shift in dynamics, his posture relaxing ever so slightly, a silent acknowledgment of the fragile truce forming between us.

Taking a cautious step forward, I sought to bridge the gap between stranger and ally. My hands tapped against my chest in a universal gesture of introduction. "Cody Jennings," I said, the name feeling somewhat inadequate in the grand scope of what was unfolding before us.

"Fedor Sokolov," the man returned, with a gesture toward himself that carried the weight of his experiences, his struggles. Then, adding a layer to the narrative, he introduced his companion with a simple, "Nikolai." The names, floating through the cold air, seemed to carry with them a host of untold stories.

"Fryar," I continued, gesturing towards my son with a sense of pride that never wavered. "My son."

"Brother," Fedor responded, the term echoing with a depth of loyalty and affection as he pointed at Nikolai. It was a simple word, yet it spoke volumes about their relationship, their shared history, and the strength of their connection.

With a cautious approach, I displayed my Portal Key to Fedor, the metal glinting faintly in the waning light. "I am a Guardian, too," I announced, hoping the universal significance of the key would transcend the barrier of language. Krid's inability to translate, indicated by her apologetic shake of the head, left us stranded on either side of a communicative chasm, yet the gesture itself was a bridge, an offer of trust and shared duty.

The situation took a sharp turn as Nikolai, overwhelmed by his injuries, collapsed with a heavy grunt. Fedor's rush to his side was immediate, a reflexive display of concern that tore through the remaining vestiges of tension between us. Fryar and I, moved by a common humanity, stepped forward to assist without hesitation.

"We need to take them to Belkeep," I declared, turning to Chief. The urgency in my voice was unmistakable. "Nikolai's wound is serious." The reality of the situation was clear; immediate action was required if Nikolai was to have any chance of survival.

Fryar, drawing upon his diverse experience from sea voyages, where quick thinking and resourcefulness were often the difference between life and death, took command of the situation. His actions, confident and decisive, were a testament to his character, his upbringing, and the unspoken code of responsibility we shared as Belkeepans.

In this moment, the lines between friend and foe blurred, united by a common cause. The act of extending help to Fedor and Nikolai was a declaration of our values, a testament to the belief that, despite the complexities of our worlds, compassion remained a universal language.

As Brogyin and the other Belkeepans arrived, their voices echoing behind, armed and braced for a conflict that wasn't there, the tension momentarily spiked. "There's no battle to be fought," Chief's voice, steady and commanding, cut through the chill air, redirecting the group's preparedness towards a more pressing need. "But they do need urgent medical assistance." Watching the men rally to assist, a testament to their adaptability and compassion, I felt a brief flicker of pride amidst the worry.

Pulling Fryar aside, the urgency of the situation settled heavily between us. "I need you to go with them. Find out as much as you can," I said, my voice low, imbued with the weight of our predicament. The request was clear: to glean any information about our unexpected guests. Fryar's nod, a silent acknowledgment of the weight of his task, was a silent testament to his maturity. "And what about you?".

The scene before us, where Nikolai and Fedor were receiving the urgently needed medical attention, was a stark backdrop to our conversation. "I need to find Jeremiah. These men are wounded, and Fedor is a Guardian, which means..." My voice faltered, the implications of Fedor's status as a Guardian unravelling a slew of possibilities, each more concerning than the last.

"Jeremiah could also be in trouble," Fryar concluded, his insight cutting through the uncertainty. His words, a mirror to my own fears, solidified the course of action I needed to take. "Yes," was all I could muster, an acknowledgment steeped in worry.

"Okay," Fryar agreed, his determination clear despite the uncertainties. "I'll learn what I can. Although unless by some miracle we have someone in Belkeep that knows Russian, I'm not sure how successful we'll be."

At that moment, Krid's potential to bridge our communication gap became clear. "Krid," I called her over, seeking to leverage her unique connection to the mysteries surrounding us. "Krid," I repeated, ensuring her attention was fully on the implications of my next question. "Are they still safe?" The query was loaded with the weight of our shared secrets.

Fryar's watchful eyes, filled with unspoken questions, observed our exchange.

"The Portal Keys?" Krid sought clarification, her understanding of the stakes reflected in her solemn demeanour.

"Yes," I confirmed.

"Of course," Krid assured, her response a beacon of hope in the chilling blizzard of our current dilemma.

"Good," I told her, ignoring my son's questioning gaze. Getting to our feet, I ushered Krid in Fryar's direction. The lingering questions burned in Fryar's eyes, but he respectfully left them unspoken.

With a nod of satisfaction, I sidestepped Fryar's unasked questions, the urgency of the situation propelling me forward. "Take Krid with you," I instructed Fryar, a directive that melded strategy with necessity. As I pulled my jacket tighter around me, a gesture more of readiness than defence against the cold, I stepped away from the group, the path to the Portal Cave beckoning me forward.

4338.211

(30 July 2018)

HAPPENSTANCE

4338.211.1

Arriving at Luke's house felt like crossing the threshold into a domain fraught with tension and unanswered questions. The atmosphere, charged with the unspoken, reflected my inner turmoil—a mix of determination and the gnawing uncertainty that had taken root in my mind. The failed attempts to contact Jeremiah since yesterday weighed heavily on me, each unanswered call amplifying the sense of urgency and concern for what lay ahead.

The mystery of Fedor's arrival, his sudden and inexplicable integration into my Guardian team, swirled in my thoughts like a persistent fog. Jeremiah's choice—a Russian with barely a grasp of broken English—posed more questions than it provided answers, adding layers to an already complex puzzle. *Why him? What unseen threads connected us in Jeremiah's mind?*

Gladys's house, once a haven in the tumultuous journey I found myself on, had offered no solace this time. Its walls, usually resonant with warmth and guidance, now echoed with a profound silence that mirrored the emptiness in my heart. The absence of her presence, her wisdom, left a void that I found increasingly difficult to fill.

The tension that enveloped the room seemed to thicken with each step I took, the air almost shimmering with the weight of my apprehension. My sigh, a futile attempt to dispel the growing sense of unease, barely echoed in the quiet before being swallowed by the charged atmosphere.

"Where is Luke?" The voice, unexpected and resonant with an Arabian accent, cut through the silence, startling me into a defensive stance. My heart raced as I turned, instinctively ready for confrontation, only to find myself facing an intruder whose presence was as imposing as it was unexpected. Tall, lean, with the starkness of a shaved head, he stood with an air of calm assurance, his non-aggression signalled not just by his open posture but by the unmistakable sight of a Portal Key in his hand.

"Who the fuck are you?" The question burst from me, a reflexive demand for answers, edged with the tension that had knotted itself within me. My gaze fixed on him, searching, assessing, the wariness in me coiled tight as a spring.

"I'm not a threat," he responded, his voice a blend of reassurance and firmness, the Portal Key he held serving as a silent testament to his claim. The air between us, charged with my initial suspicion, seemed to shift slightly, a tentative step towards understanding.

"Who are you?" I found myself repeating the question, my tone now tempered by curiosity, yet the undercurrent of caution remained undisturbed. The balance of trust was fragile, each word exchanged a weight added or removed from the scales.

"I'm Leigh Trogaris," he declared, his name a new variable in an equation that was becoming increasingly complex. "I'm a friend of Jeremiah's." The statement, intended to reassure, instead added layers to the mystery, weaving his presence into the intricate tapestry of concerns that already plagued me.

A sinking feeling took root in the pit of my stomach, a tangible response to the unfolding scenario. The revelation of a new Guardian, wounded and in need of help, had already set the stage for unease. Now, the introduction of Leigh

Trogaris, claiming affiliation with Jeremiah in Luke's living room, compounded the apprehension. It was a convergence of unknowns that seemed to herald a deepening of the crisis, a widening of the web of intrigue that surrounded us.

The urgency in my question, "Where's Jeremiah?" carried the weight of my growing apprehension, my voice tinged with a concern that felt like a tight band around my chest. Leigh's response, "He's not so good," was like a punch to the gut, his words offering more questions than answers, cloaked in a vagueness that did nothing to ease my worry.

"Take me to him," I found myself insisting, the words propelled by a surge of urgency, a need to act, to do something—anything—to aid Jeremiah. But Leigh's admission, "I can't. He's back in Strechna," hit like a cold wave, reminding me of the frustrating limitations that bound us as Guardians. The inability to use each other's Portals was a barrier I had momentarily forgotten, a restriction that now loomed large in the face of crisis.

"What—" My attempt to grapple with this information, to find some sliver of a solution, was cut short by Leigh's interjection.

"I don't know exactly what happened," he said, the tension in his voice painting a picture of confusion and urgency. "He was with Winston, another member of his Guardian team, when they were attacked."

"Attacked? By whom? Where?" The questions spilled from me, a torrent of concern and the need for answers.

"I don't know!" Leigh yelled, his frustration spilling over, a storm in his eyes. "I received a distress signal from him, and when I arrived at his location, he was covered in blood."

"Shit," was all I could muster, a succinct summation of the dread that settled heavily upon me.

"He was simmering close to losing consciousness, but he was determined to speak with me before he returned to

Clivilius to recover," Leigh continued, drawing me further into the unfolding drama. Motioning for him to continue, I was captivated by the dire narrative. "He kept rambling about Winston and Luke, something about critical intel."

As Leigh's revelations unfolded, my world seemed to tilt on its axis, a maelstrom of confusion and betrayal swirling within me. "What the hell is going on?" The words slipped from me, a verbal manifestation of the chaos that gripped my thoughts, the room itself seeming to sway in response. The realisation that Jeremiah had not sought me out in his moment of need pierced me with a sharpness that felt all too real, a sense of betrayal that cut deeper than any physical wound.

"Why you?" The question emerged, laden with a mixture of hurt and disbelief, a challenge thrown into the thickening air between us.

"I guess he thought I could get to Luke the quickest," Leigh answered, his words offering a thin veil of explanation.

As I glared at Leigh, struggling to anchor myself in the rapidly shifting reality, his next words served as a lifeline amidst the storm. "I'm Luke's Guardian Atum," he clarified, his tone grounding, offering a beacon of understanding in the tumult. The relief that followed was a balm to my frayed nerves, the logic of Jeremiah's actions becoming clearer, yet no less painful in its necessity.

"I gave a second Portal Key to Beatrix Cramer. I believe you are close with her sister," Leigh added, injecting another layer of complexity into the unfolding narrative.

Another sharp pang hit my chest, and I scowled at Leigh. If Gladys knew that Beatrix was a Guardian with Luke, my chances of convincing her to join me were almost non-existent. They could only meet safely on Earth, and those opportunities, it seemed, were quickly fading.

"Did you know that we've been trying to persuade Gladys to accept Jeremiah's final Portal Key?" I accused.

"No," answered Leigh, his response carrying a note of helplessness. "Jeremiah shares very little details of his Guardian life with me."

"That makes two of us," I retorted, the bitterness of being kept in the dark a sentiment now shared between us. This shared experience of exclusion, of being peripheral to Jeremiah's deeper strategies, did little to ease the sense of isolation that had taken root within me.

The sudden prickle at the back of my neck, an instinctual warning of danger, was the only precursor to the ominous thump that echoed through the hallway. A chill, sharp and sudden, coursed through me, the air heavy with a sense of dread that seemed to seep into the very walls of the room.

Leigh's warning, "Get ready for a quick exit," cut through the thickening atmosphere, his words a beacon of clarity in the growing fog of unease. With my senses heightened, every nerve end alert, we moved towards the hallway, our steps measured, the tension between us a tangible force.

The sight that greeted us was one ripped straight from the pages of a horror story. A man, his body battered and bleeding, stumbled from the bedroom, his fall against the hallway wall not just a physical collapse but a manifestation of the nightmare scenario we found ourselves in. The heavy thud of his body, the trail of blood he left behind—it was a scene etched in violence, a vivid reminder of the dangers that lurked just beyond our realm of understanding.

"Winston?" Leigh's voice, laden with both concern and urgency, broke the stunned silence that had enveloped me. Watching him crouch in front of Winston, the immediacy of the situation became undeniable. "Help me!" Leigh's command pulled me from the inertia of shock, propelling me into action.

Breaking free from the temporary paralysis of shock, I hurried up the hallway. As I crouched beside them, Winston's condition was dire, his lifeblood painting a grim picture on the hallway floor. His hand, coated in blood, reached out to me, pressing a small USB into my palm. "Take it," he gasped, the weight of his plea evident in his strained voice and the desperate plea in his eyes.

While Leigh worked frantically to stem the flow of blood, a futile battle against the tide of Winston's injuries, I found myself grappling with the urgency of the situation. "What is it for?" The question fell from my lips, a desperate attempt to grasp the significance of the USB now in my possession.

Winston's struggle for each breath, the blood that marked his words, lent a chilling urgency to his message. "Get the data to Luke Smith," he managed, the desperation clear in his gaze. "You must." The imperative, delivered with such intensity, left no room for doubt. This was not just a request; it was a mission, one that bore the weight of consequences far beyond the immediate danger.

Leigh's demand for the identity of the assailant, "Who did this?" was met with a revelation that seemed to hang in the air, heavy with implication. "Enemies of Killerton," Winston's response, though brief, was loaded with meaning, casting a shadow of larger, unseen forces at play.

As the reality of Winston's revelation sank in, my mind was momentarily hijacked by the tumultuous memories of the attack at Killerton Enterprises. The vivid recollections of chaos, the clash with Amber and her Guardian team, played out with sharp clarity against the backdrop of my current predicament. A shiver of doubt crept through me, the lines between friend and foe blurring in a haze of uncertainty. Amber, who had once appeared as an ally, had her own clandestine motives within Killerton, complicating the narrative further. The revelation that she, too, was navigating the murky waters of espionage and subterfuge within the same battleground we found ourselves entangled in added layers of complexity I hadn't fully considered until now.

"The blueprints?" The question cut sharply through my spiralling thoughts, a focused attempt to anchor the conversation back to the tangible, the here and now. Winston's strained response, "I don't know what that is. This contains the instruction for resetting a Portal Key," thrust us into uncharted territory, the weight of the implications momentarily staggering.

Leigh and I shared a look of shock, the potential of what lay within our grasp dawning on us both with the force of a revelation. The possibility of resetting a Portal Key, of potentially altering the very fabric of our Guardian dynamics, was a concept that both excited and unnerved.

Winston's agonised groan, a painful reminder of the human cost already paid in this shadowy war, drew our focus back to the grim task at hand. The minutes stretched out, laden with tension and unspoken fears, until Winston's struggle ceased, his passing marking a solemn moment of silence that felt heavy with significance.

Leigh's question, "Could it really be possible? Could we really reset a Portal Key and create a new Guardian?" echoed my own whirlwind of thoughts. The idea, fraught with both opportunity and risk, was a beacon of unknown potential in the murky waters we navigated. "I guess anything is possible," I responded, my voice tinged with the caution born of experience. My mind raced with the implications, the strategic advantages, and the moral quandaries that such a power could entail.

Steering the conversation back to Winston, I said, "We need to take him back to Clivilius."

Leigh nodded. "I'll take him with me, and make arrangements with Jeremiah."

"Good," I replied, a weight lifted at the thought of not having to add the disposal of another corpse to my list of urgent actions. "I'll make sure Luke gets this."

As Leigh activated his Portal, the hallway was momentarily illuminated by a wave of colour that seemed to dance across the wall, a brief interlude of light in an otherwise darkened space. Leigh, with a heavy grunt, lifted Winston beneath his shoulders, his actions a testament to the solemnity of the moment. "Be careful, Cody. I'll be in touch soon," he said, his words imbued with a sense of finality and a warning of the uncertainties that lay ahead. Watching them disappear, the hallway returned to its previous state of darkness, a visual echo of the void left by their absence.

Alone with my thoughts, I murmured, "Does Killerton Enterprises know that the Portal Keys can be reset?" The question, softly spoken, was more a reflection of the swirling jumble in my mind than an expectation of an answer. My internal dialogue provided a shrug in response, an acknowledgment of the fragmented knowledge that had come to define the Clivilian legacy over generations. The realisation that it was impossible to discern who knew what anymore settled over me, a cloak of uncertainty.

With a sigh, I returned to the living room, the weight of the USB in my fingers a constant reminder of the secrets it held. The decision to sit and wait for Luke's return was one born of necessity, a pause in the relentless pace of revelations and decisions that had marked the day. The discovery of another Killerton Enterprises access card in my pocket was an unexpected jolt, a gasp escaping my lips as I pulled it out. "Where the hell did that come from?" The question hung in the air, unanswered.

The answer, it seemed, lay in the memory of my escape from Killerton Enterprises, a moment of closeness with Amber that had gone unnoticed at the time. The realisation that she must have slipped the card into my pocket was a silent acknowledgment of her role in the intricate web of alliances and secrets that enveloped us. It was a piece of the puzzle that I hadn't anticipated, a silent gesture that spoke volumes.

Armed with the access card and the USB containing the potential to alter the very dynamics of our existence, I returned to Belkeep, the events of the day a maelicstorm of implications and responsibilities. The revelations carried with me, the secrets now in my possession, were both a burden and a beacon, the potential for change as daunting as it was invigorating.

SHADOWS OF COLLABORATION

4338.211.2

The cavern's chill, pervasive and unyielding, seemed to claw at my very soul as I stood waiting for Krid, the shadows around us deep and conspiratorial. The Killerton Enterprises access card, heavy in my pocket, served as a constant reminder of the path I had chosen—a path fraught with secrecy and burdened with decisions that felt larger than life.

Handing over the USB to Krid, my voice was barely above a whisper, "Keep this safe." The act, simple in its execution, was monumental in its implications. This small device, now transitioning from my hands to hers, carried with it the potential to alter the very fabric of our reality.

Krid's acceptance of the USB was marked by a solemn understanding, her young eyes capturing the dim lantern light, reflecting a wisdom far beyond her years. The silence that enveloped us seemed to carry the weight of our actions, the air thick with the weight of the knowledge now entrusted to her care.

"Children have secrets too, Cody," she whispered back, her words weaving through the cold air, carrying a depth of meaning that resonated within me. The USB vanished into her jacket, a testament to the trust I placed in her, and a reminder of the intricate web of secrets we both navigated.

Her gaze lingered on mine, a silent pact forged in the dimness of our clandestine meeting place. The chill of the cavern seemed to intensify as we exchanged unspoken promises, each aware of the intricate dance we were now part of.

I nodded solemnly, a shared mystique grounding us in the midst of our secretive collaboration. The USB, a tiny device with monumental implications, would find a temporary refuge with Krid, nestled alongside Sylvie and Randal's Portal Keys. The plan, as dangerous as the cavern's depths, was on the precipice of unfolding.

Once Gladys assumed her role as the final Guardian of Belkeep, the USB would find its way back to me. My purpose, clear but shrouded in uncertainty, was to ensure Belkeep's ongoing safety, even if it meant rewriting the destinies entwined in my wake.

CONCISE, BUT EFFECTIVE

1338.211.3

Pacing the Portal Cave for what felt like the hundredth time, the mantra in my mind was a relentless echo: *Concise, but effective*. Each step I took on the cave's ancient, uneven ground was a physical manifestation of the turmoil churning within me. The final Portal Key, now almost a part of me, twirled continuously between my fingers—a nervous habit that mirrored the relentless spinning of my thoughts.

Glancing down at the Portal Key, its innocuous appearance belied the weight of its power—a weight that seemed to press directly on my soul. The urgency of the situation was a sharp, constant presence, goading me into action, into decision. "If Gladys goes with Luke, it'll likely be much harder to maintain contact with him," I mumbled into the void of the cave, verbalising the thoughts that had been circling like vultures in my mind. This wasn't just another hypothetical to ponder; it was a tangible complication in the already intricate web of my life—a complication that added depth to my resolve to persuade Gladys to embrace her destiny as a Guardian of Belkeep.

Concise, but effective. The mantra repeated itself, a guiding principle amidst the doubts of uncertainty. It was a reminder that in the coming confrontation with Gladys, every word would count, every argument would need to be both sharp and compelling. The stakes were too high for anything less.

As the Portal ignited, its brilliance a contrasting against the dim, natural luminescence of the cave, I couldn't help but pause. The dance of light across the walls, a mesmerising display of power and beauty, served as a momentary distraction from the weight of my thoughts. It was a vivid reminder of the extraordinary world I was a part of—a world where the lines between the mundane and the magical blurred, where decisions carried consequences beyond the immediate, beyond the visible.

This radiant display, though enchanting, reflected the responsibilities that rested on my shoulders. It underscored the urgency of my mission, the need to ensure Belkeep's safety, and the pivotal role Gladys had to play in it all. The brilliance of the Portal, while awe-inspiring, was also a beacon of the challenges that lay ahead, of the paths that we would soon need to navigate.

❖

Exiting the fridge, the hush of the kitchen enveloped me. I paused, my senses heightened, attuned to the silent narrative of the house. The sudden clang from the bathroom acted as a beacon, pulling me with a sense of urgency towards its source.

As I entered the hallway, the sight that greeted me was one of vulnerability and surprise. "Cody!" Gladys's voice, laden with shock, broke the silence, her movements to secure the towel around her adding a layer of frantic energy to the moment. "What are you doing here?" Her question, a mix of alarm and confusion, hung in the air.

"Gladys," I responded, the confidence in my voice belying the complexity of emotions stirring within me. Pulling her into a warm embrace, I sought to offer comfort, a form of physical reassurance.

The softness of Gladys's lips against mine was an unexpected solace, a moment of connection that transcended the urgency of the situation. The kiss, firm and filled with an unspoken yearning, was a balm to the whirlwind of responsibilities and dangers that lay just beyond the confines of this moment. Relishing the closeness, I allowed myself to momentarily forget the world outside.

The kiss ended all too soon, Gladys pulling away with a whisper of reluctance. "Cody, you can't be here. It's not safe," she said, her voice trembling with the weight of her conviction. The quiver in her tone, a mirror to the fear and uncertainty that shadowed her words, underscored the gravity of what we were up against.

With a resolve that matched the seriousness of her warning, I replied, "I know." My voice was steady, a declaration of the risks I was willing to take. "I've come to take you to Belkeep." The statement was a pledge, an avowal of the lengths to which I was prepared to go to ensure our collective safety.

Gladys's reaction, a mix of disbelief and panic, painted a vivid picture of the internal conflict she faced. Her wide eyes, reflecting a tumult of emotions, and the slight stumble as she clutched at her towel, spoke volumes. "I need more time," she pleaded, her hands pressed together in a gesture of entreaty.

"Gladys," I echoed her name again, a soft insistence in my voice as I reached for her hands, feeling the tremble of her resolve beneath my touch. My fingers gently coaxed hers apart, a tender gesture amidst the storm of emotions that surrounded us. Into the opened sanctuary of her palm, I placed the final Portal Key, its weight symbolic of the monumental choice that lay before her. As her fingers slowly closed around it, a silent acceptance of the burden it represented, I locked my gaze with hers, finding a tumult of defiance and fear within their depths. "We're running out of time," I whispered, the words heavy with urgency yet softened by the undercurrent of my feelings for her.

Her nod, silent and fraught with unspoken words, was punctuated by a solitary tear that traced a path down her cheek—a silent testament to the decision she faced. The sight stirred a deep well of emotion within me, my own eyes betraying the turmoil I fought to keep at bay. The saline threat at the brink of my eyelids was a battle of its own, my mantra, *Concise, but effective,* echoing as a reminder to maintain composure, to be the anchor she needed in this tempest of uncertainty.

"I'll leave you to make your final preparations. I'll return for you and Snowflake tomorrow," I promised, laying down the path for our imminent departure. The words, a blend of assurance and farewell, were a beacon for the next steps we would take together.

The surge of emotions threatened to breach my carefully maintained façade, each heartbeat a drum of impending change. Without lingering for a response, for fear of unravelling before her, I turned away, retreating to the kitchen. The familiar, vibrant colours of the fridge door offered a momentary distraction, a brief respite from the intensity of our parting.

Stepping through, the transition was a physical and symbolic crossing, from the turmoil of our shared moment back into the solitude of my own company. The act of leaving Gladys in that hallway, with the fate of Belkeep resting in the balance, was a testament to the trust and faith I had in her decision. It was a moment of profound connection and separation, a nexus of past and future where the choices made would echo far beyond the confines of that silent house.

4338.212

(31 July 2018)

TIME'S UP!

1338.212.1

The day had evaporated into a blur of responsibilities and concerns back in Belkeep. Freya's relentless worry over Krid had become a focal point of our conversations, her protective instincts flaring in the wake of Krid's recent experiences. Despite Krid's assurances of her wellbeing, Freya's anxiety refused to be quelled—a sentiment I understood but struggled to pacify. "I've known Krid her entire life!" I had found myself asserting to Freya, a hint of frustration bleeding into my voice. The insistence that Krid was fine should have been enough, I reasoned; yet, the paternal instinct in me knew all too well the depths of concern that could not be so easily assuaged.

The complexities of maintaining communication between Belkeep's leadership, myself, and Fedor—the enigmatic new Guardian—had morphed into a taxing ordeal. Each exchange felt like navigating a minefield, my patience fraying at the edges as I sought to maintain a semblance of control and coherence amidst the confusion.

Sanity, or what was left of it, dangled precariously as I recognised the urgent need to bring Gladys into the fold in Clivilius. The weight of these compounded pressures found me in the dim light of the kitchen, where frustration finally boiled over. A curse escaped my lips as I nearly lost my footing, the sudden movement causing me to lurch forward. Instinctively, I grabbed the kitchen bench, steadying myself against the potential fall. The moment served as a pointed reminder of the physical toll these stresses were beginning to exact. "I really need to stop using this bloody fridge as an entry point," I grumbled under my breath, a mix of irritation and self-reproach colouring my tone. The fridge, once a novel means of transition, now felt like an emblem of the turmoil that had come to define my days.

Regaining my composure, I ventured forth from the kitchen into the living room, each step carrying a weight of determination that seemed to anchor me amidst the swirling uncertainties. "Gladys?" My voice, softer than intended, hung in the air, a testament to the tension that pervaded the space. The silence that greeted me was almost tangible, pressing down with an oppressive force that seemed to slow time itself.

My gaze, drifting almost involuntarily towards the world outside, snagged on the sight of a dark car stationed ominously across the road. A pulse of instinctive caution surged through me, propelling me into action as I ducked out of sight. The quiet of the room was now charged with a silent alarm, my heart thudding against my ribs as I crawled towards the window for a closer inspection.

Peering out, I could make out the figure of a man seated in the car, his head bowed in a manner that suggested his attention was anchored elsewhere. A small part of me wanted to believe he was just another passerby, perhaps lost in thought or waiting for someone. Yet, the tension that had taken root within me refused to be dismissed so easily.

My vigil at the window stretched out, minutes ticking by as I watched the stranger with a hawk's eye. Then, as if on cue, the man lifted his head, binoculars in hand, sweeping the façade of Gladys's house with a scrutiny that sent a chill down my spine. A flicker of relief passed through me as I considered my advantageous position. The street's incline and the house's setback location provided a natural cover, a small mercy in a situation that felt increasingly like a chess game with unseen players.

The realisation that, even armed with binoculars, the man's efforts to surveil the interior would be thwarted by the layout of the land was a small victory in the grand scheme of things. Yet, it underscored the ever-present need for caution, for vigilance against the threats that seemed to multiply with each passing day.

"Gladys, are you here?" My voice, a mix of concern and caution, echoed softly through the hallway as I crouched, navigating the familiar yet now foreboding space. The gentle patter of Snowflake's paws against the floor offered a sliver of normalcy in the otherwise tense atmosphere, her emergence from Gladys's bedroom a small, comforting presence in the unfolding mystery.

After a brief moment of connection with Snowflake, offering her a gentle scratch behind the ears, I turned my attention back to my search for Gladys. "Gladys?" My whisper, sharper this time, cut through the silence as I entered the darkened room. The act of standing, stretching my back with a soft crack, was a momentary release from the tension that had built up. "I'm getting too old for this stealth crap," I murmured to myself, a half-hearted attempt to lighten the situation with humour.

The drawn curtains added a layer of gloom to the room, compelling me to cautiously let in what little daylight remained. As the dim light filtered in, my eyes quickly adjusted, taking in the details of the room. The sight of an open suitcase on Gladys's bed, half-packed with neatly folded clothes, was a silent testament to intentions unspoken, plans halted midway.

"Where were you going, Gladys?" The question slipped out in a whisper, more to myself than anyone else. "And why didn't you finish packing?" The unfinished state of her packing spoke volumes, suggesting haste or an unexpected interruption. The possibilities that raced through my mind were numerous and unsettling—police, Luke, her parents' house, another Guardian—each scenario carrying its own set of implications and dangers.

"Not the police," I muttered, trying to eliminate options. The idea of law enforcement seemed unlikely, considering the sustained surveillance. A disheartening realisation struck me. "Assuming it's the police watching the house," I mumbled, reluctantly re-adding them to the list, alongside a new spectre—an "unknown entity."

"This is ridiculous," I confided in Snowflake, who seemed blissfully unaware of my growing paranoia, comfortably nestled among the clothes. Her serene demeanour was a stark contrast to the storm of thoughts whirling through my mind. "Where is your mother, Snowflake?" I asked the dozing cat, half-expecting an answer or a sign.

The idea of heading to Luke's house crystallised in my mind, a clear point of action amidst the swirling maelicstorm of questions and fears. "I have to go to Luke's house anyway," I found myself saying aloud to Snowflake, as if the cat could comprehend my words. The hope that Gladys might be there, that this piece of the puzzle would fall into place and alleviate some of the worry gnawing at me, was a thin thread of optimism in the dense fog of my current state of mind.

Turning my attention back to Snowflake, who seemed the very picture of tranquility, I couldn't help but voice a plea, half-hearted as it was. "Let Gladys know that I am looking for her, that I'm worried about her, won't you, Snowflake?" The words slipped out, a blend of earnest concern and the kind of desperate hope that had me speaking to a cat as though it could carry my messages. The moment the request left my lips, the absurdity of it struck me. Conversing with pets was one thing—a comforting habit acknowledged by many—but tasking them with messages, as if they could understand and act upon them, was another level of folly.

"I really have lost my sanity," I muttered to myself, a self-deprecating acknowledgment of the situation's effect on me. Exiting the room, I left Snowflake to her comfort amidst the half-packed suitcase.

❖

The transition from the vibrancy of the Portal's exit to the engulfing darkness of the room was jarring. The once animated hues that had filled the space with an almost ethereal light now gave way to an oppressive gloom, a stark reminder of the uncertainty that lay beyond the familiarity of the Portal's embrace. I paused, a brief concession to the need for my eyes to adjust, to shift from the brilliance of the Portal to the murkiness of reality. The hesitation was fleeting, my resolve propelling me forward with steps that felt both determined and wary.

Passing through the doorway, I turned into the tiny enclave. "Gladys," the name escaped my lips sharply, a call into the uncertainty before me. In the same breath, the Portal Key slipped from my grasp, an unexpected loss of control that mirrored the suddenness of Gladys's appearance. My arms, acting on instinct, reached out to steady her, to prevent her fall—a physical response to the unexpected collision of our paths. "What are you doing here?" The demand was sharp, a reflexive response born of surprise and concern, momentarily forgetting that it was her presence I had been seeking. "And where's Luke?" The question lingered, an additional layer of worry adding to the already tense atmosphere.

There was an urgency in Gladys's eyes, a palpable fear that seemed to dance in the dim light. "There's an intruder. You need to get out of here," her words, whispered with a fervency, cut through the confusion, a clear and present warning that shifted the dynamics of our encounter. Her hands, pushing against my chest, were not just a physical urging but a desperate plea for action, for escape.

In that moment, the room, the house, and everything within it transformed from a place of potential safety to a zone of danger. The intruder, an unseen yet palpable threat, cast a long shadow over our reunion, turning it into a confrontation with an immediate risk that neither of us had anticipated.

The urgency of Gladys's warning resonated deeply, a clarion call to action that overrode any lingering questions about her whereabouts or Luke's. The need to protect, to respond to the danger she had alerted me to, surged to the forefront of my thoughts. The darkness of the room, the fear in her eyes, and the unknown threat that lurked somewhere within the confines of the house coalesced into a singular focus—safety.

As Gladys urged me backward, her warning echoing in the charged air, the reality of our situation became starkly clear. We were not just caught in a web of mysteries and hidden dangers; we were actively being hunted, our every move possibly watched, our every decision potentially a matter of life and death.

As we retreated into the darkened confines of the downstairs living room, a mix of protective instincts and adrenaline coursed through me. Grasping Gladys's arm, I guided her with a sense of urgency that matched the pounding of my heart. "Do you know who it is?" I whispered, my voice low and steady despite the tension building around us. My question, while simple, was laden with implications, the answer holding the potential to drastically alter my next move.

"It's Detective Karl Jenkins," Gladys responded, her voice a hushed echo of fear and uncertainty. The name, spoken so tentatively, seemed to hang in the air between us, a harbinger of complications we could ill afford.

Ignoring the questioning look she gave me, I ushered Gladys toward the cramped storage space beneath the staircase. The darkness of the closet beckoned, offering a temporary haven from the imminent threat that loomed just beyond our sanctuary. "Wait for me in here," I instructed, my tone leaving no room for debate. "I'll deal with Karl."

Gladys's eyes, wide with a mix of fear and confusion, met mine. "What do you mean, deal with?" she asked, a hint of apprehension colouring her words. The question was valid, the implications of my statement not lost on either of us. But before further explanations could be sought, a creak from the floor above acted as a sharp reminder of the immediacy of our predicament.

"Just keep quiet," I whispered, a final plea for her to trust me as I guided her into the darkness of the closet. The door closed with a soft click, sealing her away from the danger that encroached upon us.

Cloaked in the dark attire that had become almost a second skin, collecting my Portal Key from where I had dropped it when I bumped into Gladys, I blended into the shadows cast by the moonlight filtering through the window at the top of the stairs. Each step I took was measured, a balance of caution and determination as I ascended. Fear, though a stranger to me in moments like these, was replaced by a calculated resolve. The thought of escape to Clivilius lingered in the back of my mind, a silent reassurance amidst the uncertainty. Gladys's reluctance to embrace her destiny in Clivilius was a known factor, yet the unfolding events might leave her with little choice. The dichotomy of her future—as a Guardian alongside me or as a free Clivilian—was a decision that loomed large, yet it was one that could only be addressed once the immediate threat of Detective Jenkins was confronted.

There is another option, a soft, emotionless voice murmured in my mind.

There is? I found myself questioning the silent suggestion, intrigued despite the high stakes of the moment.

Karl, came the response, immediate and devoid of emotion, yet it ignited a spark of realisation within me. The idea of dealing with Karl in such a final manner, making him disappear without leaving any trace behind, was a thought that both alarmed and emboldened me. *Of course!* The idea blossomed with a mix of triumph and trepidation. The prospect, though dark, offered a solution that was as definitive as it was daunting.

However, as I reached the final step and emerged into the main living area, the grim contemplation was abruptly severed by the immediacy of the situation. My body acted on instinct, driven by a determination that had been honed over countless encounters of a similar nature. Striding confidently into the room, every sense heightened, I launched myself at Karl, hoping to leverage the element of surprise.

"Shit!" The expletive slipped through my teeth as my attempt at stealth proved futile against Karl's seasoned reflexes. The detective's agility in evading my lunge spoke of his experience, a reminder of the calibre of opponent I was facing. His quick manoeuvre into the dining room, his grasp on a chair, and the subsequent thrust of it towards me was a testament to his readiness for confrontation.

The dining chair, an unexpected projectile, forced me to reckon with the reality of the confrontation I had initiated. Karl's actions, defensive yet aggressive, underscored the perilous dance we were now engaged in—a dance that could end with dire consequences for either of us.

Sidestepping Karl's initial assault came naturally, my body reacting with honed instinct. My hand, quick and sure, found the leg of the chair he wielded, and with a precise yank, I disarmed him, the chair clattering to the floor. The brief triumph was cut short as Karl, anticipating my next move, launched himself at me. The collision was unexpected, the force of his head against my chest a shockwave of pain that sent us both tumbling to the ground with a thunderous crash.

Pain flared across my body as I lay half-bent on the floor, one arm cradling my aching belly, the other acting on its own accord, seemingly indifferent to the agony that screamed through my nerves. My fingers wrapped around Karl's foot as he scrambled to his feet, aiming for the hallway door. With a surge of adrenaline fuelling my actions, I yanked back on his leg, toppling him once more, the satisfaction of regaining control fleeting as we continued our struggle.

Back on my feet, the rush of adrenaline somewhat cushioning the pain, I seized Karl, dragging him across the floor towards the stairwell. The wall at the top was my target, a portal to Clivilius my goal. Yet, the plan was abruptly derailed as Karl, in a desperate bid for freedom, executed a semi-roll and a flip kick that tore his leg from my grasp. My balance lost, fear etched my features as my ankle twisted beneath me, the edge of the landing betraying me as I teetered on the brink of a fall.

In that split second of terror, Karl's hand found mine, a grim lifeline in the momentum of our descent. But there was no relief in the contact, no shared moment of reprieve. Instead, his weight only served to hasten our fall, my back slamming against the stairs with a force that drove the air from my lungs, Karl's elbow adding injury to insult as we somersaulted downwards, a maelstrom of limbs and plaster.

The descent was a tempest of agony and confusion, the world around us collapsing into a chaotic maelstrom of our entangled bodies and the debris cascading in our tumultuous wake. Then, an abrupt silence—a devastating crack thundered through my consciousness as my skull met the unforgiving edge of the doorframe. It was a sound that seemed to echo into infinity, a distinct, final note in the dissonant cacophony that had engulfed us. In that fleeting moment, as darkness clawed its way across my vision, a cascade of vivid memories flashed through my mind. Images of Gladys, her face a beacon of strength and vulnerability, mingled with the vibrant, beautiful faces of Freya and Fryar, their lives intertwined with mine in a tapestry of love, fear, and hope. The sharpness of reality dulled, the pain began to ebb away, replaced by an encroaching darkness that wrapped around me like a shroud. The edges of my vision frayed, the last vestiges of light and sound fading into a profound silence that promised no return, leaving behind a haunting echo of what was, and what could never be again.

THE END

Printed and bound by CPI Group (UK) Ltd, Croydon, CR0 4YY
01/04/2024
03757241-0004